PRAISE FOR
THE MIDNIGHT RIDE

"*The Midnight Ride* is one hell of a trip, a whirlwind tale of murder, mayhem, secret history, and the greatest art heist of all time. I'm a huge fan of Mezrich's nonfiction books, and I totally devoured his foray into fiction. The guy is just an all-around amazing writer—and Hailey Gordon is a fabulous character. Highly recommended." —Douglas Preston, #1 bestselling coauthor of *Bloodless*

"Cinematic, immersive, and completely entertaining! With *The Midnight Ride*, Boston gets its own *Da Vinci Code*, and after you race through these irresistible pages, you will never look at the city the same way again. Impeccably researched and captivatingly told. Standing ovation for this terrific thriller!"

—Hank Phillippi Ryan, *USA Today* bestselling author of *Her Perfect Life*

"A fast ride, with casino hijinks, art heists, a college student looking for trouble, and a dangerous secret from the past. Talk about tense! Mezrich's book is fun with every twist and turn!"

—R. L. Stine, author of *Goosebumps* and *Fear Street*

"A plot to savor. Witty, smart, detailed, and highly entertaining. *The Midnight Ride* is exactly what you'd expect from a master storyteller."

—Steve Berry, *New York Times* bestselling author of the Cotton Malone series

THE MIDNIGHT RIDE

ALSO BY BEN MEZRICH

STAND-ALONE NOVELS

The Midnight Ride
Seven Wonders
The Carrier (as Holden Scott)
Skin
Skeptic (as Holden Scott)
Fertile Ground
Reaper
Threshold

NONFICTION

The Antisocial Network
Bitcoin Billionaires
Woolly
The 37th Parallel
Once Upon a Time in Russia
Straight Flush
Sex on the Moon
The Accidental Billionaires
Rigged
Busting Vegas
Ugly Americans
Bringing Down the House

MIDDLE GRADE

Charlie Numbers and the Woolly Mammoth (with
Tonya Mezrich)
Charlie Numbers and the Man in the Moon (with
Tonya Mezrich)

NOVELLAS

Q

THE MIDNIGHT RIDE

BEN MEZRICH

GRAND CENTRAL

New York Boston

Grand Central Publishing
Hachette Book Group
1290 Avenue of the Americas, New York, NY 10104
grandcentralpublishing.com
twitter.com/grandcentralpub

Originally published in hardcover and ebook by Grand Central Publishing in February 2022
First mass market edition: August 2023

Grand Central Publishing is a division of Hachette Book Group, Inc. The Grand Central Publishing name and logo is a trademark of Hachette Book Group, Inc.

The publisher is not responsible for websites (or their content) that are not owned by the publisher.

Grand Central Publishing books may be purchased in bulk for business, educational, or promotional use. For information, please contact your local bookseller or the Hachette Book Group Special Markets Department at special.markets@hbgusa.com.

ISBNs: 9781538754641 (mass market), 9781538754658 (ebook)

Printed in the United States of America

OPM

10   9   8   7   6   5   4   3   2   1

For my dad and mom, for being my first readers and my biggest supporters—but mostly for making me read two books a week when I was a kid before I was allowed to watch TV.

THE MIDNIGHT RIDE

PROLOGUE

And behold, there arose a great tempest in the sea...

    The sensation was sudden and unexpected, so wild and intense and ferocious that Robert "Bobby" Donati actually gasped out loud. He could feel—really *feel*—the wooden deck rising up beneath his feet as the massive waves crashed against the stern of the reeling boat. He could *see* the dark, violent storm clouds billowing over the shattered mast, as the bow careened toward the jagged rocks that would surely kill them all. He could hear the screams of the huddled passengers behind him—most caught up in mindless panic, some still holding oars or reaching up to desperately try to fix the mainsail—frantically trying to do something, anything, save for one man, in the center of the deck, who peered out at the storm with a calm patience that could only be described as Christ-like, because, *well*—and then Bobby's own voice tore him out of the moment, his thick Boston accent sounding vaguely tinny in his ears.

"Get over here and help me get this off the wall."

Bobby stepped back, almost surprised to feel marble beneath his leather police boots, rather than the damp wooden slabs of a seventeenth-century sailing vessel. The boat and the waves and the storm weren't any less impressive because they were behind thick glass, embraced by a five-foot-high gilded frame that looked like it must have weighed fifty, sixty pounds. Bobby wasn't sure what had made him stop in front of that particular painting as he'd made his way across the darkened gallery—the lavishly decorated Dutch Room was lined with masterpieces, gratuitously ornate frame after frame speckled along the embroidered walls, beneath candelabras and chandeliers dripping tears of crystal as old and sad as the silken drapes hanging by the arched windows that overlooked the courtyard two floors below. But for whatever reason, the boat had called out to him, and Bobby's inner voice had joined right in for the chorus; despite every rational bone in his body telling him that it was the wrong thing at the wrong time—that the smart, cautious, and safe way forward was to stick to the plan—Bobby had never been able to ignore that damn little voice.

He glanced over toward his partner, standing halfway across the gallery. Four inches taller than Bobby and twenty pounds heavier, Richie Gustiano looked ridiculous in his uniform, which was two sizes too small and bulging so much in the middle, Bobby was worried the shiny brass buttons running up the center might fly off at any moment. Worse, Richie's mustache was hanging half off his upper lip and his hat was on backward; the only thing about him that looked real was his badge, which thankfully had been more than enough to get them from their red hatchback parked in an alley a block away and into the museum through the side door.

"You hear me?" Bobby asked, and then repeated himself, louder. "Get over here and help me with this."

"Are you serious?" Richie finally responded, that

mustache dancing in tune to an accent even heavier than Bobby's own. "We ain't even supposed to be in here."

That was true; Richie might have been big, but he wasn't stupid. Well, he was big and stupid, but the plan had been simple enough that even Richie could follow it without so much as a dress rehearsal. Contract gigs were often like that; every step spelled out in intricate detail, paint by numbers—all you had to do was keep your brush within the lines.

Bobby turned back to the storm, and the waves, and the boat.

"Yeah, I'm serious."

"This ain't the job," Richie tried again.

"Yeah," Bobby responded.

But he was already reaching for the frame.

————

Once that damn little voice started speaking, Bobby had never been very good at keeping the brush between the lines. Lack of impulse control—that's what the teachers and the priests and the social workers who were eventually brought in had called it, when Bobby was growing up in East Boston; sometimes he just *did* things. Probably the reason, by the age of fifty-one, his arrest record was as long and varied as his debt ledger.

Bobby grinned, as he drew his box cutter down the length of the canvas that was now splayed out on the floor in front of him. The feel of the blade against the painting was strange and unique. The chips and dust from the paint sprayed up against his gloved fingers, filling him with a sense of gravitas. He knew that paint was old—even older than the building around him, which itself looked like some sort of Venetian palace that had been airlifted out of nineteenth-century Italy and dropped into a leafy suburb of Boston. But it wasn't just the age of the canvas, already halfway out of the gilded frame and beginning to curl up at the edges, like a bit of a newspaper held too close to a flame—Bobby knew that the decision he had made wasn't just spontaneous, it was, quite possibly, *historic*.

He kept his knee steady against the bottom of the frame as he worked, ignoring the beads of sweat dripping down the back of his neck and staining the stiff collar of his borrowed police uniform. He could hear Richie's grunts as the bigger man worked on his own painting a few feet away on the floor—a much smaller frame, maybe two feet wide and tall, the canvas depicting some sort of seventeenth-century parlor scene involving a guy with a stringed instrument, two women, and a piano. It hadn't taken much to convince his partner to join in on the fun, once they'd gotten the big one off the wall. Richie had always been more of a follower than most of the hoods Bobby had grown up with on the streets of Revere, which was why Bobby had tapped him for the job in the first place. No matter how simple a gig looked on paper, there was always the possibility of unexpected complications— and the last thing you needed when things went off script was a partner who liked to think for himself.

As Bobby slid the box cutter down toward the final corner of his own canvas, he finally surveyed the room around them. "Off script" was an understatement. It wasn't just the painting of the boat, and the one Richie was digging into; there were now a half dozen empty frames splayed out across the gallery, each beside a little pile of shattered glass. Some of the canvases were already rolled up and piled in a corner by the door, while others were still spread out near where they were working. Bobby didn't have tubes to put them in, but he had plenty of tape and zip ties in his duffel bag, which was just outside the Dutch Room, in the second-floor hallway leading to the rest of the museum. Tubes would have been better—Christ only knew how much these things were actually worth— but the tape and the ties would have to do.

This wasn't Bobby's first art heist, though it was certainly his strangest, mainly because it wasn't really supposed to have been an art heist at all. But he'd stolen paintings before, and he knew that art this old often went for millions. Then again, with paintings like this, it wasn't so much about how much they were worth, it was more a question of finding someone willing to pay for them. Even the most eccentric billionaire couldn't exactly hang a Rembrandt on his living room wall.

But a little after 1:00 a.m., dressed as a cop working a box cutter through the last few inches of the border of a four-hundred-year-old painting, Bobby didn't concern himself with potential next steps. One of the benefits of acting on impulse was you really got to feast on the moment, and looking across the violated gallery, it was clear that Bobby and his partner had served themselves quite a buffet. Bobby actually felt bad for the feds who would undoubtedly try to piece together what was now a chaotic crime scene. To be fair, even before Bobby had deviated from the plan, none of it had really made much sense.

Case in point, the two security guards who had first let them in the side door after seeing their badges, who were now taped up and handcuffed in a boiler room three floors below. If it had been up to Bobby, he

would have taken the box cutter to them first, because
he was a pro, and pros didn't leave witnesses. Then
there was the amount of time they'd already spent in
the museum; a quick glance at his watch told him
they'd already been there an hour—an insane amount
of time, though in this Bobby only had himself and his
impulsive nature to blame. If he'd followed the plan,
they'd have been in and out in minutes.

But despite how confusing it would look to the
feds, Bobby wasn't concerned about the time, any
more than he was worried about the security cameras
they had passed on their way from the basement,
where they'd taped up the security guards, to the
second floor of the gargantuan building. The security
system was nearly as dated as the gallery around him;
on the way out, they'd have no trouble grabbing the
tapes from the VCR in the first-floor security booth.
Likewise, even if they'd spent the entire night taking
frames off the walls of every room in the place, it was
unlikely any real policemen were going to show up to
interrupt them. There was a reason the people who
had hired Bobby for the job had chosen that particular
night—March 18—which also happened to be the
tail end of St. Patty's Day. Every self-respecting cop in
Boston was either off duty and drunk, or on duty and
dealing with drunks.

Bobby finished with the massive painting and rose
to his feet, sliding the box cutter back into his pocket.
Richie joined him in the center of the room a few
minutes later, sizing up the scene with a resolved look
in his thickset eyes.

"I guess we should get what we came for," Richie
finally said, and Bobby nodded, as he began scooping
up the rolled canvases. As he started for the door,
he noticed his partner had paused in front of a low

shelf containing a handful of sculptures; the bigger man seemed particularly intrigued by an old-looking vase, something foreign, maybe Chinese or Arabic. The object didn't seem that impressive to Bobby, but for whatever reason, Richie shrugged and grabbed it from the shelf.

Bobby smirked, as he led his partner out of the gallery and back into the second-floor hallway. They had a pile of paintings worth millions, and Richie had stopped for a vase that would look right at home in the back corner of their neighborhood pawnshop. At least the big mug was getting into the spirit. Hell, maybe the vase would pay for the parking tickets they were surely collecting in the alley down below.

———

Five minutes later Bobby was two steps ahead of his partner as they entered a much smaller exhibit— more of a hallway than a gallery, cluttered with period furniture and lined with drawers filled with portraits and drawings. This time, the walls sported only a handful of ornate, gilded frames. Still, Bobby counted more than a few that might make nice additions to the canvases he'd already accrued.

But his partner was focused on their target, affixed to the wall above a mid-eighteenth-century cabinet halfway across the room. Not a painting—nothing as intense as the boat in the storm that had first caught Bobby's eye, or even as pretty, if staid, as the parlor scene Richie had grabbed from the Dutch Room. An object, something old, but nowhere near as ancient as the Chinese or Arabic vase. And it wasn't in a frame, but even so, it was going to be difficult to remove. No box cutter, this time—Richie already had a screwdriver out of his jacket pocket and was judging the cabinet below the object with his eyes, trying to decide if it would really support his weight.

Then he paused, looking back at Bobby.

"They want the flag, too?"

Bobby shook his head. They didn't want the flag.

They didn't want the paintings.

They had hired Bobby — paid him a ridiculous amount of money — to get one thing from this museum, and one thing only. A ridiculous amount of money, to follow a plan that didn't make much sense, to steal an object hardly worth anything at all.

Bobby glanced around the room, at the drawers filled with portraits and drawings — and then he grinned.

Impulse control.

As Richie took his screwdriver to the object attached to the wall, Bobby headed toward the drawers. He wasn't Irish, but tonight he was going to celebrate like he'd been born in Southie, not Revere.

Paint by numbers was always the smart play; kept you safe, smooth, and under the radar.

But it was the Impressionist masterpiece that got you into the history books.

CHAPTER ONE

It was a little after 2:00 a.m. on a Wednesday, and Hailey Gordon was on the run of her life.

She gripped the cushioned edge of the blackjack table with both hands as she tossed a purposefully nonchalant glance at the cards spread out across the green felt. Christ, it was hard to keep her emotions in check, push down the excitement coursing through her veins. She wanted to leap from her chair, bear-hug the nice old man sitting two seats down from her, lift him up in the air, and swing him right out of his orthopedic clogs. Instead, Hailey painted her face with a bored look, then waved a manicured hand over the table, letting the dealer know she didn't want any more cards.

Next it was the old man's turn, down at third base, the last chair at the table. It had just been Hailey and the man for the past hour, because it was so god-damn late and the middle of the week, and because the limits in this particular corner of this particular casino were way too high for its zip code. Hailey had no idea how the man could afford a hundred-dollar minimum; from his clogs to his resort-wear linen suit, the man's look screamed pension. Then again, Hailey knew better than most—looks could be pretty deceiving. She'd been using her looks to deceive for a really long time. And at the moment, she was about to deceive her way into a tidy little fortune.

The dealer wasn't paying attention, and the pit boss—gnarled, mildly overweight, belly pushing precariously against the buttons of his uniform as he chatted up a cocktail waitress on the other side of the blackjack pit—was otherwise engaged, so Hailey let her glance linger a little longer across the table. The brightly colored metropolis of chips spread out across the felt nearest to her was a thing of pure beauty, and judging from the dealer's revealed card—a six, a wonderful, incredible, palpably sexy six—things were about to get even better. Hailey had eight thousand dollars behind her four hands, another six thousand in yellow chips, *bananas*, already safe next to her drink, a light brown mixture in a scotch glass that smelled like apple juice if you got close enough. Because, in truth, it *was* apple juice.

Looks, again, deceiving.

But moving her eyes from the table to the surrounding casino, Hailey knew she had nothing to feel guilty about. The entire place—this entire industry—was built on sleight of hand. The table gaming room was vast and very beige, other than the felts; beige, from the tables themselves to the thick carpeting to the curtained walls. In stark contrast, there were velvety red chandeliers hanging from the high ceiling—matching the crimson tide that blanketed every inch of the nearby slots parlor, and soft, soothing music pumping in from speakers hidden somewhere in the corners. The air was cool and, if rumors held true, slightly over-oxygenated. And everything smelled slightly floral. To be sure, the place was rife with flowers. A seizure-inducing botanical excess, from the fifty-five thousand different blooms spanning the walkways out front of the lavish casino's entrance, to the four thousand potted plants spread through the gaming areas and hotel rooms, to the multitude more intertwined in the working carousel that dominated the foyer. But the scent in the air didn't come primarily from the colorful plants, it was manufactured by teams of aroma therapists and pumped in along with the oxygen. Everything, from the decor to the lighting to the air, was *designed*, by people much less interested in art than commerce.

There is a reason there are no clocks in casinos, and that it is always hard to find your way back to the front entrance. There is a reason Vegas doesn't have minibars in the hotel rooms, and there is a noticeable lack of windows anywhere near the gaming areas. Heck, there is a reason that the carpets in casinos are usually ugly and discordant; the idea is to keep your eyes up, on the flashing lights of the slots and the deft flight patterns of the dealing cards. The visual cues, the design of the building, the smell in the air—it's all there to get you gambling and keep you gambling. Because the more you gamble, the more, on average, you lose. And it doesn't matter if the casino is smack-dab in the middle of the Vegas strip, or here, three thousand miles away on the edge of Boston Harbor; a casino is one big act of deception, a reverse ATM masquerading as an entertainment facility, where everything and anything is aimed at separating you from your money.

Encore Boston Harbor was as pretty and twinkling as anything they'd ever cooked up in Nevada. From the $30 million Koons sculpture of Popeye—Popeye!—in the front hallway to that flowered merry-go-round in the lobby—complete with a unicorn, a Pegasus, and a hippocamp, because why not?—the place felt a lot like Vegas. And during the early evening hours, the clientele was well-heeled, professionals in sports coats mingling with club-attired millennials from the city. But the later it got, the more the patronage turned local, Chelsea and Everett and Malden, and that suited Hailey, because deep down, beneath her streaked blond hair, and the preppy-collared tennis shirt and matching skirt she was wearing, and her polished fingernails, and the fake jewelry on her fingers and throat, she *was* Chelsea and Everett and Malden. The clothes and the jewelry and even the hair were an act, something she'd carefully put together in the little bathroom she shared with two roommates in Central Square, Cambridge. Even the way she was sitting, bottle-tan legs crossed at the knee, tennis shoes bumping up and down, fingers absentmindedly curling twists of her golden hair—all of it was part of the act. *Pretty blond trophy girlfriend, blowing through her boyfriend's stacks of chips, not a care in the goddamn world.*

None of it was real. The money on the table was basically everything she had to her name. There was no boyfriend, she'd never held a tennis racket in her life, and her hair was naturally brown. *A magic act within a magic act.* Anybody looking her way—from the pit boss to the men in the security booths attached to the "eyes in the sky" monitor above the blackjack felt to the little old lady at the end of the table—would see what she wanted them to see: *pretty blonde trophy girlfriend.* Not an applied math PhD student at MIT who was paying her way through life with the one attribute that was *real* about her: her facility with numbers. And right now, the numbers were telling her that she was about to walk away from a long night of cards with enough money to pay her rent, a semester of tuition, and most of her outstanding bills.

The old man finally asked for another card on top of the hard fourteen he had in front of him, which the dealer wearily obliged, revealing a four. Hailey added one to the running count, adjusting the true count in her head: *Plus fourteen*, two-thirds into the deck, a really deep deal, probably because the dealer, mid-fifties, balding, with glasses fogged by hours in the over-air-conditioned room, looked bored out of his mind and at the end of a long shift. A count that high so deep into the deck meant the cards left to deal were heavy with faces and aces; the dealer's showing six would likely lead to a busted hand, which meant the four hands in front of Hailey would pay out.

Even if it sounded complicated to the uninitiated, beating the game of blackjack was actually simple math. You kept track of the low cards and the high cards as they came out of the deck; the more low cards that came out, the higher your count, and the better the deck became. The deeper into the deck you went, the more significant that number was—the difference between the running count and the true count. And the higher that number went, the more money you wanted to have on the table.

Hailey's original bet had been two thousand dollars, and she'd been dealt two face cards. The dealer had turned over a six. She'd split the faces, which was an unusual play. At the level she was playing, you'd expect a move like that to get attention from the pit boss, but the cocktail waitress was way more interesting than a dumb, drunk blonde throwing her boyfriend's money away after a day on the tennis court. Then both of Hailey's split hands had hit faces—a jack and a queen—and she'd split again.

Even the dealer had raised his eyebrows above his foggy glasses at the eight thousand dollars she now had laid out in front of her, but she'd only laughed and made some comment about how mad her boyfriend was going to be if she lost.

Now, as the dealer reached out to turn over his hole card, she did her best to keep the tension out of her cheeks and eyes, keeping that smile light and unconcerned—and there it was, a ten, bright red and perfect, for a dealer sixteen. Which meant he needed another card. His fingers sped to the shoe in pure mechanical fashion, gears in a machine, and then the next card whizzed onto the felt, faceup. Another ten.

A dealer bust at twenty-six.

Hailey fought the fireworks in her chest as the dealer began pushing equal stacks of yellow chips next to her bets, another eight thousand dollars to add to her fourteen. *Twenty-two thousand dollars.* The old man at the end was clapping his hands together, his hundred-dollar bet doubled, and Hailey was about to congratulate him when something caught her eye. Past the old lady, all the way across the beige room, a door had opened and two men were coming through. Big men, big and burly, one with a crew cut and the other with a dye job that wasn't fooling anybody. Both were wearing dark suits, and the one with the crew cut had an earpiece and was talking into something attached to his lapel.

"Nice win," the dealer said, scooping up the cards, but Hailey was barely listening. The two men had made it a few yards before pausing, the crew cut still speaking into his lapel. And then he looked up— right at Hailey. Before she had a chance to react, they had locked eyes, and she *knew*.

She had been made.

CHAPTER TWO

Thanks," Hailey said to the dealer, uncrossing her legs and rising quickly from her chair. "I better get back to my room and hide this from my boyfriend, or he'll give it all back on the roulette wheel."

She grabbed the chips with both hands and swept them into her purse, which was open on her lap. Her roommate Jill's purse, actually, tiger print, with bronze clasps worn down from many nights spent clubbing in Kenmore, makeup applied and reapplied in bathrooms jammed with BU girls. The lipstick and compact had been replaced with a fake ID and a half-empty juice box. All part of the routine—heading to the bathroom early in the evening, dumping out the scotch she'd ordered when she'd first sat down and refilling the glass with apple juice. Nobody betting two thousand dollars a hand at blackjack was playing sober, and no matter how late it was, no matter how inattentive the pit boss seemed, in a casino you had to assume someone was *always* watching.

Obviously, that assumption bore true again, because the two suits were now heading in a straight line for Hailey's table. She jammed the last few chips into the purse and clicked the wonky clasp shut.

"You don't want me to color you up?" the dealer asked.

"I like the sound they make rattling around in my purse," Hailey responded.

And then she was away from the table and moving fast toward the hallway leading out of the gaming area, toward the interior of the resort. She would rather have gone straight for the front entrance, but the two suits were closing quickly and she wasn't sure she could make it in time.

Card counting wasn't illegal, and the fake ID was a minor crime, not the sort of thing you'd find yourself in handcuffs over. But like every practiced card counter who played the sort of stakes she was playing, she'd had run-ins with casino security before, and she knew they'd try to "back room" her if they caught her. Which meant a trip to somewhere deep in the bowels of the hotel, where they'd threaten to call the police, threaten to take her chips, and then make her sign some sort of "trespass" act—basically saying if she returned to the Encore, she'd be trespassing. And then, most likely, they'd fingerprint her before they'd let her leave with the chips.

And that was what she had to avoid. Because the fingerprints wouldn't match the fake ID; nor would they match the *real* ID she had sewn into a pocket in her skirt, where she kept her apartment keys and her credit cards. And it certainly wouldn't match the name on those credit cards, or the rental agreement she'd cosigned with her roommates, or the identification materials at the registrar's office at MIT. Being good at math wasn't going to earn her a PhD if she was facing multiple charges of fraud, no matter how innocent her motive.

Bottom line was, she had a lot more at risk than twenty-two grand in chips.

She skirted between two more blackjack tables, dodged a waitress carrying a tray loaded with vodka

Red Bulls, then nearly upended a planter bristling with something that looked like a botanical experiment gone horribly wrong involving bamboo, a rosebush, and a miniature weeping willow. Then she was out of the gaming room and pushing her way through a more crowded hallway. Weaving past a group of bach-elorette partiers with matching T-shirts and blinking bunny ears, cutting between two Instagram-worthy women in the midst of a selfie by a spitting fountain shaped like a clamshell, then nearly slamming head-first into a pair of young men in shirts that were a little too tight and much too shiny. She finally dared cast a look back down the hall, hoping against hope— and her heart froze, because the two suits were still coming fast, the one with the crew cut pointing right at her as his thick thighs propelled him forward.

Damn. She sliced hard to the right, moving faster down another hallway until she reached a wide-open juncture with a marble floor adorned with brightly colored gigantic butterflies, beneath a high, recessed ceiling—dripping more of the gargantuan insects, poised midflight in a way that was probably supposed to elicit whimsy, though to Hailey seemed a bit more predatory. In the center of the juncture, beneath and between the huge bugs—that glistening, stainless steel statue—the cartoon sailor Popeye—proportions in tune with the swarm. Hailey had seen photos of the Koons sculpture in magazines months before the casino had opened—she knew Steve Wynn had paid $28 million for the garish, if amusing, monstrosity, and had bought it specifically for the Boston Harbor outpost of his casino empire because to him, at least, it evoked something playful and nostalgic. But in person, the six-foot-five, two-thousand-pound sculpture— polished to such a reflective sheen it made Hailey's eyes water to look at it—seemed more intimidating than inviting. To her, it didn't shout nostalgia; it screamed testosterone, which, in a casino—no matter how floral—was pointedly redundant.

But the sort of people milling about the Encore at 2:00 a.m. on a Wednesday didn't seem to care. Hailey quickly slid into the glut of tourists gathered around the sculpture, ducking and weaving between extended cell phones and the odd, actual camera. For a moment she thought she might have lost the suits as she reached the opposite side of the juncture— but then a flash of reflected motion in one of Popeye's bulbous, shiny shoes caught her eye. The two men were moving along the outskirts of the crowd, searching—any minute they were going to see her, and then they'd be right on top of her.

Keeping the statue between herself and the suits, she worked her way back through the crowd and into another hallway, then sprinted the last few yards to a bank of elevators leading up into the hotel. There was a keypad next to the buttons, but she was prepared. She yanked a room key from her purse—the key she'd lifted from the back pocket of a middle-aged salesman so engaged in video poker in the slots parlor she could have taken his belt and shoes, too—and hit the button.

Thankfully, the elevator doors opened right away, a young, drunken couple sharing a bottle of champagne stumbling out. Hailey leapt past them, hit a random floor, and slammed the door close button with the heel of her hand. There was a painful pause— and Hailey cursed to herself, as the two suits saw her from the end of the hall and rushed forward. She hit the button again and the doors started to slide shut, but slow, too damn slow. The suits were at a full run, the closest crew cut with his hand outstretched to stop the door—when someone drunkenly stumbled into him from the side, causing his hand to miss. Hailey caught a brief, blurred glimpse of the drunk—dressed mostly in denim, apologizing in a slur of words—but then the elevator doors slid shut and she was moving upward, breathing hard.

A minute later she was out on the sixth floor of the hotel, quietly pacing the long hallway, her tennis shoes sinking into the thick carpeting. *Beige, more beige.* She knew she didn't have much time—the security goons would figure out what floor she was on, and they would be there within minutes. She scanned the doors on either side of her as she went, looking for a fire exit. There might be cameras in the stairwells and halls, but if she was fast enough, maybe she could get outside before anyone got to her. Her face on a camera wasn't going to be a problem; a fingerprint went back a lot further in time than facial recognition software, because by the time she'd grown into this face, she'd become the person on her ID. It was unfortunate that her fingerprints hadn't changed at twelve, like the rest of her body. Puberty had its limitations.

She was halfway down the hall, still scanning doors, when she heard the metallic ding of the elevator behind her. Someone was coming to her floor. Could the security goons have found her that fast? She began to panic, rushing forward, looking at door after door after door. And then she saw it: one of the hotel room doors about three feet ahead of her was slightly open. As Hailey leapt forward, grabbing at the knob, she saw why. The keypad above the knob was hanging off the door by a spaghetti twist of wires. *Someone broke into this room, and recently.*

Hailey paused for the briefest of seconds, wondering now if this was such a good place to hide. But then she heard the elevator doors whiffing open at the end of the hall, and she made the only decision she could. She dashed inside the room, shutting the door as well as she could behind her. Then she turned, her back against the knob, and tried to catch her breath.

The room was large, with a big picture window overlooking the dark and undulating murk of the Mystic River. The decor of the room was more beige upon beige, from the oversized bed to the thick curtains by the window to the walls. There was a framed print above the bed, a colorful, comic-strip drawing of a blond woman looking into a hand mirror—assuredly something expensive, rare, and mostly ignored by the type of people who would stay overnight in a casino overlooking the Mystic—and a flat-screen TV on a dresser directly across. But Hailey's attention was immediately drawn to a chair in the corner by the window, because it was facing the door and because it was also occupied.

The man in the chair looked to be about fifty and disheveled, wearing a suit jacket too small for his rounded shoulders and gray pants that didn't match. His belt wasn't around his pants, which was odd. Stranger still, the belt wasn't gone; it was, in fact, tied tightly around the man's left wrist, pinning the man's hand against the arm of the chair.

"Sorry, the door was open," Hailey started to say, then paused, as her mind digested what she was seeing. The man was staring right at her, eyes open, but the look on his face wasn't right.

"Are you...OK?" she said.

The man didn't answer. It was then that Hailey noticed: he didn't answer because there was a two-inch bullet hole in the middle of his forehead.

CHAPTER THREE

As the elevator doors whiffed open and Nick Patterson stepped out into the carpeted hallway bisecting the sixth floor of the Encore Boston Harbor hotel, he felt something sweeping through his chest that he hadn't felt in so long, it took him another step before he realized what it was.

Hope.

A smile broke across his angled, somewhat sallow face, because the feeling was so foreign and absurd and impossible. *Like a flower-covered unicorn on a goddamn carousel.* For nearly nine years, he'd had nothing to look forward to. Even in the last few months, as the end of his time at MCI-Shirley had neared, there had been no sense of optimism, and no sense *in* optimism. A guy like him, with no family to speak of, no skills beyond what had gotten him inside in the first place, no money or prospects—what the hell did he have to be optimistic about? What did he have to look forward to on the *outside* that wasn't going to get him right back *inside*?

The elevator doors shut behind him and his heavy work boots sunk into the carpet, each step pushing him forward. He patted the inside pocket of his jean jacket for the hundredth time. Of course, it was still there, stiff and square beneath the denim, wrapped in a plastic sandwich bag for extra security. Nuts, how something so small and mundane could be so valuable. More valuable, in fact, than everything Nick had ever stolen, more valuable than anything he could have stolen in a dozen lifetimes. So valuable, in fact, that it might very well make the nine years he'd spent locked up worthwhile.

Because if he hadn't been locked up, he'd never have met that damn skinny kid with the mop of red hair and the freckles.

He began searching the doors on either side of the hallway as he went, looking for the right number. It still seemed crazy to him, setting the meet in a place like this. Sure, he liked casinos as much as the next guy, but even at 3:00 a.m. it seemed too high traffic, and there were cameras everywhere. Having a record didn't get you banned from a casino; half the degenerate gamblers in the country had records, and without the degenerates these places could never afford all those chandeliers. But it seemed sloppy to start this sort of transaction in such a public place. Of course, there was nothing illegal about meeting a guy in a hotel room, showing him something in a little plastic bag, in exchange for a nice fat down payment. But if nine years at MCI-Shirley had taught Nick anything, it was that the less attention you drew to yourself, the better. He'd have been much happier to set the meeting in some bar in Southie.

Unfortunately, it wasn't up to him. Hell, none of this was really his plan. It was all—*inherited*. No doubt, the kid with the mop of hair that matched the velvet in the slots parlor had picked the casino precisely *because* it was loud, brash, and flashy. Everything about that damn kid had been loud. The minute the kid had walked off the bus from the clearing center in Walpole, cursing at the screws as they went through the admission routine at Shirley, jawing with any inmate near enough to catch his attention, the cons had begun taking bets on how quick the kid was going to end up in the infirmary, or worse. Nick himself had been on the over at four days. And maybe that was the real reason Nick had approached the kid in the TV room on his second day inside; not some internal need to help out, some unaccustomed sense of empathy, but to protect his wager.

Still counting doors as he moved down the hotel hallway — 621, 623, 625 — Nick could picture the look on the kid's face as he'd laughed away the hoots and catcalls from the other inmates in the day room, the shouted threats and promises. In that, he was right; it wasn't the noisy, pumped-up idiots and short-timers he had to worry about. Sure, they might throw a punch to earn some cred from their buddies, but they weren't out to do any real damage. It was the quiet ones, the ones who wouldn't even look at you as they stuck you with a shiv. Not for cred, not to make a name, but to keep order, keep things quiet and smooth. The redhead and the short-timers were just visiting. For the cons, Shirley was *home*.

But the kid had just laughed, bragging that his lawyer was going to get him out in three weeks, tops, and everything was going to change after that. Because he had something big planned after he was out, something *monumental*. And that's when the kid had taken something out of his shirt pocket and showed it to Nick.

Nick touched the plastic bag through his jacket again. Truth was, when the kid had first placed it gingerly on the dayroom table like it was some sort of irreplaceable Fabergé egg, Nick had thought it was a joke. It wasn't until the next morning, when he'd taken the time to do a little research on the computer terminal in the cellblock library that he'd fully realized what he'd seen. And by then, of course, it had been too late—for the kid. All his heavy plans, his one shot at something monumental—gone because someone didn't like the way he had mouthed off in the shower or neglected to wipe down a weight in the yard or forgotten to courtesy flush during his time on the john. Whatever the reason, big or small, the kid had gotten a shiv in the kidney while lining up in the chow hall at breakfast, and Nick was suddenly left with a decision.

Let it go, forget what the kid had shown him, go back to his routine, his hopeless life. He himself was only looking at another couple more months at Shirley before he was up for parole. He could have gone back to the mindless rote, day in, day out. Or he could try something new.

Take a chance. Stick his neck out for the first time in nine years and see where it led him.

627. 629. 631.

He stopped in front of the door, mentally checking the number against what had been written in the redheaded kid's little notebook. Nick had found the notebook rolled up and jammed into the hollow aluminum leg of the kid's bunk, along with what Nick now carried in the bag in his jacket pocket. Once Nick had made the decision to take that chance, it hadn't been hard to follow through; bribing a screw to get into the kid's cell during lunch hadn't been difficult, and although they'd already bagged the kid's belongings to send to his next of kin, nobody had done a thorough search yet, the kind of search that only a con could properly conduct. See, to a con, every item of furniture, every fixture, every bit of molding was a place to hide something. Nine years in, you could put a cell phone in a bar of soap or inside a biscuit from the canteen. Nick hadn't known exactly where to look, but he'd known *how* to look.

And now here he was. He reached out to knock on door 633, his knuckles hitting wood more solidly than he'd meant—before he realized with a start that the keypad above the knob was hanging out of its mount by wires.

What the hell? But the door was already swinging inward.

CHAPTER FOUR

The first thing Nick saw was the girl. Blond and slim and preppy, tan legs sprouting from a tight white skirt. The same girl he'd seen running into the elevator in the casino lobby, being chased by security. At the time he'd figured it was nothing more than a dine and ditch; maybe she'd stolen a coin cup from an aging drone draped over a slot machine and was making a run for it. Bumping into the security guards had been more instinct than anything else: *someone running, someone chasing.* He'd certainly never expected to see her again, and definitely not here.

She was standing with her back to him on the other side of the hotel room, facing a chair. As she heard him enter, she swung around, and he saw her face, which he hadn't gotten a look at in the elevator. Pretty, but much paler than the legs, porcelain even, and the look in her eyes was pure terror. Then his attention moved to the chair, and the body sprawled across it, still mostly in a sitting position, one arm belted to the wood.

"Christ," Nick murmured.

The girl took a step toward him. Her whole body was trembling, and something slipped from under her arm—a purse. It hit the floor with a clatter, its clasp breaking open, casino chips spurting out across the carpet.

The girl dropped to a knee and started scooping at the chips.

"This isn't what it looks like," she said, as she jammed handfuls back into the purse. "I mean, I found him like this."

"He's dead," Nick said.

He'd stopped in the doorway, the door still open behind him.

"Yeah, I figured that much out myself."

Then she paused, looking up from the floor.

"You're not hotel security."

"He's been shot," Nick said, ignoring her. "Somebody shot him."

The girl paused. She was reading his face in a way that made him instantly uncomfortable.

"You know him," she said. It wasn't a question.

Yes, Nick knew the man in the chair. Not personally, but he knew him. He'd spoken to him on the phone twice from prison, and once since he'd gotten out. The first time to explain that he'd "inherited" the deal from the red-haired kid, and that he needed to push back the meeting a couple months. And then right after he'd gotten his parole.

"Jimmy O'Leary. Jimmy the Lip, they call him. I mean, because of, well, you know."

The girl then noticed for the first time, the dark discoloration on the man's lower lip. A birthmark that went from one corner halfway to the other.

"And you're here to see him," she said, rising back to her feet. "Well, I think you got here a little late."

And suddenly she was heading for the door. She was a good four inches shorter than Nick's six feet, but she didn't seem intimidated by him at all. Nor, in retrospect, did she seem as thrown by the man with the bullet hole in his head. The girl's face was pale, she was trembling, but she hadn't fallen apart, as most "civilians" might. No question, this wasn't her first dead body. Nick's either. Even though he was mostly a B&E guy, and had never carried a piece, he'd seen a body before. His second night at Walpole, before getting the transfer to Shirley. Piece of crap dealer hung himself in the cell next to Nick's, and he'd had to spend six hours next to the body, listening to it bloat and leak. Something he'd never forget.

He thought about stopping the girl as she passed him, but instead stepped aside. His mind was churning. *This isn't good, not good at all.* This meeting, originally set up by the red-haired kid, was supposed to change everything. And now Jimmy the Lip was dead, and Nick was standing there, just a few feet away. He couldn't begin to count the parole violations.

"You're not waiting for that hotel security to arrive?" he asked. "The ones you called?"

"I didn't call them," she said. "And I don't want to be here when they arrive."

"And the police?"

"You can stick around if you'd like. This doesn't involve me at all."

And then she was through the door. No question, she had her own problems; Nick didn't think she had anything to do with Jimmy the Lip's death, but he had no idea what she had been doing in his room. The fact she hadn't called the police was a big red flag, the sort of flag that maybe made her a more likely ally than adversary. Nick took one last look at Jimmy the Lip, then followed the girl, quickening his step to catch up. She was heading away from the elevators, toward a door at the end of the hall marked "Emergency Exit."

"Hold up. I'm coming with you."

"Like hell you are," she said, quickening her pace. "I'm getting as far away from this, and you, as I can. Like I said, this doesn't involve me—"

"I find you in a room with my dead fence. That makes you involved."

She looked at him.

"Fence? Like in the movies?"

"Whatever. Look, when they find the body, they're going to look at the cameras from the casino, from the elevator, from wherever else they've got them. And they're going to see you, and they're going to see me. And they are going to put us both on this floor, maybe entering that room."

She'd reached the emergency exit door, put her hand against the wood.

"So?"

"So they are going to think one of us had something to do with the dead guy in the chair. That makes you my alibi. And me, yours."

The girl put her weight against the door—and then a brief look of panic crossed her face, when it didn't budge. Nick pulled a security keycard from his pocket. The girl raised her eyebrows—seemed to take in his jacket for the first time.

"You swiped that from the guards. Downstairs, outside the elevator. That's why you bumped into them."

Nick shrugged, used the key on the fire door. When it clicked open, the girl edged past him.

"Well, I don't need an alibi. And, no offense, but you don't look like much of an alibi. You look like you just got out of jail."

They were in a cinder-block stairwell heading downward. No alarm, but that didn't mean there wasn't something buzzing in some security booth somewhere. They had to move fast.

"I did. And I don't intend to go back, not for murder. If I'm going back, it's going to be for something worthwhile."

They were taking the steps two at a time, her in front, him right behind. As he went, he reached into his jacket and retrieved the little plastic bag. He tapped her shoulder, then handed it to her. She looked through the clear plastic, at what was inside.

"What the hell is this?"

"This is what I was bringing to Jimmy the Lip. He was going to give me a hundred thousand dollars for it, as a down payment."

She stopped, one tennis shoe above the next step.

"This is a Polaroid picture. He was going to give you a hundred grand for a Polaroid?"

"Look closer."

She squinted through the plastic.

"Looks like a picture of a picture."

"A painting, yes."

"Looks old," the girl said. "A woman playing a piano, next to a guy with a guitar and another woman singing. It's nice, I guess."

"Nice?" Nick said.

"What? It's not nice?"

He took the Polaroid in the plastic bag from her and jammed it back into his jacket. Then he started forward again down the stairs, taking the lead. Now she was a step behind him, but he could tell she wasn't just heading the same way, trying to get away from hotel security, or the police, or the casino. He was leading, and now she was following.

"It's not a piano, it's a harpsicord. And it's not a guitar, it's a lute."

It sounded funny even to Nick, the word "lute," in his Dorchester accent. A few months ago, he'd never heard of a lute. And he'd never seen that painting before. But since that day in the TV room at Shirley, he'd done his research. This girl didn't know it yet, but that painting was incredibly valuable. And famous. Maybe, Nick thought to himself, as he quickened his pace down the stairs, famous enough to get someone a bullet hole in the middle of his forehead.

In some ways, you could say, it was the most famous painting in the world.

CHAPTER FIVE

Professor Adrian Jensen didn't try to hide his distaste as he carefully undid the clasps of his professional-grade, polystyrene bicycle helmet, pulled it off his head, and shook free his glorious halo of reddish-gold hair. Even though he'd managed to find a table as far back from the bar that ran the length of the crowded tavern that squatted—as it had, for nearly two and a half centuries—in the heart of one of Adrian's least favorite suburbs of Boston, he could barely hear himself grumble over the clatter and din of the two dozen blazer-clad, khaki-draped academics clustered together about that aging parapet of oak, enthusiastically chattering, laughing, carousing, as they toasted one another over the conclusion of what had to be the three longest days of Adrian's professional life.

Placing the helmet on the empty seat next to him, he kept his eyes low so as not to attract the attention of any of the beaming blowhards at the bar, should they look his way. The sad truth was, he only had himself to blame. One of the many maxims that had guided his life through a world so continuously inhabited by a surging sea of lesser minds was the tired-to-the-point-of-cliché belief that nothing good ever came from being out past midnight. And here he was, a quarter past two in the morning, having barely survived a seventy-two-hour conference put on by the Historical Society of Charlestown, Massachusetts—of which, by no fault of his own, Adrian had inherited a charter membership as part of his tenure at Tufts—adding precious moments of insult to already unbearable injury, in the quest for a bit of food in the one place left open after the city's official closing time.

At least the table in front of Adrian was set precisely enough. A glass of barely adequate white wine, which he'd ordered from a passing waitress, stood to the left of a bowl of slightly stale buttered rolls. If he could just keep his head down long enough for the kitchen to complete his citrus and beet salad—the only item he was willing to risk ordering off a menu that included kielbasa and something titled "Fenway egg rolls"—he might just escape with some level of dignity intact.

The fact that most of the crowd surrounding the bar—and scattered about the tables to Adrian's left and right—wore lanyards displaying mostly respectable college affiliations did nothing for Adrian's mood. The many faces he recognized belonged to scholarly circles he dutifully avoided. Part of the reason he'd traded his own blazer for one of his cycling jerseys for the short bike ride over from the conference hall was to inhibit the sort of unavoidable collegiate camaraderie that might easily be interpreted as a brief moment of mutual respect. Adrian suffered fools rarely, and the fact that this lot held advanced degrees from fine universities around the Northeast only made them a slightly better breed of fool.

But again, Adrian was there by his own misguided choice. Eyes still lowered, he lifted his glass, revealing a kitschy coaster emblazoned with the Bunker Hill

Monument, one of the area's most familiar, if overly phallic, tourist attractions, then took a sip from his wine, letting the warmth of the second-tier alcohol—if not the taste—cushion his distress. At least the bar itself had history; it was no accident the historical society had thrown its after-party at one of the oldest taverns in the country, certainly one of the most famous Revolutionary-era watering holes in a state littered with eighteenth-century tourist traps. From the signs imbedded on doorposts and chiseled into sidewalks all over Massachusetts, it often seemed that the Founding Fathers had spent as much of their time touring pubs, restaurants, and charming inns as they had planning their war with the British. But at least the Warren Tavern in Charlestown was one of the handful of authentic stomping grounds of famous names like Washington, Franklin, and Revere—which almost made Adrian forgive the kielbasa, if not the Fenway egg rolls. And though the place had been "restored" more than once, it still looked much as it had 240-odd years earlier, when it had first opened its doors in 1780. Mostly oaken tables, glass steins hanging from fixtures above the bar, Revolutionary paraphernalia along the walls. If Adrian could have only traveled back in time along with the decor—and away from the noisy, self-inflated crowd of blowhards who shared his academic occupation, if not his refined sensibilities—he could have forgiven the bland vintage currently swirling past his tongue.

But the fixed chronological nature of his misery was only made all the more evident, as a new burst of laughter emerged from the area of the bar; then Adrian heard a voice rise above the rest, and his ears reddened in tune with his hair.

Raising his head more out of reflex than will,

Adrian caught sight of Charles Walker—short hair, mild jowls, starting to succumb to a bit of middle-age bloat—standing in the midst of the crowd, which could now be described as adoring. As usual, Charles was holding court, his hands waving in the air in front of the shiny brass buttons of his double-breasted suit. No doubt, the buttons were antiques, most likely bought at auction, perhaps once belonging to some minor Revolutionary officer. There would likely be a story tied to them, which Charles would tell at cocktail parties and academic gatherings, over and over; the more drinks he'd imbibed, the more dramatic the tale, and by the end of an evening like tonight, Adrian could imagine those buttons would have already crossed the Delaware and deflected a bolt fired by King George himself.

To many of his colleagues, Adrian might have seemed the peacock; but in Adrian's mind, Charles Walker leaned heavily into the second syllable of the adjective. Somehow stiff and bombastic at the same time, with a flair for the fantastic. Everything Adrian hated about the current state of his profession—

"Professor Jensen, is that you?"

Adrian felt his stomach drop as he realized Charles was looking his way. Adrian quickly lowered his eyes—but too late. Charles separated himself from the crowd and was suddenly bounding across the tavern. A moment later he was leaning over Adrian's table, so close Adrian could smell the alcohol on his breath.

"The whole point of a conference is to confer," Charles said, through a grin. "And what better way to confer than over a few drinks—"

"I prefer to drink in the company of my intellectual equals."

Charles looked at the empty seat next to Adrian,

and his eyes dimmed a bit. But he was still smiling. It might have been the booze, but Adrian could see something in the man's rounded face; a level of confidence that seemed out of character, even for someone as pompous as Charles.

"We're in the same sandbox, Adrian. You should learn to play nice. I didn't see you at my lecture this morning. Though it was hard to pick out faces in such a crowd. Quite the reception."

Without asking, Charles reached forward and grabbed one of the rolls out of the bread bowl. Adrian watched in disgust, as Charles spoke between bites, flecks of grain leaping from his lips.

"Boston is big enough for both of us. It doesn't always need to be a competition—"

"There's no competition. I simply don't like you. You're a flawed and foolish fantasist. So why don't you go back to your fan club at the bar, maybe regale them with another wonderful tale brimming with muskets, triangular hats, and wild, unverifiable theories."

"Always the charmer," Charles said. But then he leaned even closer over the table. "Tonight, I'll let it slide. Because I'm not here to tell stories. I'm here to celebrate."

Adrian rolled his eyes.

"Your lecture wasn't that impressive."

"Not my lecture. Tomorrow, I'm submitting a new paper for publication. And it's going to change the world."

Even for Charles, that seemed overly dramatic. Adrian scanned the man's bulbous face, but saw no edge of sarcasm, nothing but that pure, unadulterated, annoying confidence.

"More wild theories," Adrian said. "More science fiction."

But Charles only winked, took another bite of the roll, then placed it back in the bread bowl. As he turned and headed back across the tavern, he threw a final look in Adrian's direction.

"Even the flawed and foolish get struck by lightning now and then."

Adrian watched the man as he was once again engulfed by the lanyards at the bar. *Ridiculous.* A paper that was going to change the world? Like Adrian, Charles was a professor of eighteenth-century American history. Harvard, not Tufts—but still, who did he think he was? Even the most revolutionary academic paper published by someone in their profession barely caused a ripple in the mainstream world; outside of academia, most people's interest in eighteenth-century American history peaked somewhere between the seventh and eighth grades.

But watching Charles, once again surrounded by his doting peers, it was obvious the man was bursting at the seams. He was clearly celebrating *something*. And his happiness appeared to be infectious, not only among the gathered lanyards; farther down the bar, Adrian noticed a woman—tall, angled, dark hair held together by ivory chopsticks—clearly out of Charles's league, and yet she seemed to be intrigued by the buffoon, even smiled at him.

Adrian shook his head. Again, after midnight— *he only had himself to blame*.

He turned away from the display at the bar. Then he grabbed the molested bowl of buttered rolls, leaned over to place it on the next table over—to the surprise of the couple sitting there—and went back to his barely passable white wine.

CHAPTER SIX

It was the perfume that hit Charles Walker first, bringing him out of the deepest and most satisfying hours of sleep he'd experienced in the years since his divorce. A blend of grapefruit and vanilla that at once stung slightly as it hit the back of his nostrils and was also somehow instantly sensual, causing a dull throb to ignite in his boxer shorts. And even before he opened his eyes, he felt a smile crawling across his lips.

He took a deep, openmouthed breath, inhaling that incredible scent, letting it dance across the tip of his tongue. He was still in the fog of that in-between state, not fully awake but no longer catatonic, his memories of the night broken into visual flashes— like images on shattered glass, of soft, slender, wonderfully curved body parts and of furious, physical, *gymnastic* sexual acts. He knew it was a night he'd never forget, even though he still couldn't understand exactly *how* it had occurred. In truth, nights like that didn't happen to Charles, not since the divorce—and certainly not before. Twelve hours ago, he'd have bet his last dollar that nights like that didn't happen in real life to *anyone*.

He rolled onto his back, stretching his arms above his head, getting the kinks out of his aching shoulders. It was then that he also noticed the music;

soft, classical, mostly violins with the hint of a viola, drifting through the air around him in gentle waves. He recognized it immediately—a Bach concerto, recorded in 2007 by the Philadelphia Orchestra— because it was from his own collection. Not digital, of course, not bastardized by some computer software, but real, the vibration of a needle against vinyl on the record player in his living room one floor down— the way God, and the Philadelphia Orchestra, had intended music to be played.

His smile grew, and he opened his eyes. He was lying in his bed in the bedroom on the upper floor of his town house two blocks from Harvard Square, but still everything around him looked foreign. His sheets, normally stiff and tucked into the corners even after a night's sleep, were mussed and twisted. His pillows were in even worse shape, like they'd barely survived a hurricane. The one under his head had mostly escaped its pillowcase and was leaking down feathers all over the bed. The other pillow, which usually remained untouched on the opposite side, was bent nearly in half, and in the middle of the pillowcase he could see an unmistakable, two-inch lipstick stain. Bright red, hell, *blood* red, like something you'd see on the cover of a cheap, pulpy romance novel. Evidence, Charles realized, that it hadn't just been a dream. It was all real; *she* was real, and if the music was any indication, she was still in his house.

He quickly rose to a sitting position. His head pounded at the motion, and he felt cobwebs at the back of his mouth. He looked over at his bed table, searching for his phone, which might tell him the time; but the device wasn't where he'd usually left it, and he had no idea where it might be—or even if he'd brought the damn thing home with him the night before. Another lost phone—it was beginning to become a habit.

Before his divorce, he'd never been more than a casual drinker; maybe once a week, he'd ended his evening with a glass of red wine from the cabinet in his study. But in the years since, he'd rediscovered an affinity for the grape—which had slowly evolved into a full-blown affair. And in recent years, like his ex-wife, he'd begun to side-step beyond his monogamous nature: wine had given way to vodka, then gin. Even tequila, in a pinch. Usually, even on an off night, he'd find his way back to his town house before anything eventful happened. Lost cell phones aside, there was only so much trouble a professor of history could get into, in the social world he lived within.

But last night was different. Even before he'd met her, sometime after 2:00 a.m., he could recall—last night had *felt* different. Even before the conference had ended, he'd begun celebrating—starting with a glass of champagne in the speaker's green room at the convention hall, then continuing on at the tavern after-party.

Sitting up in his bed, he heard a noise from downstairs: high heels against the imported slate tiles that covered most of his kitchen. The tiles had been his ex-wife's choice. She'd had expensive tastes in everything from home decor to her choice of divorce lawyer. On a tenured professor's salary, Charles had been able to pay off the tiles, but he'd be paying for the divorce lawyer for years to come.

The tiles, for their part, now seemed worth the cost, just for the click of those high heels against the slate. Charles quickly slipped out from under the comforter and crossed his bedroom to the hook by his closet, where he kept his bathrobe. The bedroom was bright for 5:30 a.m.—either she'd opened the shades that covered the single window overlooking quiet, tree-lined Brattle Street before he woke up, or they'd left the shades open the night before. Charles seriously hoped it was the former; his neighbors were almost entirely professors like him, and at least three houses had a good view of his bedroom. He'd have a hard time walking into the faculty dining hall if he thought any of his stiff, overeducated neighbors had witnessed even a portion of last night's activities.

He made sure the bathrobe was tied tight, then exited the bedroom. The stairs leading down to the first floor were cherrywood and polished so smooth he could see his reflection in the banister. His ex-wife had always made fun of his proclivity for cleanliness and order; to be sure, he knew in most things he was just as stiff—and certainly as overeducated—as his neighbors. Harvard professors were a breed, and especially those in the history department. Last night wasn't just a giant leap for Charles, but a Neil Armstrong moment for his entire profession.

He was grinning by the time he reached the first floor. To his right was the kitchen, those slate tiles, the Italian marble island, and the chrome appliances glowing in the morning sunlight streaming in from the double glass doors that led out to the yard. The distinct aroma of freshly ground coffee swirled in the air, but to Charles's surprise, the kitchen was empty. His attention shifted to the left, through the open archway that led to his study. He heard a new clicking sound, but this wasn't heels on floor. This clicking was fingernails against a keyboard.

His smile faded a bit as he made short work of the last few steps and entered the study. Most of the furniture was leather and old, in stark contrast to the kitchen and bedroom. That was because the study was *his*, had always been his, even when he was married. The reclining chair in the corner by the record player— still spinning, waves of violins rising and falling like summer tides—was worn from years of use, and the thick oak shelves climbing every wall were filled with books, even more worn and old, mostly antiques and first editions he'd picked up in quaint bookstores over the years. All of the titles had to do with history; specifically, American, mid-eighteenth century. And throughout the study, there was more evidence of his life's obsession. A print above the record player of Paul Revere's famous engraving of the Boston Massacre. A glass-enclosed, full-scale copy of the Declaration of Independence set on an oversized coffee table in the center of the room. And a replica of a Minuteman's trusty musket standing in a polished wooden frame in the corner by his desk.

The desk itself was mahogany and vintage, remi- niscent of the writing desk Thomas Jefferson used to draft the original Declaration; Charles had picked it up at an antique fair upstate, along with certification papers proving its provenance. It had been crafted in a woodworking shop on a street that was now part of the flats of Beacon Hill; a family-owned business that had traced its lineage back to the *Mayflower*, and had been active during the Revolutionary War, pivot- ing at the time to make casts for cannons and gun barrels instead of desks and armoires. Over the past two years, Charles had filled the drawers of that desk with papers—mostly original letters and documents pertaining to his research, some incredibly valuable, wrapped in protective sleeves and cases.

So, it was no surprise that a sharp dagger of concern pierced his stomach as his gaze shifted from the desk to the chair behind it; in retrospect, the fact that the woman had put a record from his collection onto the turntable without asking was presumptuous enough. But now seeing her stretched out in his chair, his laptop computer open on the mahogany in front of her, a mug of coffee next to her fingers, which were caressing the curves of his computer's mouse, Charles found himself at an uncharacteristic loss for words.

CHAPTER SEVEN

H ope you don't mind," the woman said, sweetly. "I'm an early riser. I needed to check my email, and my phone is out of battery. But I made you coffee. Right there, next to the Declaration of Independence."

Charles saw the mug on the table—thankfully on a coaster—by the glass case. He still didn't know quite what to say, so instead he retrieved the coffee and took a little sip. It was the deep roast he'd gotten from Trader Joe's in Central Square, with just the right amount of cream and sugar. There was also something spicy in the sip—maybe nutmeg? Cinnamon?

"Two sugars and a cream, and a little surprise I whipped up myself. Just how you like it."

He flushed a bit, snippets of conversation from last night at the tavern echoing in his ears. Right after she'd come up to him by the bar, startling him, and told him he looked just her type, she'd asked how he liked his coffee in the morning. Such an aggressive approach; he'd surprised himself by not excusing himself and running for the door. But he'd already been many glasses of wine deep, not counting the champagne from earlier. And he *had* been celebrating.

Looking at her, even lounging at his own desk like she'd picked it out from the antique fair herself, he realized he'd never really had a chance. Five-nine at least, with legs that seemed almost too long for her body, bare all the way to the edge of the skirt that hugged her perfect thighs. Her hair was jet black and tied up in a ponytail, held together by a pair of ivory white chopsticks—though the night before he distinctly remembered it loose and wild, spread out across the pillows of his bed. Her cheeks were angled high and sharp, and her lips were full, still bloodred and turned up at the edges. But it was her eyes that were her most distinct feature; dark like her hair, but perfectly elliptical, like a hieroglyphic you'd expect to find on the cornerstone of an Egyptian pyramid.

In short, she was way above his pay grade. Fifty-two-year-old, divorced professors of mid-eighteenth-century American history didn't pick up women like her in taverns; they certainly didn't get *picked up* by women like her, well, anywhere. It was unnerving, seeing her at his computer, drinking his coffee, using his record player—but maybe he was overreacting.

He took a deeper sip of his coffee. The warm liquid felt good against his dry throat, the vapors battling the slight pounding in his skull. It really was foolish to drink so much on a weeknight—usually he kept the real benders for the weekends—but then, he hadn't had many occasions to celebrate like that. Sure, he'd finished papers before, had published many, all the way back to his PhD thesis that had ended up in the *Cambridge Historical Journal*, leading to his recruitment by Harvard's history department. But that paper—a detailed exploration of the relationship between John Hancock and Samuel Adams based on a trove of original letters he'd discovered tucked into a notebook of Ben Franklin's on loan to Widener Library from a collector in London—wasn't even in the same league as what he was about to accomplish.

Thinking of what was coming—what was just a handful of days away—buoyed him as he stepped deeper into his study. He could only imagine what his colleagues were going to say when they read his paper. The surprise, the utter awe, even better—the *envy*. Charles felt himself start to tremble with joy, even through his hangover, at the thought of the thunderclap that would move through the various universities. And then, the icing on the cake—Adrian Jensen, that foppish, haughty, egotist—

His thoughts paused as he noticed the woman had gone back to the computer, and as he continued toward the desk, she turned the laptop so that he could see the screen.

To his surprise, it wasn't open to an email server. It was open to something he instantly recognized. He stopped, halfway past the coffee table, right beside a shelf lined with books about the Boston Tea Party.

"That's my paper," he said.

She nodded, tapping her long fingernails against the mouse.

"Yes. Really interesting. I stumbled onto it while looking for my emails. It's fascinating. I've always considered myself a Revolutionary War buff, but I've never read anything like this before."

He looked at her, then at the screen. Although it was possible he'd left the paper open in some task bar on his computer, he couldn't imagine she'd read much of the fifty-page document, unless she'd been awake much longer than he'd thought. He wasn't surprised she'd found it interesting. Even though most people glazed over a bit when he told them his focus—the Revolutionary War era and the interrelationships among the Founders—he knew that the paper on the computer screen between them was something different. As he'd told that narcissist Adrian, Charles's research, *his discovery*, was certain to make worldwide news. No matter what journal he sent it to, once it was out in the world, he was certain it would find its way into the mainstream. For a history professor, it was a once-in-a-lifetime shot. Which was probably why he hadn't already published the paper; in fact, the only people who'd seen it, other than this woman who had picked him up the night before, were the handful of Revolutionary War obsessives who frequented an obscure Reddit chat stream he'd started a few months earlier. He'd just posted the synopsis the morning before to see what they thought. He hadn't yet logged on again to see the response, but he was certain the four or five followers of the subreddit he'd gathered over the months would have a lot to say. People who dreamt about the works and deeds of Thomas Jefferson and Ben Franklin were easily incited.

"I've always been fascinated by Revolutionary War heroes," she continued. "Men like Patrick Henry, George Washington, and of course, Paul Revere."

Charles swirled the coffee in the mug with a shake of his wrist.

"Revere wasn't actually a war hero," he said, feeling the need to correct her. "Though he is, arguably, the most famous name of the period, especially in this region. But the tourists who regularly visit his carefully preserved house in the North End, or his gravestone in the Granary Burying Ground by Downtown Crossing, have no idea who he really was."

If she had read through the paper on the computer, or much of it, she must have gathered that Charles was arguably the foremost Revere scholar in the country — or at least, one of *two*. His memory of the night before was sketchy, but that might even have come up in conversation. It wasn't his best opening line, and it tended to land pretty flat, but he usually dropped it at some point. Although to be fair, last night she'd done most of the talking, while he'd done most of the staring.

"In fact," Charles continued, "Revere was pretty much a failure at battle. Court-martialed in 1779 and dishonorably discharged after a botched siege of a British fort in Maine—the most disastrous battle in the Revolutionary War—that left most of his battalion killed or captured."

"But that's not how he's remembered," she said.

Charles sipped the coffee again. His smile returned, because now they were solidly on his turf.

"Listen, my children, and you shall hear, of the midnight ride of Paul Revere."

"Right, the poem. Longfellow, right? The British are coming."

"Revere certainly had the best PR of any of the Revolutionary heroes," Charles said, repeating a line he'd used, sometimes successfully drawing a laugh, when he'd taught a freshman core class to undergraduates on the period, "but most of what people think they know about Paul Revere, and his famous midnight ride, is completely wrong."

"He didn't ride his horse across Boston, warning the people that the British were attacking?"

"It wasn't *his* horse, and no, he wasn't warning the people of Boston of an impending attack. And most of his ride took place outside of Boston, on the way to Concord and Lexington. He also took the first part of his journey—across the Charles River—by boat, and he wasn't alone, there were three riders working together. And during the ride, Paul Revere was actually captured by the British, roughed up a bit, and then released."

She tapped the computer screen with a red fingernail.

"This paper goes a lot deeper than that."

So she had read that much, at least. For some reason, Charles got the immediate and strange feeling that she was humoring him, getting him to expound on information she already knew. He realized that he'd never actually asked her what she did for a living, or who, really, she was. In fact, he wasn't sure he even knew her name. Something that started with a *P*, but he was afraid to make an attempt, considering what they'd already done together—the lipstick on his pillow. In all of that, he felt so awkward, so unsteady; so, he stuck to the arena he knew best.

"That's correct. The true reason behind that midnight ride. But before we can even begin to understand what Revere was *really* up to, we need to understand who the man actually *was*."

The woman hit the mouse with her other hand, and then tapped the lines of text in the first paragraph of his paper.

"His family was French; his father owned a silver shop. Revere was a craftsman, a silver worker. One of the most technically gifted of his era. He also worked at dentistry, but he probably didn't make George Washington's wooden teeth."

"He was a technologist," Charles said, feeling his face flush. A little embarrassing, how excited he could get over Revere. "An innovator. He worked with silver, but also bronze and wood. And copper—it was Revere's shop that first covered the Boston State House dome with copper. He was also one of the most talented engravers of his era."

He glanced at the print of Revere's famous engraving of the Boston Massacre on his study wall, made just three weeks after the actual event itself. The drama of the piece was palpable; the viciousness of the redcoats and the misery of the injured and dying colonists engraved with such passion, it was no surprise that the work had helped incite a nation.

"He was also a Freemason," the woman said, looking at the screen.

Again, it did not appear she was reading something she did not already know. Which was odd. *Who was she, exactly?* A fellow historian? He didn't want to be judging her by her appearance, but she didn't look like any American history buff he'd met before. And he'd met plenty.

"He was a founding member of the Massachusetts chapter of Freemasons, correct. Many of the Revolutionary names were Freemasons. Ben Franklin, of course, but also Hancock, and Revere. But Revere's connection to the Freemasons was really besides the fact."

Most people knew about the Freemasons; they'd been the subject of numerous pop novels and movies, and why not? A mysterious organization, or private club, dating back hundreds of years, with secret rituals and symbols, shadowy clubhouses and influential, often wealthy members, some famous, some infamous—wonderful grist for the conspiracy theorists. But Charles knew: *Paul Revere's relationship to the Freemasons paled in comparison to his true affiliation.*

"Revere wasn't just a Freemason," Charles said, lowering his voice. "He was part of something much more mysterious and ancient than Freemasonry."

He almost continued, then stopped himself. If she'd read through his paper, she knew where he was going—but if she hadn't, well—he took another sip from his coffee, while watching her face. Those incredible cheekbones glowed in the light from his computer. He supposed it didn't make any difference. He was going to be submitting his paper within days. And then his research, his discovery, would be everywhere.

"And now we're at the gist of it," she said. "That midnight ride."

Charles was happy to shift from the revelation of what Revere *really* was, to the facts of that fateful night.

"It was, at its heart, an intelligence mission. On top of whatever else Paul Revere was, he was one of America's first spies. He'd founded a group he called the Mechanics, and a faction of that group called themselves the Sons of Liberty. The Mechanics were tasked with keeping tabs on the British. That particular night—April 18, 1775—the Mechanics had uncovered that a team of British soldiers was on its way to Concord."

"To arrest John Hancock and Sam Adams," the woman said.

"That's what we learn in high school. Hancock and Adams were the de facto leaders of the American rebels; Hancock, a wealthy merchant—the richest man in Massachusetts—and Adams, a failed young businessman but a real rabble-rouser, a fan of mob violence, and probably one of the leaders of the Boston Tea Party. They were arguably the most dangerous men in the colonies. So, it seems understandable that the British might want to send a detachment of men to go find and arrest them. But describing the British mission that way, well, it's not entirely accurate. The British did intend to arrest Hancock and Adams, but that wasn't the main focus of their raid, or of Revere's ride. When Revere was captured by the British, and then released, he continued on to where Hancock was hiding, even though he knew his compatriots had already warned the rebel leadership. He continued on for one purpose."

Charles waited a moment, to make sure her focus was entirely on him.

"To retrieve Hancock's trunk."

Charles said the words with a flourish, maybe a little too much volume. As he did, he felt himself nearly stumble, and reached out for a nearby bookshelf to steady himself. Perhaps he was still a little drunk from the night before. But he was too engaged now to slow down.

"After Hancock and Adams made their escape, Revere retrieved the trunk — a heavy, leather-covered, four-by-two, locked wooden chest — and carried it off into the woods. It was that trunk that the British were searching for, that trunk that caused Revere to ride, at great personal danger, across Massachusetts that night."

"The trunk," the woman prodded. "I've read about it before. It contained letters, contracts, things like that, communication between the Revolutionary leaders. Political and maybe sentimental value."

Charles shook his head so violently he nearly toppled over again. His mind was swirling a bit, so he took another sip of the coffee to try and steady himself. Again, he tasted something spicy.

"Is that cinnamon? Or tamarack?"

"Something like that," the woman said. "The papers in the trunk, Charles."

"Yes, the papers in the trunk. Revolutionary documents, yes. But that wasn't all that the trunk contained."

And now he was there, his discovery, the thing

that was going to change his life. *Hancock's trunk*. It had survived Revere's adventure back in April 1775, survived the many years, decades, centuries, and had ended up, rather ignominiously today, in a museum in Worcester, Massachusetts, where it was kept in a hermetically sealed basement storage unit, and annually put on display for local schoolchildren. It hadn't been easy for Charles to get permission to run a radiological study on the case—first an X-ray, then a CT scan—but what he'd discovered had made all the red tape he'd had to cut through worthwhile.

Because what he'd found was bigger than a cache of Revolutionary War documents. Bigger than Revere's connection to the Freemasons, or the importance of his spy network, his Mechanics. What Charles had discovered was a secret that, had the British succeeded in capturing Hancock's trunk, wouldn't just have changed the course of the Revolution—but of *human history*.

While Charles's thoughts were racing backward to the moment when he'd first seen it for himself on that portable CT scanner, the woman at his computer scrolled through his paper to that very image. And now there it was, on his laptop screen, in stark black and white. A radiographically enhanced image from a piece of parchment, hidden within the wood of the back wall of Hancock's trunk.

And yet, as incredible as that image was, it wasn't the whole story, not by a long shot. Because what the woman at his computer couldn't possibly know, was that the paper on Charles's computer wasn't complete. He'd purposefully kept the very best part to himself, something he would reveal after the paper made its rounds and turned the world upside down. *His second discovery: one that rivaled, and surpassed, his first.*

He turned his attention from the screen to the woman, wondering what she was thinking, what that image meant to her. But her eyes, those dark, perfect ellipses, those *hieroglyphic* eyes, told him nothing. In fact, as he stared into them, they began to shimmer, shiver, *swim*.

"I don't feel right," Charles finally mumbled.

And then he noticed that his tongue felt abnormally large. His shoulders seemed to stiffen, and a tingle moved down the skin of his legs. Was he really still drunk? No, it was more than that. *Was he having a stroke?*

"What's wrong with me?" he stuttered.

He tried to take a step, but his legs wouldn't move right. His hand opened and the mug fell to the floor, hitting the carpet with a thud. Then Charles was falling, too. He reached out to catch the coffee table—but his arm was as weak as his legs. He hit the floor next to the mug, shoulder first. He fought hard to twist his body so he could still look upward, toward his desk.

The woman had come around from the other side and was now standing over him. Her high heels were inches from his face, her long legs rising up for what seemed like forever.

"Other than the Reddit group," she said, her voice barely audible through a strange rushing sound that was now filling Charles's ears. "Did you give this paper to anyone else?"

The part of his brain that was still thinking logically realized it was a very strange question. What did that matter?

"What's happening to me?" he gasped, his tongue barely forming the words.

"It's a paralytic," the woman responded, from atop

those long, long legs. "It comes from the Brazilian rainforest. It doesn't have a name, actually, but it's derived from the skin of an indigenous yellow frog. I put it in your coffee. That doesn't matter now. Charles, concentrate. Did you give this paper to any-one else?"

A paralytic? From a frog? Charles blinked, realizing his eyelids were the only thing that still felt normal. His arms and legs couldn't move, and his chest, his chest was growing heavier by the second.

"Paralytic. My coffee."

"Yes. The effect starts in the skin, you felt the tingling? Then it moves to the muscles. First the big muscle groups, the legs, the arms. Eventually, makes its way to the lungs. I can reverse it, but we really don't have much time. Did you give this to anyone else? Or send it to anyone? A friend? A colleague? Anyone?"

She's poisoned me. Why? It didn't make any sense. He'd never met her before. He was a history professor. An expert on Paul Revere. Why would anyone want to poison him?

Paul Revere. His paper. His groundbreaking, life-changing paper.

She knew about the Reddit group, so she must have found it there. But how? The Reddit group was small, three or four scholars from universities around the world, the type of people who spent evenings searching obscure message streams for conversations about Paul Revere. How had she stumbled into that world, how had she found his paper, which he'd only emailed to the group the morning before? Or had she been monitoring the thread the whole time? Read the paper, then come to Charlestown to find him?

Seduce him?

Poison him?

"Please," he tried, his words crashing together like a train derailed from its track. "Help me. I can't breathe."

And at that moment, he suddenly realized—he *had* sent the paper to one other person. Yesterday morning, after he'd emailed it to the Reddit group. But not via his computer, not even through his phone. A hard copy, via the postal service, of all things. Because he'd wanted the recipient to feel the weight of the thing in his hands.

Not a colleague, or a friend. And not for advice, not like with the Reddit group. He'd sent it to one other person—*out of pure spite*.

He opened his mouth to try to tell her—but it was too late. Now his jaw wouldn't move. His lips were open, but his face was frozen in place. The woman watched him for a second longer, then turned and headed back to his computer. As he stared, unable to blink, she held something small and metallic against the base of the keyboard, and suddenly the screen blurred, then went blank.

The woman turned back to look at Charles one last time, splayed out on the floor.

His eyes were still open, but the pupils were growing larger, and wider, and rounder.

And then everything went dark.

CHAPTER EIGHT

W ell, what have we got here," the burly, pug-nosed
homicide detective growled, as he caught sight of
Zack Lindwell entering the sixth-floor hotel room
from the crime scene staging area that now took up
much of the hallway outside. "You must have gotten
off on the wrong floor, Lindsy. This one is way below
your pay grade."

Zack faked a smile as he picked his way between
two CSI rats in white smocks and matching gloves
who were on their knees on the beige rug, measuring
shoe prints. Another half dozen of the Boston area's
finest hair-follicle and carpet-fiber collectors were between Zack and the state police detective, who was
over by the body in the chair, but they didn't look up
from their work.

"I don't know, Detective Marsh. There's a Koons in
the lobby and a Lichtenstein about two feet from where
you're standing. I think I'm right where I belong."

Marsh glanced at the cartoonish painting above
the bed, then snorted, unimpressed.

"That thing qualifies for a visit from Quantico?
Well, it's still on the wall. You can head back to your
buddies at Art Crimes and tell them to stop wetting
their pants. And if the ME finds a Picasso rolled up in
this guy's intestines, I'll be the first to let you know."

This got a laugh from the closest lab rat on the floor, who was carefully bagging what looked to be a yellow casino chip that had rolled under the foot of the bed. Zack stepped over the smocked man's leg as he moved next to Marsh. Close enough to the body, now, that he could see the waxy sheen growing in patches across the man's skin, and the blisters already forming in the outer epidermis. Based on this, and the general stiffness apparent in the man's limbs—even the arm strapped to the chair—Zack put the time of death somewhere before midnight, but later than 11:00 p.m., between six and seven hours ago. He knew from the case call that the body had been discovered around 3:00 a.m. by hotel security, who had been checking doors on a different matter and had found the broken lock outside. Surprising, that the ME hadn't arrived yet—but then again, it wasn't even six in the morning, that hazy hour between night and day shifts. From the look on Marsh's face, no doubt the detective was at the tail end of a long night, which meant he'd likely be even more unpleasant than usual.

"I'm not here looking for Picassos, Detective. And I highly doubt Jimmy the Lip here would have been able to tell a Picasso from a C. M. Coolidge."

Marsh raised a wary eyebrow.

"Dogs playing poker," Zack explained. "Prints were real popular in the suburbs in the 1970s."

"Yeah, thanks for the art history lesson, Lindsy, but I couldn't give two shits about how well you know your painters. I'm more curious about how you know our rapidly bloating friend. And, for that matter, what you're doing here in the first place."

It was about as cordial a welcome as Zack had ever received from the rough-and-tumble state detective. They'd worked together twice before—though "worked together" was a very liberal description. Four years ago, a month after Zack had taken over the Art Crimes desk of the FBI's Boston field office, he'd consulted on a murder-robbery at a resort on the Cape, involving an antique Cartier watch that had been lifted from a private collection a week before. The minute he'd entered the crime scene, Marsh had been on top of him, shouting about chains of command and jurisdiction. It wasn't just the usual back and forth between state law enforcement and the feds; Marsh had a real disdain for the Art Crimes desk. He saw Zack as a book-smart dilettante who'd spent more time at some elite university studying paintings than in the streets with the dirtbags who stole things and killed people, and thought that he had no business sticking his nose into real police work.

Zack's FBI training aside, Marsh hadn't been entirely wrong; Zack's classmates at Yale, where he'd gotten his PhD in art history, focusing on the European Impressionists, had been equally surprised when he'd applied for the opening in the FBI Art Crimes division. What neither Marsh nor his colleagues at Yale knew was that Zack had grown up around cops. His father and uncle had both walked beats in New Haven, Connecticut, where Zack had grown up. He was also well familiar with the sort of people Marsh put in handcuffs every day; his two favorite cousins had gone from stealing car radios in junior high school to stealing the cars themselves after their father, the beat cop, had died young of a heart attack, leaving the family struggling on a police officer's pension. Both were in jail now, but Zack had remained close to them, visiting them at the medium-security lockup they called home in Western Mass.

But it certainly hadn't helped matters with

Marsh when one of Zack's informants had quickly solved the case, pinning the Cartier theft on a local mobster. Nor did Zack and Marsh's relationship improve a year later, when Zack had solved a shoot-out robbery at an auction house in Marlborough, back-tracing the steps of one of the thieves, and eventually leading Marsh and his colleagues to the case's unsavory conclusion—the two hapless art thieves bleeding to death all over a Renoir.

Now, another year gone by, they were together again, flint and steel on the sixth floor of the Encore Boston Harbor. Zack had a feeling he wouldn't be mending his relationship with the ornery homicide detective anytime soon.

"Jimmy O'Leary," Zack said, nodding at the dead man in the chair. "He's a midlevel fence. Loosely connected with the Dominel family in Southie, but pretty much an independent businessman. Usually moves low-level product. Silver candlesticks stolen from someone's estate. A painting grabbed off a wall in some university dining hall. Once he tried to sell a Tiffany chandelier that fell off the back of a truck when they were renovating the old Four Seasons in the Back Bay."

"Jimmy the Lip," Marsh said. "Charming. You've got nice friends, Lindsy."

"More of an acquaintance. Hadn't heard from him in years. Then a couple of days ago, his name came up. Seems he had something to fence. Something that was way out of his usual league. He was asking around because his usual buyers couldn't handle something like that. Not even close. Some of the people he asked reached out to my office."

Marsh looked at him.

"They reached out to the FBI?"

"Because of the sizable reward."

Marsh's angry demeanor seemed to fade a bit, as he became genuinely interested.

"How sizable?"

"Ten million. Immunity from prosecution. That sizable."

Marsh whistled, and a couple of the nearby CSI rats looked up.

"That's a serious number. What kind of candlestick is worth ten million dollars?"

"Not a candlestick," Zack said. "Paintings. Eleven of them. And two other items. Stolen more than thirty years ago. March 18, 1990—"

"Don't tell me," Marsh said.

"Yep. The Gardner paintings."

CHAPTER NINE

Detective Marsh laughed out loud.

"The Gardner theft. It's like herpes. Flares up every couple of years. You feds get some hot tip from a phone line, or some drug dealer gets pinched and tries to talk his way into a lighter sentence by throwing up a bunch of bull about this guy he knows, who knows a guy, who knows a guy—when the hell are you going to give up on that pipe dream already?"

The truth was, Marsh wasn't wrong. The Gardner Museum theft remained the most famous unsolved art heist in history, the subject of countless theories, tips, investigations, and dead ends: On March 18, 1990, shortly after one in the morning, two men posing as police officers had talked their way into the small museum outside of Boston, tied up the two guards, and made off with eleven paintings—including *The Concert* by Vermeer, one of only thirty-four existing paintings by the Dutch Baroque master, and now perhaps the most valuable missing painting on earth. None of them had been recovered. On top of the Vermeer, the thieves took a number of Rembrandts, including *The Storm on the Sea of Galilee*, and others including works of Degas and Manet. In a strange twist, along with the eleven valuable works of art, the fake cops had also stolen two objects that seemed decidedly random: an ancient Chinese "gu," a vessel or vase used for liquids such as wine, and a bronze finial in the shape of an eagle that had once sat atop one of Napoleon Bonaparte's flags. Neither of these two items were particularly valuable, which made their addition to the looted works more mysterious. But the paintings themselves were worth hundreds of millions, if not more; recent assessments had put the value of the theft at over half a billion dollars, making it the biggest unsolved heist ever.

For many a federal agent over the past four decades, the Gardner paintings had been the investigative equivalent of Melville's white whale; so many leads had brought agents so close to solving the case that announcements had been drafted and discarded multiple times. Scenarios had abounded, involving Boston gangs rising all the way up to Whitey Bulger himself, the most famous mobster in local history. Many books and articles had followed trails both strong and obscure, eventually veering toward a plot involving a second-tier gangster named Bobby Donati, who might have hoped to use the paintings as leverage to get a colleague out of prison. Donati's gangland murder a year after the theft made it a difficult theory to prove, though the investigations surrounding a number of Donati's associates had kicked up many promising leads. And yet, for all the investigative efforts, the paintings, the finial, and the gu were still missing—and the $10 million reward the museum and the FBI had offered remained unclaimed.

When the calls had come in from one of Agent Zack Lindwell's contacts that Jimmy the Lip was inquiring about that reward, Zack had assumed it would be another dead end, like all the rest. In fact, he might not have even followed up, had Jimmy the

Lip not ended up strapped to a chair, with a hole in his forehead. Six hours ago, Zack could easily have written the calls off to fantasy, mere tall tales. But in the light of the early morning streaming in off the river, things looked a little different.

People didn't usually get shot in the head for making up stories about missing valuable art. And the bullet hole in Jimmy's head wasn't even the worst part of the crime scene.

"Two fingernails," Zack said, changing the subject as he drew Marsh's attention to the corpse's hand, still pinned to the chair by the dead man's belt. "Torn off clean. Probably with a plier. Someone was looking for information."

Marsh nodded. The expression on his face hadn't softened, but as much as he disliked Zack and the FBI, he did like solving cases. No doubt, Zack had already saved him time at the computer by identifying the corpse, and that was welcome; Marsh didn't seem like the type who was particularly adept with a keyboard.

"Security cameras put two people in the vicinity of the room, within spitting distance of the time he got whacked."

Marsh gestured toward one of the CSI guys, who brought over a pair of black-and-white photographs, culled from the security footage. Both photographs were from cameras at the end of the hallway, above the elevators. The first was of a man of indeterminate age, with narrow features and light brown hair. The guy's face had a weathered, tough look to it, and his build was tall and athletic, but there was a slight hunch to his shoulders. He had been caught in motion, and from the way he walked—confident but wary, arms loose enough that if he needed to move quickly he could—

Zack could tell he was no stranger to the worlds both Zack and the detective knew well. If Zack had to guess, the guy was a criminal, a cop, or a convict.

The second photo was a bit more of a surprise.

"Is that a tennis skirt?" Zack asked. The detective only shrugged.

The girl was pretty, probably late twenties, with streaked hair and too much jewelry on her fingers and throat. Her face was round, her cheeks flushed, even in black and white. She had also been caught moving down the hallway, but her gait was much faster, and she was looking back over her shoulder. No doubt, she was running from something.

"Yeah," Marsh said, noticing Zack's look. "Hotel security had chased her into the elevator on the gaming floor. Apparently, she's a card counter, made a bundle at a blackjack table and then booked it up to the sixth floor when they came after her to throw her out."

"They checked her ID at the table?"

"They did, but turns out it was a fake. Ran the name and picture, and they don't match anyone in the state. Hotel security looked back over the tape, say she's real good, had them completely fooled for most of the night. And this wasn't the first time she'd hit them. We're working on a real ID, but it's going to take time."

"And the guy?"

"Him, we know. Facial recognition software generated a match right away. A dirtbag named Nick Patterson, nine years at Shirley on a string of bank jobs all over Middlesex and Suffolk counties. Did his time quiet, out on parole just two weeks ago."

Zack turned back to the man's photo. No doubt, this was the more likely candidate for the killer. Like they always say, you hear hoofs, you don't look for zebras. Then again, it was the zebras that had always kept Zack up at night, not the horses. When he'd first studied the Gardner heist during his training at Quantico, it hadn't been the paintings that had caused him to lose sleep—the Vermeer, the Rembrandts. It had been those two other stolen items, the ones that didn't make any sense. The Chinese gu. The bronze eagle from Napoleon's flag. The gu, maybe that could be written off; it was really old and an easy grab, sitting right there on a shelf just inches from the Vermeer. But taking the eagle, that was work: The thieves had first tried to unscrew the entire flag from its frame, leaving half the screws undone. Then they had climbed halfway up the wall to unscrew the finial. It hadn't been easy, and it hadn't been quick. Why bother with it? You've got a Vermeer worth a hundred million, easy, and you stick around for a worthless bronze eagle?

"So, this Nick Patterson," Zack said. "He walks after nine years, heads to the Encore, and kills a small-time fence?"

"Tortures him first," Marsh said. Then he shrugged. "Who knows? Maybe they had some beef going back to before he got locked up. Or maybe he got wind that Jimmy the Lip was moving something valuable, came here to get a piece of it? How much was that reward again? Ten million? That's worth a couple of fingernails."

Zack didn't say anything. It seemed weak to him, that Patterson would have come here to question and kill a low-level fence. Jimmy the Lip was a middleman. He didn't steal things, he didn't hold on to things, he just moved them. A guy like Jimmy, you either sold to him, or you bought from him. You didn't kill him.

Still, it was possible—if Jimmy really did know something about the Gardner paintings, $10 million was a good incentive to try and get that information from him. There were plenty of people who would do some pretty horrible things for $10 million. Maybe Nick Patterson was one of them.

"You think whoever did this got what he was looking for?"

Zack shrugged.

"One thing is sure. Whoever came here last night knows a hell of a lot more than we do."

Marsh looked at him.

"How do you figure?"

Zack pointed to the dead man's hand.

"He only took two nails."

CHAPTER TEN

Hailey slid out of the back of the yellow cab onto the deserted sidewalk, the sea breeze from the harbor, just a hundred yards away, biting at her cheeks. She tried not to think about all the bad decisions that had led her to just that spot; if the past few hours were evidence of anything, it was confirmation of what she'd learned at twelve, when, a runaway with little to her name except a genius for numbers, she'd first set out on her own: *Bad decisions compound, like interest.*

She watched Nick Patterson come out of the taxi on the other side and pay the driver from a roll of twenties he'd pulled out of his jean jacket. Case in point, her decision to follow this ex-con to an alley lined with warehouses, so deep in South Boston she might as well have been in Dublin. Nick Patterson was one compounded lifetime of bad decisions in work boots and denim, the kind of guy she'd learned a long time ago to stay away from. Apart from math, her greatest skill was her ability to read people. Usually, she could read a face as quickly as she could game a blackjack felt, and she'd been reading Nick Patterson since they'd left the casino four hours ago.

He didn't seem dangerous or violent, but he was certainly a thief. He didn't appear sophisticated enough to be a con artist, and he'd seemed sufficiently disturbed by the dead fence in the hotel room to convince her he'd had nothing to do with the murder. But it was also clear that he was *involved*, and by following him out of the hotel and to this alley in Southie, she'd allowed herself to also get involved—something that went against every instinct she'd developed over the past sixteen years. All because of a photograph of a painting she'd never seen before, and the excited claims of a thief she'd just met.

She watched as Nick came up next to her and nodded toward the boxy, four-story building directly in front of them. The windows didn't start until the second floor, most were boarded over, and the walls were covered in graffiti, the slurs and gang tags worn down by the constant lick of harbor air. Hailey hadn't realized there were still forgotten buildings so close to the seaport, which had transformed in recent years from the kind of place you might safely stash stolen art to a bustling, overcrowded playground for entrepreneurs and twenty-somethings, bristling with outdoor restaurants, dance clubs, movie theaters, and posh hotels. No doubt, at the stroke of midnight some well-heeled developer would wave a magic wand, and this boarded-up building, too, would transform into a lab or a coworking space or a Cheesecake Factory or a P.F. Chang's.

"This is the place," Nick said. "Things might get a little dicey. The plan wasn't to show up empty-handed."

The plan. Nick had gone over the rough details in the cab ride from the casino to the all-night diner where they'd spent the last few hours waiting for daylight, and Hailey still wondered why she hadn't told the driver to pull over and dump her out right into the Ted Williams Tunnel. *Bad decisions piling up, like a chain-reaction crash on the expressway.* Hell, chancing her way on foot through the 3:00 a.m. traffic in the tunnel seemed more logical than the story Nick had been spinning. But still, she'd kept on reading that narrow, hardened face, those deep-set eyes. There was no doubt, as crazy as the story got, Nick believed every bit of it. The guy was a thief, but he was also sincere.

The photo in his jean jacket was of a stolen painting, part of a stash worth maybe a billion dollars. Though the theft had taken place thirty years ago, the paintings had finally surfaced, and were now sitting in this warehouse in South Boston, in the hands of some associates of the redheaded kid Nick had met in prison. Nick had taken over the kid's role in the scheme and had arranged to move the paintings through a fence, who was either planning to sell them himself, or turn them in for the reward—$10 million—and give Nick a hefty cut. But now the fence was dead, tortured and murdered in that hotel room.

"The guys holding the paintings," Hailey said. "They're connected to the original crime? The Gardner heist?"

Hailey hadn't recognized the painting in the photo when Nick had first shown it to her in the stairwell, but she'd definitely heard of the famous heist. She'd been rough on the details, but Nick had filled her in on the rest at the diner, while she'd picked at a stack of pancakes. Despite his rough exterior, Nick wasn't stupid, and he'd obviously done some deep digging while he was still locked up. The Vermeer and the rest were incredibly valuable, but they were also extremely recognizable, which made them almost impossible to sell. Probably why they'd remained hidden for so long, though Nick had his own theory. Apparently, the guy who most investigators had pinned the heist on—a brash mobster named Bobby Donati—had been murdered a year after the theft. Beaten, stabbed twenty times, throat cut, then shoved in the trunk of his Cadillac, which was left parked on a street in Revere. Nick's theory was that it had been a mercenary operation; Donati had been paid by someone to rob the museum of some particular works of art, and not always the most valuable. Then he'd hidden the stash, and either died before he'd been able to turn it over to whomever had hired him, or had died because he'd been *unwilling* to turn it over.

Either way, according to Nick, those paintings had remained hidden in various basements and safe houses in Boston for three decades.

"In a matter of speaking," Nick said, responding to Hailey's question as they headed up the path toward the warehouse. "According to my notebook, my redheaded friend had been clued in to the stash by the daughter of one of Donati's associates. Gail Gustiano—her father, Richie Gustiano, supposedly had had something to do with the theft, might even have been involved. Gail was too afraid to try to move the paintings herself. Red had promised he'd keep her at arm's length, and that he and his buddies—a couple of Southie hoods—had the necessary connections to move the paintings."

"And now you're along for the ride."

"*We're* along for the ride," Nick corrected. "I stepped into the easiest part in the play. The go-between; show the proof of the stash to the fence, get the down payment. Everything looks good, I bring Jimmy the paintings, and then I contact Gail and deliver her cut. She keeps her hands and identity clean, and everyone leaves happy. Or so it was supposed to go."

"There wasn't pushback when you took over for the redheaded kid?"

Nick shrugged.

"Everyone in this is here for the same reason: to get paid."

Hailey paused, letting him get a few steps ahead on the path. The door to the warehouse looked as daunting as the building itself; heavy and metal, with a peephole slot halfway up that could be opened from the inside. There was still time to get away from this; to walk away and forget that she'd ever met this ex-con or seen a Polaroid of that stolen painting. She still had that small fortune in Encore chips in her purse, which her roommate could change in for her, and even if her face was on a surveillance tape at the casino, it wasn't a sure thing they'd connect her to the murder. The cops were probably already scouring the city for Nick, a guy with a prison record who had actually been in contact with the murder victim.

Only Hailey knew that he was innocent of the murder. Not *innocent*, of course, but he hadn't killed Jimmy the Lip, and for that, she was indeed his alibi. But she wasn't going to pretend she had followed Nick to South Boston to keep him from a murder rap. At the diner, they'd come to an agreement; once they'd retrieved the paintings, they'd find a way to return them for that reward. Nick and his associates would get the lion's share, but there would be enough left over to keep her off the blackjack tables for many years. Nick was right; she, like all the rest, was there to get paid.

"Circle of life," she said, then followed him the rest of the way to the door.

Nick didn't respond, because he'd gotten there first. His body had gone strangely stiff, which made

Hailey's chest tight. When she got next to him, she saw what he was looking at—three bullet holes in the rusted locking mechanism; the metal closest to the door's frame had buckled inward, where it appeared that someone had pushed their way in, hard and fast.

"This doesn't look good," Nick whispered.

He glanced behind them; the alley seemed deserted, and save for the odd seagull, devoid of motion.

"What do we do?" Hailey whispered back, fear rising inside of her.

"The smart thing to do would be to get the hell out of here," Nick responded.

Instead, he set his jaw, pushed the door open, and headed inside.

Bad decisions, compounded.

Hailey took a deep breath and followed.

CHAPTER ELEVEN

At first the vast, open room was shrouded in darkness, save for the cone of light streaming in from the open doorway. She could make out a concrete floor and ridiculously high ceilings; what she'd thought was a four-story building from outside was actually one big open warehouse, with metal catwalks ringing the upper levels all the way to the unfinished, beam-marked ceiling. Huge shipping crates lined the walls to her right and left, stacked by machines that sat dormant in the shadows; she could see the frame of a forklift on one side of the room, and some sort of wheeled ladder contraption in the far corner, rising up almost to the ceiling.

But when Nick finally found a light switch on the wall close to where they'd entered, Hailey's attention was immediately drawn to the center of the room. First, because the crates were hard to ignore. A half dozen of them, wooden, lined up next to each other on the concrete floor. The crates were all open, and as she followed Nick deeper into the warehouse, she could see that at least the closest few were empty. Next to the nearest crate was a crowbar, and the shattered remains of one of the crates' lids. And next to the crowbar—

"Is that a shotgun?" Hailey asked.

She'd never seen a shotgun before, not in real life. You didn't see many guns at MIT. And even after she'd run away at twelve, old enough looking to pass for sixteen, even older looking when it was dark, and was living mostly in cheap motels by way of the fake ID and what money she could make at odd jobs, she'd managed to avoid the sort of people who knew a .22 from a .38. Guys like Nick, who was already kicking at the shotgun with the tip of his boot, looking it over carefully.

"Still loaded. They didn't even get a shot off."

And then she followed his gaze to the two men lying on the floor behind the last crate, right up next to each other. The strange thing was, they looked almost peaceful, side by side, arms stiff as boards. As Hailey took another step forward, she realized that everything about them was *stiff*—not just the arms, but their entire bodies, rigid and stiff like human statues. Both of their faces looked young, and so similar they could have been brothers. One had blondish hair swept back by too much gel and the other had more of a buzz cut, but their eyes were the same, blue and wide-open, frozen in place. The same as the mouths, open lips caught somewhere between a shout and a scream.

"They look paralyzed," she whispered, stating the obvious.

Nick went down on one knee to check their pulses. Then he shook his head.

"This happened fast. Someone, or a lot of some-ones, came in through the door, disarmed the twins, did something awful to them."

"But why kill them like this?"

Nick thought for a minute, still looking over the empty crates.

"Fingernails," he said, simply.

Then he rubbed a hand over his eyes.

"Jimmy the Lip worked with every two-bit criminal in every zip code within twenty miles of the Boston Harbor; he must have had some guesses as to where the twins might hide a stash like this. Not a surprise, he had enough connections in this part of town to know every seagull by the patterns of crap they leave on the sidewalk. Whoever took his fingernails found out about the warehouse from Jimmy and got a little more creative with the twins here."

"The paintings weren't enough?" Hailey asked. "What more were they looking for? Why not just take the paintings and go?"

"Whoever did this is a professional, and professionals don't leave loose ends behind. But a bullet to the skull is way easier than whatever this is."

Without another word or another look at the bodies on the floor, Nick suddenly started back the way they'd come, toward the alley. Hailey watched him—but didn't follow. She knew she should have been a step ahead of him. Working over a casino was one thing; card counting had put her in dangerous situations numerous times over the years, from confrontations with security guards who took their jobs too seriously, to late-night encounters with the sort of people who hung around casinos after 2:00 a.m. But she'd always managed to get away before things got rough.

But this—was well beyond rough. She'd seen three dead bodies in the space of a night. And yet she was still planted in place. Nick was a few feet from the door when he finally noticed she wasn't with him and gave her a look.

"The paintings are gone. This is over."

"Maybe," Hailey found herself saying. "Probably. But you don't know that for sure. These paintings are worth millions, right? If even one of them wasn't in those crates—"

"Didn't you hear me?" Nick hissed. "Professionals like this don't leave loose ends. And the two of us— we're the mother of all loose ends right now. Whoever did this could be down the street watching."

Hailey nodded.

"All the more reason to stay put until we figure this out."

"There's nothing to figure out. Someone tortured Jimmy the Lip, then came here and did worse to the twins."

"But the trail doesn't end with them," Hailey said.

Nick paused, still close to the door.

"You mean Gail."

"You said you stepped into the role of the 'go-between.' Did the twins know how to reach her?"

Nick shook his head.

"Which means," Hailey continued, thinking it through, "they couldn't have told whoever did this where to find her. These crates held paintings— maybe all of them—but maybe not. Even one of those paintings could be worth a fortune."

Nick paused in the doorway. He looked back at the rigid bodies.

"You think Gail's going to hand them over to us? After this?"

"You think she's going to want to keep them. After this?"

Now Nick was thinking, too. Then he reached into his pocket and pulled out his cell phone.

The woman was short, heavy-set, with a mop of curly hair and square features, and she'd barely made it two steps into the warehouse before her face dropped and her skin went pale. Before she could back out the door, Nick was already talking, fast, filling in the details he'd neglected to add during the short call he'd made to get her there in the first place.

"Gail, I'm sorry you had to see this, but I couldn't exactly tell you on the phone. Jimmy's dead, the twins are dead, and whatever paintings were here are gone."

Gail looked like she'd just been hit by a shovel. Her wide-set eyes were like saucers above her boxy jaw. Her shoulders were slumped—but Hailey couldn't tell if that was a natural state, or had more to do with the two bodies in the warehouse. The woman was clearly upset. But the way she was now glancing at the open crates made Hailey think her sadness also carried a healthy component of self-interest.

Then Gail looked at Nick. "The down payment?"

Nick shook his head.

The woman's shoulders slumped even farther. Hailey could imagine what she was thinking. All that stolen art, bouncing around South Boston for three decades, lost, almost forgotten. And now lost again.

"Cursed," Gail finally grunted. "Those damn things are cursed."

"It's a lot of money," Nick said. He seemed strangely resigned. "There's nothing mystical about it. People die when there's lots of money at stake. You know how they say some businesses are too big to fail? Well, some things are too big to steal."

Gail shook her head.

"That's the crazy thing about all of this," she said. "Bobby wasn't even supposed to take those goddamn paintings. He was no good at following orders. Probably why he ended up in the trunk of his car."

Gail turned and headed for the door. Nick called after her.

"Gail, wait. What do you mean, he wasn't supposed to take the paintings?"

Hailey was still digesting what the woman was saying. Bobby was the gangster who had supposedly robbed the Gardner. Gail's father was his partner. *Following orders?* Then he really hadn't planned the heist himself?

Gail reached the open door, then waved at Nick and Hailey to catch up to her.

"Bobby was hired to rob the museum. But he wasn't being paid to steal paintings. It was something else they wanted. Bobby had gone over and over it with my dad, because it had never made any sense. The thing they wanted—it was pretty much worthless. So, Bobby, with all that priceless art around him, had taken his own initiative. He'd turned a little B&E for hire that might have gone pretty much unnoticed, maybe a police report growing cobwebs in some filing cabinet somewhere, into the robbery of the century."

They exited the warehouse, back into the bright morning light. Hailey looked past the woman and saw a car parked at the curb. A Buick, at least ten years old, that needed a good wash and a new set of tires. The woman was heading for the trunk, her keys already in her hands. Hailey knew that she shouldn't have still been following, that the bodies were now compounding as fast as the bad decisions, but she couldn't turn away. It wasn't just the money anymore, it was the criminal *equation*, *the puzzle* that kept getting more complex, adding more variables, twisting and turning as the story evolved. It was baffling and irresistible.

That was the thing about Hailey and equations—she couldn't walk away until they were solved.

"Whoever had hired Bobby—my dad called them 'serious people,' and he'd only used that term when he'd really meant it, hadn't been happy about what Bobby had done. They didn't like the attention. The thing was, they'd also hired Bobby for a second job, another robbery. Something connected to the first. But that second job never happened, because instead Bobby ended up in the trunk of his car."

The woman smirked at that, because she'd arrived at the trunk of her own car. She put her keys in the lock, then looked at Nick and Hailey.

"No," she said. "Bobby wasn't hired to steal those paintings. He was hired to steal something else. Something that's pretty much worthless, in comparison. So worthless, I didn't even include it in the deal."

With that, she yanked open the trunk.

Hailey took a full beat to understand what she was looking at.

"That's—" she started, but the woman cut her off.

"Yeah. And you can have it. I don't want anything to do with it anymore."

Gail shook her head, her curly hair bouncing in the harbor breeze.

"Because everyone involved with that damn thing seems to end up dead."

CHAPTER TWELVE

"A little clichéd, Patricia," the man with the thinning blond hair and the delicate features said, as he made a show of wiping down the wooden bench with a monogrammed handkerchief. "But at least the view is nice."

He put the handkerchief back into the front pocket of his tailored, European-slim electric-blue suit, and settled himself onto the bench. He waved a manicured hand toward the placid pond in front of them, his fingernails filed and polished to the color and consistency of tempered glass.

"And very romantic. I should have suspected you would have chosen such a location, considering your training. But, of course, we need to keep this professional. This is far from a social call."

In that, the slight man was correct. In everything else, he was dead wrong. Although a park bench in the middle of Boston's Public Garden might seem an unlikely place for a clandestine meeting between two highly trained operatives in a dark, criminal trade, it was also the most logical setting. Cafés, restaurants, and bars were difficult environments to secure, and the possibility of surveillance high. A hotel room was out of the question; if things went wrong, there needed to be more than one exit, and hotels meant cameras, which necessitated disguises, which were both time-consuming and annoying. Which left the outdoors. And what could be more natural and unremarkable than a man and woman sitting together on a park bench by the pond in the middle of the Public Garden, watching the beautiful swans peck at each other just a few yards away.

"Not a social call at all," the man continued, folding his hands together on his lap. He was still staring straight ahead—perhaps actually looking at the swans. They were magnificent creatures, to be fair, even sitting quietly, pruning each other at the water's edge. A pair of them, white as snow, with wingspans of almost seven feet, proud necks rising and falling as they worked their daggerlike beaks.

"We are here, Patricia," he continued, "because the Family is concerned. I don't have to tell you; things are not going as planned."

Another thing he got wrong—her name wasn't actually Patricia, though it was a close enough approximation that she didn't feel the need to correct him. But he knew that as well. She was not deceived by his appearance, any more than he was by hers. Beneath the tailored suit his body appeared narrow and long, but she could see what others might miss; the tight cords of muscles running up his thighs and forearms. Everything he did was physically precise, because his body had been toned and trained to act with physical precision. His blond hair was thinning, yes, but because it had been dyed and pruned and changed so many times it was impossible to know its true color and form. His features were delicate, but most of them were not the features he had been born with. He had changed his face almost as many times as his hair. Even now, she could see the hint of foundation on his cheeks and forehead.

Nothing was as it seemed in their world.

"I'm a bit surprised," she finally responded. "Usually, Mr. Arthur conducts these meetings in person. Sending you seems a bit...extreme."

The man smiled. The name he had given her on the phone was Curt, even though it was every bit as approximate as Patricia.

"You're surprised. Really. After the disastrous failures of the past twelve hours."

Patricia winced, only partly because it was a fair assessment of what had transpired. Incredible, that it had only been twelve hours since she had been called into such furious action, after years of methodological investigative work and general spy craft on behalf of a massively rich boss she knew only by his first name who was brutally intolerant of failure. Even after a lifetime of training, her body was feeling the toll of the three consecutive missions. At thirty-seven, she was still in peak physical condition, but age had its limitations. When she'd first finished her "education" as an operative at the age of fifteen, she'd been able to conduct similar missions for days on end.

"The trunk has been located. It won't be a problem again. And I've put the paintings on the cargo ship," she said, straightening a line in her knee-length skirt.

It was the third outfit she'd worn in the past day. At the casino, she'd needed to blend in; a maid's uniform she'd lifted from the laundry room in the basement of the Encore had worked well, even though it had been a size too large. She could have subdued the out-of-shape fence in a straitjacket and handcuffs, if she'd needed to. The young men in the warehouse had been more of a challenge. She'd worn an athletic jumpsuit and body armor, even though there had never been much of a chance of the low-level criminals getting a shot off. She doubted either of them had ever used that shotgun other than for intimidation; they had been totally unprepared for what had hit them.

The same could be said for Charles Walker. The leather skirt and high heels she'd chosen for that job had been even more efficient weaponry than a shotgun. The high heels, she was still wearing, but the skirt was back in her hotel. If this meeting went south, that skirt would have no effect on a man like Curt. But the heels still had their uses.

"Mr. Arthur doesn't care about the paintings," Curt said. "The Family hasn't waited thirty years for a bunch of paintings."

Amazing, how easily Curt could dismiss a half a billion dollars in stolen art. But Patricia knew that, in this instance, Curt wasn't speaking for himself. The two were of a breed. Hired guns. For more than a decade, she had been drawing a paycheck from the Family, and it had all come to a head in the past twelve hours. So many starts and stops over the years, and finally, she had gotten so close.

First, the fence. It wasn't the first time one of the many sources involved in the business of "moving" contraband art she had been monitoring—via phone taps, email worms, paid informants—had begun making noises about the reward; after all, the Gardner theft was one of the most famous heists in history, and nearly every middleman, pawnshop owner, and low-level art thief in the Northeast had taken a stab at retrieving the missing stash at one time or another— all ending in various degrees of failure. So as usual, she had been skeptical; but a little digging had allowed her to put enough together to excite the Family—

after so many years, the object Mr. Arthur so coveted finally, actually, did appear to have been on the verge of surfacing. But in the warehouse, she'd been dismayed when she'd opened those crates. A half billion in paintings, nothing more.

And then, poor Professor Charles. As the Family had instructed, she had been monitoring him for months, along with a handful of his academic colleagues, for any signs that anyone had stumbled into the Family's *business*. She had been shocked to see his recent paper posted on the Reddit board he'd created. It had been easy work excising the attachment before any of his colleagues might have seen it, and even easier work gaining access to his home, computer, and bed. If she'd moved any slower, and he'd have published that paper, there was no telling what his discovery might have led to, and how the Family might have reacted. The image he'd uncovered from within John Hancock's trunk might not have been enough, alone, to inspire the sort of connective thinking that might threaten the Family's grand plan.

"Maybe so," she finally responded, now also watching the two swans. "But the paintings and the professor... There are so many threads, but the knot is beginning to unravel. It won't be long now."

It was the slightest thing, the quietly threatening way Curt shifted against the bench, one of those manicured hands drifting close enough to the material of her skirt to make her shiver. But then Patricia's training kicked in and the muscles of her body coiled, a spring pulling tight. Her mind was instinctively shifting through options. The .22 hidden in the sleeve of her blouse. Small caliber, but at close range it would do the job. The heels, of course; a two-inch blade waiting in the toe of the left, and the spring-loaded syringe of paralytic concealed in the right, along with a second syringe containing the antidote, which she'd yet to employ. The twisted bands tying her long, sable hair into a ponytail; within the material of each twist, a coil of razor wire. And there were always her hands. She couldn't be certain she could take Curt in hand-to-hand combat, but she was willing to put her training against any in the world. Curt might have spent years perfecting himself into a living weapon, on offer to the highest bidder. But Patricia had been quite literally *born* for this.

"The Family won't accept more failure, Patricia."

Patricia wasn't her name, because she didn't have a name. She had a number. *Пятьдесят*. The transliteration, "Pyats-dess-yat," was very close to Patricia. But it had never been intended as a name. She was merely the fiftieth girl born in that dormitory on the banks of the Irkut River. Of those fifty, fewer than thirty were still alive fifteen years later, when General Yakov, formerly of the FSB and before that the KGB, had been forced to close down his training facility. She would always remember the "graduation" ceremony, Yakov standing in front of his "children," bemoaning the fate of the fallen Soviet experiment, the disaster that was Yeltsin's Russia.

We are all mercenaries now, Yakov had told his *ласточки*—"swallows," the name given to the participants in the program that had begun in the 1920s, under Stalin, which had first repurposed Bolshoi dancers and movie actresses, before Yakov had the idea in the eighties of breeding his own. *Swallows*, girls, now women—trained in techniques that in the end were not so disparate: The strategies to make a man's heart beat faster were not so very different than the tactics involved in stopping it from beating altogether. *Distract, disarm, find a weakness to infiltrate and exploit, strike quickly and with great precision.* That training applied whether you were trying to make a man fall in love with you or break his neck.

Patricia forced her muscles to uncoil, as she saw that Curt likewise relaxed against the bench next to her. At the moment, at least, he was not there to replace her, or kill her.

"No more delays, Patricia. Do whatever you need to do to cut those threads and untie that knot."

перерезать эту нить. "Cut the threads." Another of Yakov's favorite teachings. Poor Professor Charles, the fence in the hotel room, the brothers in the warehouse. That left only two remaining threads. She considered showing Curt the photos she had on her phone, which she'd taken from the surveillance cameras at the casino. *The unidentified young woman, and the ex-con.* Patricia had already made inroads into finding them—an inside track, of a sort, on an investigation already in motion. Once she found them, she believed, she would be on her way to accomplishing her mission, but Curt didn't need to know any of this, because Curt was just like her. A mercenary. Nothing more.

"They have names," she said, quietly, not a hint of her Russian accent showing through. "The swans. They come back every year, right to this spot. They call them Romeo and Juliet."

Curt raised an eyebrow.

"That makes this spot even more romantic. If, again, clichéd."

"It turns out that they're both female," Patricia continued. "They're quite beautiful. But they can also be vicious. Dangerous, even."

"So I've heard. The beaks—"

"You would think so, of course, but it's not the beaks you need to watch out for. It's their wings. Beneath the beautiful plumage, the elbow joints. Strong and sharp; it's rumored that they can break a man's arm with one flick of those wings."

She turned, gave Curt a long look.

"There will be no more failures. No more loose threads."

She didn't wait for him to respond. Without another word, she rose and headed off through the park, away from the bench, the mercenary, and the swans.

CHAPTER THIRTEEN

Adrian Jensen muttered angrily to himself as he worked the combination wheel on his bike lock, pinning the lightweight, ridiculously expensive carbon frame of his cycle to the aluminum signpost jutting up above one of the most highly trafficked corners in downtown Boston. Not cursing, exactly; Adrian was too aware of the constant stream of morning foot traffic coursing by him, like a river parting around a jagged stone. But he was stammering and gabbling under his breath: a steady torrent of verbal self-affliction that had run continuously and unimpeded for the six-mile ride from his office at East Hall, 6 The Green, smack-dab in the center of the Tufts campus.

He was still talking to himself, in fact, as he removed his bike helmet—and as usual, and in dramatic fashion, once again brandished his reddish-gold hair—then hooked the helmet to the bottom of his heavy backpack. The backpack was still slung over his left shoulder, the strap digging into the thin material of yet another of his many tight cycling jerseys. This time, the jersey matched his pants, which hugged his oversized calves and thighs like a wet suit, or if you hated the look, like an oil spill on a drowning bird.

In the bright light of day, Adrian was fully aware of the image he projected, from the cycling clothes to his tanned and Nautilus-shaped form, to the ringlets and waves of that expertly coiffed hair. He knew that many of his students, and a fair portion of the other professors at Tufts—not just in the department of history but throughout the humanities—often used terms like "dandy" when they thought he was out of earshot; but other people's opinions had never bothered him. Perhaps it was his severe upbringing at the hands of his scientist parents, but he'd never had patience for the opinions of fools or rivals; in fact, the only thing he disliked more than unsolicited opinions were flights of intellectual fancy.

Which explained his current mood, as he stared up at the Georgian facade of the mostly granite building that took up much of the block, where School and Tremont streets meet. To be sure, King's Chapel, the oldest continuously used religious site in Boston and one of the oldest churches in America, was familiar to Adrian, a place he'd visited many times. As a scholar who'd dedicated much of his adult life to eighteenth-century American history, it would have been impossible for him to avoid such a high-profile location, favored by a multitude of Revolutionary War figures, many of whom were entombed in the building's catacombs, or buried in the plot of land directly adjacent to it; those heroes that were not on the grounds of the church were interred right across the street, in the Granary Burying Ground, even more popular with tourists and history buffs. But on this particular afternoon, Adrian could think of a dozen places he'd rather be than in this grand, old church.

In two hours, he was supposed to be giving a lecture to an auditorium full of freshmen about Paul Revere's role in the Boston Tea Party, one of the most famous—and much misunderstood—episodes of the

Revolutionary period. Adrian didn't enjoy lecturing freshmen; he didn't really like undergraduates as a breed and was much happier lodged in his office or in one of the university's many libraries, working on his research projects. But even standing in front of a crowded hall filled with bored, core requirement–obsessed teenagers who'd chosen a course on the Revolution because they'd thought they'd be hearing about musket battles and cannonballs, instead of taxation issues and harbor-docking rights, was preferable to his current absurd adventure—a mission necessitated by the fanciful speculations of an academic competitor.

Adrian shivered with disgust as he reached into the backpack and withdrew the bulging sheaf of papers in a manila envelope, in much the same state as he'd found the damn thing, in the mailbox in his office that very morning. "Absurd" was the right word for it; when he'd first opened the envelope and read the cover title, he'd nearly tossed the entire thing into the nearest receptacle:

THE MOST AMAZING PAUL REVERE
DISCOVERY IN HISTORY

Adrian shook his head at the audacity of such a title; but the subject line paled in comparison to the audacity of Charles Walker's thesis. Amazingly, Charles had not been exaggerating in the tavern—his paper was incredible—and *absurd*—and *insane*. The only thing that had kept Adrian from mulching it immediately were the exhibits attached at the end. Because once Adrian had finally gotten through all those pages of fantasy, speculation, nay, science fiction, he'd finally made his way to the attachments. Charles's discoveries, his *evidence*. And to be fair, as absurd as the entire project appeared, those discoveries, well, they weren't simply absurd.

They were maddening. And worse—maybe true.

Adrian's gaze shifted from the envelope back to King's Chapel. First to the columns, because they were impossible to ignore. Then higher, to the rectangle of stone with the arched Palladian windows, rising above the congested midday traffic. No steeple—the original builders had hoped for one, had even drawn up plans, but a financial squeeze had left them with just enough for the granite "tower." Dreams, as they often were, overmatched by reality.

Adrian's attention moved back to the envelope in his hands.

Maddening. Because it appeared Charles's fever dreams, in this instance, had somehow *overcome* reality.

Adrian shook his head, that mane of ringlets flashing in the sun. He and Charles had never had anything close to a good relationship. Given the differences in their personalities, they could never even agree to disagree about the arcane details of their shared intellectual focus. Even before this new, wild thesis, Charles had always been drawn to the fanciful and the fantastic. Adrian had often suggested the buffoon should have found his way to Hollywood, rather than the hallowed halls of Harvard. Leave it to the masses to picture Paul Revere as a swaggering, near mythical character; as a scholar, Adrian had always believed his duty was to reveal Revere as the man he really was— a slightly pathetic warrior, but a brilliant metallurgist, engraver, and technologist. In Revere's own words, a mechanic.

Charles Walker had always believed there was more to the man. And when they argued, his response had always been the same: Boston was big enough for two eminent experts on Paul Revere, no matter how disparate their scholarship. Adrian could spend his days in the diligent pursuit of the mundane details of Revere's life, while Charles would focus on the dramatic secrets he believed were hidden *beneath* those details.

In other words, Adrian would pursue actual academic work, while Charles would chase his flights of fancy. And up until those exhibits attached to the end of this wild paper, that's what Charles had done, in Adrian's view. Spun fantasy, wild theories, and yet…

Feeling savage with anger—and, yes, jealousy—Adrian tore open the envelope and dug into the papers, retrieving the final page. As he did so, something that had been paper-clipped to the inside of the envelope fell out, landing on the sidewalk between his feet. With an annoyed grunt, Adrian scooped it back up, barely giving it a glance. Of course, he'd recognized the object when he'd first seen it back at his mailbox: one of the coasters from the Warren Tavern, with the image of the Bunker Hill Monument on one side. He hadn't given it much thought when he'd first seen it, and even less thought now—because once he'd shoved it into his pocket, his attention was captured again by that last exhibit at the end of Charles's paper: a printed image, incredibly detailed, that was actually a photograph of an original Revere engraving. An engraving that Adrian was quite sure had never been published, or even seen, anywhere before.

Incredible. And paired with the second exhibit—the photo that Charles had included in the paper itself, from Hancock's trunk, even more than incredible.

Awe-inspiring.

What Charles had discovered within the walls of John Hancock's trunk would have been enough, alone, to set Adrian's entire profession on fire. Adrian himself had found it so compelling that he'd spent much of the morning trying to arrange his own radiological study of the trunk—to no avail. It turned out the donor who had loaned the trunk to the Worcester museum had unexpectedly sold the trunk that very morning to a private collector with very deep pockets. Though the trunk would remain on loan to the museum, the new owner had insisted on retrieving it for a period of assessment and repairs. A new radiological study would have to wait.

So Adrian had been forced to do what he'd hoped to avoid; he'd called Charles's office, hoping to see Charles's radiological evidence in person. And that's when he'd been told the terrible news.

The coroner's office hadn't yet determined if it was a heart attack or a stroke that had left Charles dead on the floor of his office earlier that morning. Judging from the man's appearance—and his breath—when he'd accosted Adrian at the Warren Tavern the night before, it was obvious the poor fool had overdone it. Now he was gone, his paper unpublished, and Adrian was left with a quandary. He'd never agreed with Charles in life, but in death, as much as he tried, he found he couldn't simply dismiss what the man had uncovered.

He stared down at the image in his hands. Like the picture Charles had included in his paper, from Hancock's trunk, this second image was of an engraving, presumably one of Revere's. Adrian was certain this engraving had never been seen before, and he also was fairly certain he knew where it was from.

Revere's time capsule. Of course, the time capsule

itself was well known, even outside of academic circles. Buried by Paul Revere and Samuel Adams in the cornerstone of the Massachusetts State House in 1795, the capsule had first been opened in 1855, cleaned and documented, and then reburied. But in 2015, a much more public "opening" had taken place, in the Art of the Americas Wing of the Boston Museum of Fine Arts. In front of the governor and multiple television cameras, the museum's curator had revealed the contents of the capsule and sent them for study, gathering together a group of experts to go over each item. Most of the contents of the capsule had been much what one would have expected: newspapers of the era, in fairly good condition. Twenty-three coins of varying denominations. One of George Washington's medals, a Seal of the Commonwealth, a title page from the Colony records. And then a final item—a silver plate, hand engraved by Paul Revere.

Although the plate seemed, of itself, unexceptional—the words engraved on it simply indicated that the cornerstone had been laid by Samuel Adams, then governor of the commonwealth—the museum had sent out a call to local Revere experts, and Charles Walker's Harvard pedigree had placed him at the front of the line.

For the first few months after the capsule had been opened, Charles had spoken of nothing else but that silver plate. And then, strangely, he'd gone silent about it and had never even mentioned it in passing, not once. Now, Adrian understood. Because he was certain that the picture in his hands was of that same plate—except it had been cut in two, sliced lengthwise, opened like the pages of a book. Adrian had no idea how Charles could have gotten permission to do such a thing; no doubt, he'd done it in secret. But that didn't matter now, not only because Charles was dead but because inside the silver plate, he'd found a *second* engraving. And the import of this engraving far eclipsed the first.

Not words, this time, but an image. Adrian could easily identify the man pictured in the engraving: Paul Revere, as he would have appeared near the end of his life. In front of Revere, across what appeared to be the floor of a workshop or metal factory, sat a dozen wineglasses, in a perfect row. Each of the wineglasses appeared to be filled halfway with liquid. And at the very edge of the engraving, beyond the last glass, sat a large bell. Vibration patterns had been carved around the bell—clearly meant to symbolize that the bell was ringing. And Revere, at the other end of the line of wineglasses, was just as clearly making notations. Looking closer, Adrian could see that beneath each glass, Revere had etched a number. And beneath it all—Revere, the glasses, the bell—appeared a date.

A date that didn't make any sense.

1814

Adrian knew, the time capsule had originally been buried in the cornerstone of the State House in 1795. It hadn't been reopened until 1855, and then reburied until modern times. The date on this engraving implied that sometime after 1795, but before Revere's death in 1818, he had surreptitiously replaced the original silver plate with a second plate, containing this bizarre self-portrait. Not impossible—in fact, Revere, as the top metallurgist and mechanic of his time, and the only person in the Americas who had figured out the art of working with copper sheeting—had been commissioned to replate the State House's dome as late as 1803, and would have had easy access to the cornerstone. But the question remained—why? What did this engraving mean? And what was so important about the picture—the wineglasses, that bell, the numerical notations—that Revere would have wanted it so artfully hidden and preserved?

Adrian shook his head again, jammed the picture back into the manila envelope, and the envelope into his backpack. He slung the pack over his shoulder, then turned his focus on the church. Even if Charles hadn't just died on the floor of his office, this was a mystery Adrian would have felt obligated to pursue. There was meaning, a secret, behind that engraving, and Adrian was one of the very few people with the knowledge to figure it out. It was that that had led him here, to King's Chapel. That knowledge and that date: 1814.

One last mutter to himself—this time, something approaching a curse—and Adrian joined the stream of tourists heading toward the church's front door.

CHAPTER FOURTEEN

Adrian found himself transported backward two hundred and fifty years the moment he stepped through the doorway of King's Chapel. He quickly worked his way by the enclosed pews—wooden booths containing red-cushioned benches and walls, separated from the aisle by hinged doors—heading toward the front of the prayer hall, which was well-lit by arched windows and a magnificent central chandelier. The tourists around Adrian seemed most excited by the pews; in the Revolutionary era, wealthy families would purchase the enclosed real estate, passing the velvety cubicles down from generation to generation. But Adrian's focus remained elsewhere. Not on the raised minister's perch, or the massive C. B. Fisk organ that took up the back balcony—King's Chapel's sixth, installed in the mid-sixties. Adrian hadn't come to the church for religion or music; he was there searching for answers.

It took him more time than he would have liked to navigate past the tourists and families milling in the aisles, but eventually he arrived at his destination, the roped-off entrance to the stone stairwell leading up to the church's bell room. The man standing on the other side of the velvet rope acknowledged Adrian with little more than a nod. The man's first name was Bevil, and that was one of two important things Adrian knew about him, other than that he was one of the half dozen caretakers of the church's grounds. They'd met twice before on previous visits; it was during the second of these, when Adrian had wanted a private tour of the vast catacombs beneath the church, that he had discovered the second fact: Bevil was paid by the hour and wasn't paid much. Fifty dollars was enough to get him to do most anything you wanted.

Today, Adrian wasn't interested in digging through catacombs. Once he showed Bevil the fifty he had stashed in the front pocket of his cycling pants, the groundskeeper unclasped the velvet rope and ushered him into the stairwell.

"Hurry up, Professor. There's a guided bell tour in twenty minutes, so we've got to be quick."

The stairwell was narrow and dark, and felt a century older than the rest of the church interior. The walls were stone, the steps wooden. Adrian had to move carefully not to trip over himself as he rushed to keep up with Bevil. A handful of narrow twists, and then they reached the top where the stairwell opened into a small room with slatted windows and more stone walls.

In the center of the room was the biggest bell Adrian had ever seen in person, hanging in a rusting, iron frame, attached to a circular wooden mechanism with a heavy rope leading downward, through the floor, into the church proper. Even in the near darkness, the bell was impressive, more so because Adrian knew the details. Over four feet across in diameter, weighing 2,500 pounds, when it rang it could be heard throughout the city. Etched across the top, in clear letters, the name of the man who'd cast and delivered it: *Revere*.

"He called it the 'sweetest bell he ever made,'"

Bevil said, as they stood in front of the bell. "Died two years after it was hung."

Adrian didn't respond. He knew more about Revere, and by extension, this bell, than this church groundskeeper could learn in a lifetime. The bell in front of them had indeed been cast by Paul Revere and hung in King's Chapel two years before Revere died, at eighty-three. Although the date carved into the bell, near Revere's name, was the date it was delivered and hung, 1816, Revere had begun molding and casting it two years earlier, when he'd first gotten the order from the church, whose original bell had cracked.

In 1814.

"His last one," Bevil continued. "He made three hundred of them. Some say he became obsessed with making bells late in life. Had a heck of a business in copper, cannons, armaments, silver, engravings. But all he seemed to care about as he got older were the bells. Kept on making 'em, until this one."

Adrian was hardly listening to the man. He knew what the textbooks said about the bell in King's Chapel, that it was Revere's last and most impressive. What was written in textbooks—and most history books—didn't matter to Adrian. Most textbooks were flawed, only as valuable as the reputations of those who had penned them. And most people who wrote history were flawed as well, spending their careers in pursuit of elusive acclaim.

Men like Charles.

Adrian reached into his backpack, this time beneath the manila folder, and retrieved a small but heavy electronic device, about the size of a hardcover book. It had a screen on one side next to a panel of knobs and buttons. He had been careful during the six-mile ride from Medford not to hit any potholes or bumps that might damage the thing; Professor Vladimir Gregor, one of the heads of the electrical engineering department at Tufts, had assured him it was much more expensive than it looked.

Gregor had been surprisingly helpful when Adrian visited him in his engineering lab earlier that day, even though Adrian had done his best to hold back as much information as he could. Not because he didn't trust Gregor, who was one of the few members of the faculty Adrian found serious enough to call a friend. But precisely because Gregor shared his sensibilities and might very well have laughed him right out of the engineering lab if he'd known the full, absurd-sounding truth.

Adrian *had* shown Gregor the engraving, which was unavoidable—and Gregor had only needed to look at the picture for a moment before he'd actually gotten excited. *The wineglasses*, he'd exclaimed, *lined up like that in front of the bell—you see what they are, don't you?* And then he'd explained—the wineglasses were an ingenious if primitive version of the device that Adrian now held in his hands.

"What the hell is that?" Bevil asked. "You're not going to damage the bell, are you? Because that's gonna cost you way more than fifty bucks."

"I'm not going to damage it. I'm just going to measure it. This is a spectrum analyzer. It measures sounds—tonal frequency, lengths of acoustic waves. Creates a pattern that can be understood mathematically."

Adrian was saying words he barely understood himself. But Gregor had been sure. In the engraving, Paul Revere had set up the wineglasses to measure the waves of sound coming off the bell. Although when a bell was rung, the human ear translated the varying frequencies given off by the curvature of the metal as a single tone, the math behind what one was hearing was much more complex. Rising and falling sine curves representing the frequency of the sound waves.

In the engraving, Gregor had explained, the surface of the wine in the glasses would have rippled because of those waves. Where each wineglass was positioned, combined with how much liquid was in each one and the shape of the glasses themselves—would capture those waves differently, giving you a surprisingly precise measure of the length of the waves. The distance between each ripple could be calculated, and with that information, you could reconstruct the sound you were hearing mathematically. At least you could if you were brilliant at such things, like Gregor—or Paul Revere.

The numbers beneath the glasses represented Revere's calculations based on the readings from the ripples in the wine. Those numbers, in that particular sequence, gave you the mathematical signature of a specific "tone"—the sound emanating from the bell. According to Charles's paper, Revere had been experimenting his way to a particular tone: *a tone with, as insane as it sounded, world-changing ramifications*. According to the paper, it had taken Revere three hundred bells to get it right, but with his last bell, he had succeeded. Achieved the impossible, made a bell whose tone could— It was so insane, impossible, Adrian couldn't even put the thought into words.

Gregor had been able to calibrate the device that Adrian was now holding with the data Revere recorded. Which meant that, over two hundred years after Revere had hung his sweetest bell, Adrian was about to conduct the very same experiment pictured in the engraving.

"Ring it," Adrian said. Bevil looked at him.

"You're kidding, right? That bell gets rung three times a week. Sundays, Wednesdays, and Saturdays. And you don't ring it from here, you ring it from downstairs. That's what the rope is for."

"But you could. Ring it from here. Right now."

Adrian cradled the spectrum analyzer in one hand, pulled a second fifty-dollar bill out of his cycling pants, and held it out along with the first. Bevil stared at the two bills for a moment, then shrugged.

"I do get my days mixed up sometimes. All the allergy medicine I take. Like they say, don't operate heavy machinery when you take antihistamines."

He grinned, snatched the two bills, then made his way to the heavy rope leading down below. He took the rope in both hands and looked at Adrian.

"Might want to cover your ears."

Adrian ignored him, instead hitting a switch on the spectrum analyzer, powering it up. The screen turned green, with a bright line running across the middle. Beneath the line was a row of numbers.

"Ring the damn bell, Bevil."

Bevil put his weight into the string, pulling down. The giant bell stirred, slowly at first, then rocked forward in its frame. Adrian could feel the wind from the great beast against his face, and then the bell reached the highest point of the arc, swung downward, and from it emerged a clang so loud and powerful it nearly knocked Adrian off his feet. The stone wall behind him shook; hell, the entire church seemed to vibrate with the noise. Adrian could imagine the tourists in the pews below and out on the street—and across the city—looking up. Then his focus was entirely on the device in his hands.

The green line on the screen was no longer straight, it was suddenly curving up and down like a slithering snake, undulating like ocean waves, moving from one side of the device to the other. Beneath the curves, a sequence of numbers began to appear, one after another. One for each of the calibrations Gregor had entered into the machine based on the etching. *A mathematical code for the noise coming from the bell.* Adrian's face flushed as he looked from the curve to the numbers, hardly believing that it was working, that Gregor had been right, that Revere in the engraving had been using the glasses to measure the bell—when suddenly he noticed something.

The numbers were wrong. They didn't match the numbers in Revere's engraving.

Either Gregor had miscalculated, which seemed unlikely, given the man's background and ability. Or the numbers were wrong because this wasn't the sound that Revere had been measuring in the engraving. This wasn't the sound—the tone Revere had been chasing, the powerful, world-changing tone—because this wasn't the bell.

But that didn't seem possible. The date on the engraving was 1814. Revere had made this bell in 1814, or around then, just a couple of years before he'd died. He'd made three hundred bells, worked obsessively building them up until his death. The King's Chapel bell wasn't just supposed to be the sweetest bell Revere had ever made. It was supposed to be his last.

"But it wasn't," Adrian suddenly said. "It wasn't his last bell."

The bell slowed in its frame, the sound receding just enough so that he could be heard. "The textbooks are wrong."

Bevil looked at him, hands still on the heavy rope.

"That's not true. The King's Chapel bell was Revere's last. It's right in the brochures we give out downstairs."

Adrian shook his head. With Charles's death, he was now the singular, preeminent Revere scholar in the nation. He hadn't realized it before—but if Charles's thesis was right, and the engravings he'd found were authentic—*there had to be another bell*.

Adrian had a sudden thought. Balancing the spectrum analyzer in one hand, he reached into his pocket with the other, and his fingers felt stiff cardboard. Slowly, he pulled the coaster from the Warren Tavern free, and then gazed down at the picture emblazoned across its surface.

"What's this all about, Professor?" Bevil asked. "What were you trying to measure with that device?"

Gregor had asked something similar, back in his lab. *What was Revere up to, with those glasses? What was so important about that bell in the picture, and the sound it was supposed to have made?*

Adrian hadn't been able to answer Gregor then, and he certainly wasn't going to answer this groundskeeper now. Not because Adrian didn't know the answer; that, in short, was the entire thesis of Charles's paper. The last paper he'd written before he'd died.

An insane, absurd, fanciful thesis, about who Paul Revere really was, and what he was trying to achieve. And what, if the engraving meant what Charles thought it had meant, Revere *had* achieved.

Adrian took one last look at the coaster, then shoved it, along with the spectrum analyzer, into his backpack and headed for the stairs leading down into the church.

"Where are you going, Professor?"

Adrian didn't answer. His mind was already somewhere else. Across the city, to a place where he might find more answers.

CHAPTER FIFTEEN

'll be there in twenty. Keep the bodies warm for me, Detective."

Agent Zack Lindwell hung up his cell phone and slipped it back into his jacket pocket, right next to his badge. The phone felt warm through his jacket and shirt, which made sense, because it hadn't been a short phone call. Getting information out of Danny Marsh over a cell phone was like trying to pry a renaissance masterpiece out of its gilded frame; eventually, you just had to take a razor to it to get the damn thing loose.

It had taken ten minutes just to get the detective to give him the most basic details of the new crime scene at the South Boston warehouse, and that was before the detective had even gotten around to mentioning the unique state of the two victims. This time, the ME was already on the scene, but from what Marsh had told Zack, the ME wasn't going to be much help until he'd gotten the results of his toxicology reports. The way the bodies were piling up, by then they'd all be finding themselves dodging national news vans and network television anchors.

Zack rubbed at his tired eyes. He knew he needed to head to South Boston, to see the scene for himself, but he wanted a little more time to contemplate what he'd already uncovered. So, for the briefest moment, he stayed where he was: sitting on the edge of a twin bed in a small, stoic bedroom in a third-floor walk-up two blocks from Mass Avenue in Central Square. The furniture in the room was mostly utilitarian, painted in calming pastels. Across from the bed was a small, converted card table serving as a desk, propping up a cheap laptop computer and a few blank notepads. Next to the computer was a wooden bookshelf that might have come from a garage sale. Between the shelf and the single window overlooking a parking lot was another card table, and then a dresser. Zack had already gone through the drawers. Mostly cheap dresses and jeans, a few T-shirts, nothing remarkable. No stash of money or casino chips had been found, but then, Zack hadn't yet brought in the state CSI team, or the fiber-and-hair bloodhounds. Somewhere in this room, he assumed, was a loose floorboard, ceiling tile, or false shelf bottom. Maybe a stack of bills, maybe more yellow chips, maybe even a computer memory card full of records. Good card counters always kept meticulous records, whether out of ego, or efficiency; in that, they were very similar to professional art thieves.

Zack finally rose from the bed, casting a quick glance out the window to gauge the time. Midafternoon, now, but the parking lot below was only half full. This part of Central Square had so far avoided full gentrification, but the rent was probably still pretty high, being so close to the MIT campus. Most of the apartments in the building were filled with students, a lot of them, presumably, math and science whizzes like Hailey Gordon. The roommate—Jackie something—who was still in the apartment's kitchen two doors down talking to one of the investigators Marsh had sent by, was studying quantum physics. A pretty girl, friendly, and very smart. Zack had already gone through her bedroom, which had been filled with family pictures, stuffed animals, high school and college paraphernalia. On her desk he'd noticed a framed photo of her boyfriend, a student at Emerson. On her shelf, next to the books on physics, a row of shot glasses emblazoned with various local sports teams' logos.

But this room, *Hailey Gordon's* room, was a different story. Apart from the few pieces of furniture, there was hardly any proof that someone actually lived here. No family photos. No signs of high school, college, or sports allegiances. No picture of a boyfriend, no teddy bears. The books in the bookshelf were mostly math texts, physics, a little chemistry. The laptop was protected by a password that the techs at the field office would eventually be able to crack, but Zack didn't expect they'd find much of interest within those bytes and bits.

The only thing in the room that offered even a hint that someone had been here in the past week was spread out across the second card table: a half-finished puzzle. At least a thousand pieces, which in itself was unremarkable. But the pieces were all white— no pictures, no color, not even a slight variation in shade. When Zack had first walked into the room, he'd turned a few of those pieces over, assuming they were upside down.

Hailey Gordon was certainly an enigma. Not the least because her name wasn't actually Hailey Gordon. Although the facial recognition software at the casino had led Zack to this apartment, hers was a carefully crafted identity that went back many years. She had succeeded for all these years as someone who didn't actually exist.

The girl who'd occupied this room and had been at the Encore casino twelve hours ago in the room of the murdered fence had been born Katie Allenbeck, in a small town near Fitchburg, by the New Hampshire state line. The staties had gotten one fingerprint off the yellow casino chip they'd found under the bed where Jimmy the Lip had been killed, and that fingerprint had been the first page of a memoir that tended almost entirely toward tragedy. Zack's researchers at the field office had been able to fill in most of the pages.

Katie had been orphaned at the age of four when her parents had been killed in a car accident. No other family to speak of, she'd ended up in the system, bouncing from foster home to foster home, never quite finding the right fit. But at the age of ten, that had changed for her; she had been taken in by an older couple who'd raised dozens of foster kids. Dr. Lawrence Pinter, a retired engineer and scientist who spent his time collecting and repairing antique crystal radios in the basement of his rural home, aided by his wife, Martha Pinter, who had been a kindergarten teacher at the local public school. Good people, who'd never been able to have children of their own.

But there was no happily ever after. Six months after taking Katie in, Martha Pinter died of a heart attack, and things went quickly south. Dr. Pinter began to have episodes of what would later be described as dementia. Local police were called a half dozen times, finding him wandering in the neighbors' yards, or stumbling along the side of a nearby highway. Child services began to get involved. Then one morning, Dr. Pinter was picked up on a freezing winter day, in a field two miles from his home, half-dead from hypothermia. A judge decreed that he needed to become a ward of the state. Katie was going to have to be moved again, placed with a new family.

And that's when the next tragedy struck. When child services arrived at the Pinter home to pick up Katie, they found the house engulfed in flames.

Zack had read through the file from the Fitchburg Fire Department, who had been called in when the fire had grown too large for the local crew. According to forensics, the fire had started in the old man's workshop; apparently, a crystalized stone called pyrite, used in the workings of the doctor's antique radios, had set off the blaze. It turned out pyrite could be highly flammable, under the right circumstances.

At the time, it was never clear what had happened to the girl, whether Katie had died in the fire or run away as the flames swallowed up the house. At first, she'd been listed as a missing person, but as time passed and no sign of her materialized, she'd been forgotten, like the hundreds of other untethered kids her age who disappear every year. Technically, her file was still open, but nobody had been looking for Katie for a long, long time.

Hailey Gordon's file, at least the one kept at the admissions office at MIT, where she'd attended as an undergrad and was now a graduate student, was much more pleasant reading. She had written her own story there, and it was a good one. Zack had always enjoyed fiction over nonfiction. In fiction, the story went wherever the author chose to take it.

A con artist of a familiar kind, yes, but Hailey Gordon was also plainly a genius. Faking an identity, let alone a high school record, good enough to get her into MIT was a feat in itself; succeeding at such an elite university, and surviving this long on her own was even more impressive. According to the roommate, Hailey had usually paid her rent and bills in cash, and though she was often late, she had never missed two months in a row.

Card counting, odd jobs, petty schemes—however Hailey had done it, she'd managed pretty well. She'd focused on her studies, stayed under the radar—until now.

If Zack had to guess, she'd stumbled into this murderous mess by accident; but since she hadn't come home to the apartment or shown up to her classes that morning, it appeared she was at least along for the ride, either under duress or as a player. Marsh's detectives were scouring the city for Nick Patterson, the much more likely candidate for the murder itself, but it was clear from the evidence they'd already gathered that Hailey might well be a willing participant in whatever was still going forward.

Witnesses had placed Hailey with Patterson in the taxi that had taken them from the casino to the warehouse in South Boston—now, a second brutal crime scene. After a fair amount of verbal fingernail pulling over the phone, Marsh had described to Zack the open, empty crates; enough crates, of the right size and shape, to have once contained the Gardner paintings. But the crates were just crates; the bodies were something else.

According to the ME on the scene, it was certainly a double homicide, but it was unclear exactly how the two young men had died. A toxicology report would take time, and even that might not be conclusive. Zack knew there were plenty of toxins that didn't show up on a toxicology report; chemistry was a fickle sport. A piece of crystal could power a radio, but it could also start a fire big enough to burn a house down.

Zack crossed the small bedroom, taking a pair of gloves out of his jacket pocket and slipping them on over his fingers. He unplugged Hailey's laptop, retrieving it for the techs back at the field office, who would make short work of the device's password protection. He'd already called them from the bedroom, bringing into play an even more sophisticated technical weapon from the FBI's arsenal. Now that the roommate had provided Hailey's cell phone number, they could both use it to place her location and also begin the process of getting a warrant for a remote wiretap. Not only would they be able to listen in on any calls she might make, but they could also attempt a "phishing" expedition: call the phone, remotely disable the ringer and any screen indications that a call was coming in, and force a connection. Hailey's cell phone would become a listening device, a remote bug. Zack had used the tech before to varying degrees of success. If the phone was in a coat or a purse or a deep pocket, you didn't get much. But if you were lucky, if the phone was out in the open, it was like you were right there, along for the ride.

Nick Patterson might have been the key to the murders, but Zack had a gut feeling that Hailey— Katie—was the key to cracking the case. As he turned to head out of the bedroom, he took a last look at that unfinished puzzle, those unblemished, unpainted puzzle pieces.

Hailey might be the key, but they'd have to move fast. From what Zack could tell, Hailey Gordon might be good at solving puzzles, but she was even better at running from them, leaving pieces in her wake.

———

Two hundred yards away, across the sparsely filled parking lot, Patricia sat behind the steering wheel of a black Escalade. Even from that distance, she could see the FBI agent making his way through Hailey Gordon's bedroom. Patricia knew she only had a few minutes before the agent worked himself down the three stories to the back entrance of the apartment building, then out into the parking lot where his own government-plated sedan sat waiting. But Patricia was in no rush.

She turned to glance at the small, rectangular device on the empty seat next to her. The device was about the size and shape of a small toaster oven and was connected by a twist of wires to a concave speaker she'd suction cupped to the bottom of the Escalade's dashboard. At the moment, the sounds emerging from the speaker were mostly the rustling of material, and the rhythmic patter of shoes against carpet. No doubt, the FBI agent had put his cell phone back in his jacket pocket, which would muffle anything he might say. No matter—Patricia had already heard everything she needed to hear.

The IMSI-catcher—or StingRay, as it was more commonly known—was much more impressive than it looked; it could mimic a cell phone tower, forcing mobile phones within a fixed distance to connect to it, capturing audio, text, even video. With the knowledge of Zack Lindwell's specific phone signature, Patricia had been able to use the device the same way the FBI agent hoped to use Hailey Gordon's phone—as a remote transmitter. Not only had Patricia been able to listen in to the agent's conversations with the FBI field office and the state detective, but she'd been able to access the camera on the man's device, getting a clear view of Hailey's bedroom.

The StingRay itself hadn't been easy to acquire, but the family she worked for had impressive resources. Even more difficult had been working her way into the FBI field office to keep tabs on the agent in charge of the investigation; but that was a part of a much longer project, one that Patricia and the Family had been engaged in for some time. The FBI had entirely taken over the Gardner theft investigation within days of the robbery back in 1990, so the Family had been forced to extend its tendrils in that direction from very early on. Of course, had Bobby Donati followed the Family's orders, and only taken what he'd been paid to take, there would never have been much of an investigation, and the FBI would never have been called in. The Family would have acquired what they had been seeking—what Paul Revere had crafted and hidden centuries ago—and so much could have been avoided, so many unnecessary deaths over the years. Bodies in trunks of cars, supposed heart attacks and strokes, corpses in hotel rooms and warehouses. There were more bodies tied to the Gardner heist than Zack Lindwell would ever know.

The FBI agent couldn't be blamed for his igno-rance, Patricia thought; he seemed fairly competent, actually. The fact that he had followed the trail to the girls' apartment was a sign of outside-the-box thinking, which would undoubtedly serve better than investigating by the books. Nick Patterson was a professional thief and was the premier link to what Patricia was seeking; but Nick Patterson was a simple cog. On his own, he would not be a threat. Left to his own devices, he would eventually slip up.

The girl was different. She was brilliant, unpre-dictable, a wild card. Given enough time, enough information, she might figure out what was actually going on around her — and that made her dangerous.

But with their remote wiretapping, Zack Lindwell and the techs at the FBI had made things much easier for Patricia. They were leading her right to Hailey Gordon.

The agent's footsteps continued reverberating through the speaker attached to the dash, as Patricia hit the ignition button, the car's engine rumbling to life. She had no more time to waste.

There were aspects of Hailey Gordon's background that reminded Patricia of herself. Molded by a difficult childhood, a broken toy who had fixed herself. The girl was gifted, and she knew how to disappear. Even more unnerving, given the current situation: Hailey Gordon was the type of genius who loved nothing more than to solve a puzzle just by its shapes and pattern.

CHAPTER SIXTEEN

When things go sideways—you go forward...

Nick Patterson was moving fast down the tree-lined stretch of Massachusetts Avenue, fighting to keep up with the strange young woman in the tennis skirt. She'd been two steps ahead of him the entire journey from the alley in South Boston, her tan legs churning at a thousand RPMs. Dodging parking meters, bike racks, the odd pedestrian—no question, she was on a mission now, and Nick was along for the ride.

They'd gone the six miles almost in silence, despite the brief efforts Nick had made to engage her in conversation. Along the way he'd learned her name—Hailey—but little else. Certainly, she was wary of him, and she had every right to be. But Nick knew there was something else going on with the sudden change in her demeanor. Before the warehouse—and what they'd found in the trunk of Gail's car—she'd been reluctant, reticent, despite her outward bravado, a little scared. Now she seemed possessed.

When things go sideways... It was something Nick's father used to throw at him, on the few occasions the man was home and lucid; the sort of philosophy lesson you expected from a guy who spent most of his time under a table at the local pub. But at the moment, it seemed to apply.

Things had certainly gone sideways. Nick's hope for the sort of easy score that would set him up for a lifetime had been pretty much shattered in the past twelve hours, replaced by three dead bodies and the threat of the sort of criminal charges that would make his past indictments look like petty indiscretions. And yet instead of wallowing in the turn of events, they were indeed moving forward, at a pace that had him breathing hard.

It had helped that most of the sprint had taken place underground and by way of subway cars; the Blue Line from Southie to Government Center, a short hop to Park, then the Red Line to Kendall. Nick had known all the stops, because the T had been a lifeline to a kid who'd grown up with little money and even less of a home life, but he'd never taken the stops in this order. Even though it was only a few miles, there was an enormous distance between the stoops and concrete playgrounds of Dorchester and this spot, a long stone's throw from the Mass Ave. bridge.

Just looking at the people brushing by them on the sidewalk brought some of Nick's old insecurities into his shoulders. College-age kids in sweatshirts with letters on them. Professorial types in slacks and blazers. So many people with glasses. When Nick was a kid, hardly anyone he knew wore glasses. You didn't see well in Dorchester; you squinted.

As Hailey took a hard right into a crosswalk, playing toreador with the sparse traffic, Nick's discomfort multiplied. The immense limestone building rising up from the sidewalk across the street seemed both intimidating and a little arrogant, from its colonnade of ionic columns to the massive windows climbing up the walls. Of course, there was a dome on top— and the building behind it had even more columns and an even larger dome, modeled after the Greek Pantheon. Boston and its surrounding neighborhoods liked domes; Nick had always suspected it was because domes made people like him feel particularly small.

When they reached the other side of the crosswalk intact, Nick cast another glance toward Hailey. She was about to take the first stone step that led to the entrance of the imposing building, but had paused, and was now looking up and down the curb behind them, searching for something.

Nick had to admit, watching her, that she was growing on him, even as he wondered why she was still willing to be part of his dangerous game. Then his attention shifted to the object under her right arm—the object from Gail's trunk, wrapped in a checkered towel.

The towel had been in the trunk as well; God only knew how long that thing had been bundled up that way. *Years, maybe decades.* As Hailey continued to search the curb, a section of the towel moved as well, revealing a glimmering hint of what was beneath. In the morning sun, it shined like gold.

Except it wasn't gold, it was bronze, gilded and shaped over two hundred years ago.

"The eagle," Nick had exclaimed, when Gail had first opened that trunk. "The finial, from the top of one of Napoleon's flags. This is it? Donati was only supposed to steal the gold eagle?"

"It's not gold," Gail had responded. "And yes, he'd been paid—an insane amount of money, actually— to steal that damn eagle."

Hailey had lifted the object out of the trunk. It was about ten inches tall, maybe three times as long wing tip to wing tip. Weighed a couple of pounds. Bronze, not gold, so it couldn't be worth much beyond the historical value. Not the kind of money you risked your life or freedom for. *Or killed for.*

It was then, while Hailey had been running her fingers over the wavelike curves of the eagle's wings, that Nick had noticed the other object in Gail's trunk, wrapped in a smaller, similarly checkered towel. Gail had shrugged at him.

"And that's the second thing Donati was paid to steal."

"I thought Donati never took the second job. I thought he ended up in the trunk of his car."

Gail nodded again.

"He didn't do the second job. My father did. After Bobby was murdered, my father couldn't help himself. Donati had told him the details, and he was curious. So, one night, he went ahead. It wasn't difficult. It wasn't an art museum. But it was a museum, of sorts. In a house. The oldest one in Boston, in the North End. Nineteen North Square. The house is still there."

Hailey had looked up for the first time from the eagle in her hands.

"Your father robbed Paul Revere's house?"

Nick had thought the address had sounded familiar. Growing up in Boston, especially if you'd made it through middle school, some landmarks were hard to avoid.

"Not the whole house. Just a basement library."

Gail had reached into the trunk and handed Nick the second object. When Nick had unwrapped the towel, he'd found himself holding a small book, the size of a child's diary, bound in a leather cover.

Stranger still, when he'd opened the book, he'd discovered that the pages weren't paper. Or not simply paper—each page was gilded in what appeared to be sheets of copper. As he'd leafed through the pages, he'd also found that they were all completely blank.

"Your father was commissioned to steal a book filled with blank pages?"

But Gail had already slammed the trunk shut, heading for the driver's-side door.

"You two are on your own," she'd said, as she'd gotten into the car. "And don't take this the wrong way, but I hope I never see either of you again."

Now, forty minutes later, four subway cars and one crossed river away from that warehouse in South Boston, the two-hundred-year-old bronze eagle was under Hailey's arm, and the strange book with blank copper pages was tucked in Nick's back pocket. And they were standing at the front entrance to one of the top math-and-science-focused universities in the country, a veritable mecca for the types of people Nick had pretty much avoided all his life—and Nick had no idea why they were there. But from the moment Hailey had taken the eagle from Gail, and started to inspect it, wings to claws—she'd suddenly changed.

She'd seen something on that eagle that had made her eyes widen and made her breathing go a little funny. Something that had gotten that mind of hers churning and set them off on the six-mile sprint to this place. And no matter how hard Nick had tried, she hadn't yet let him in on whatever it was.

Nick shifted his gaze back to the stone building.

"You don't exactly fit the profile," he finally said.

"What do you mean?"

"No offense, but you don't scream MIT."

Hailey smiled.

"Is it the hair?"

"Maybe the way you react to dead bodies."

"Trust me, I'm crying on the inside. You're not

exactly breaking down, either. And you knew those people."

"I don't like this any more than you do."

She didn't seem convinced. Nick felt his cheeks flush. He didn't mind being judged—professionals in robes had done it to him more often than he'd liked to admit. But for some reason, he didn't want Hailey to get the wrong impression.

"I take things. But I don't hurt people."

"Taking things hurts people."

Nick didn't have an answer for that. He could have pointed out that he'd found her hiding in a casino, that she hadn't called the police on him after three dead bodies, and that she'd been by his side ever since she'd seen the photograph of the stolen Vermeer. But the truth was, her words cut deeper than he wanted to admit. He'd always drawn a stark line between himself and the sort of criminals he'd found himself locked up with at Shirley. He was a thief, sure—he'd gone from being a teenager who'd broken into the neighbors' homes when they were away to a young adult knocking over ATM machines and parking meters. And then the short hop to real B&Es—gas stations, convenience stores. But it wasn't until he'd moved onto banks that he started to realize sooner or later, lines get crossed no matter how well you planned things out, or how careful you tried to be.

Case in point, the job that had gotten him sent to Shirley for a medium haul. He'd hit five banks in six weeks, all without a hitch—because he'd worked fast and had never gotten greedy. All of them, sleepy branches after hours, outdated safety systems and underpaid security guards with shift changes so predictable, you could use them to set your watch. He'd kept to the teller drawers and avoided the vaults and deposit boxes—gotten in and out in under ten minutes each time, avoiding cameras and silent triggers with ease.

Job number six should have gone just as smoothly. And in fact, it had been going smoothly; Nick had come in through an underground parking garage, disabling two separate alarm systems, and had emptied the teller drawers, avoiding the packets of big bills with the dye charges and the oddly rigid-looking twenties stacked on the pressure alarm triggers. He'd been about to make his way back through the garage—when he'd nearly run headfirst into a portly security guard coming out of the bank manager's private bathroom. The guy had still been working his belt closed when he'd seen Nick and realized what was happening. Then they'd both gone for the guard's holstered .45.

Nick still didn't know whose finger had touched the trigger. But the guard had ended up in intensive care with a bullet in his thigh, inches from the sort of artery that would have put Nick in prison for the rest of his life instead of five years. And the noise from the firearm had ended Nick's string of good luck, alerting a passing patrol car. Not that Nick would have left the security guard to bleed out on the floor of the bank—or at least, he liked to think he wouldn't have. Half a decade in prison made those sorts of calculations hazy.

In any event, as much as he'd liked to have been able to hit down at Hailey from the moral high ground, he knew it was a losing proposition.

Instead, he pointed at the building ahead of them.

"Are we going in? I assume we're here for a reason."

Hailey nodded but made no move to continue up

the steps. Instead, she kept scanning the curb. Nick realized she was looking at the cars parked at the meters. Most were new models, probably expensive. Then her eyes settled on an older make—a nineties model Ford Taurus covered in bumper stickers beneath a bowed birch tree.

Hailey headed toward the car, gesturing for Nick to follow. As they got close, she looked around them to make sure nobody was nearby. Then she opened her purse, started digging through the contents. Nick caught sight of casino chips—lots of them. Mostly yellows. *Christ, there had to be more than ten grand in there.* But Hailey pushed past the chips and retrieved a flask.

As Nick watched, she opened the flask and dumped the contents on the sidewalk. Nick got a whiff of something familiar in the breeze.

"Is that apple juice?"

Hailey handed him the flask, then pointed toward the Taurus.

"I bet you're good with cars."

"My dad worked on them a little between jobs, and he used to take me with him."

His dad had always been between jobs. The longest gig he'd held was when Nick was seven or eight. Roofing work at some construction site at Fort Point Channel. Until he'd gotten canned for drinking on the job. Which was great—it gave him more time to drink at home.

"Not fixing them," Hailey said. "Breaking into them."

Nick eyed her.

"You looking for a new stereo?"

"Not the stereo. The battery. I need about twelve ounces of battery acid."

Nick raised his eyebrows.

"It's a thermal flask," Hailey continued. "I like my apple juice cold. So, it's lined in glass. The acid won't be a problem. And I'm guessing these older cars are easier to get into, easier to tinker with."

"You want me to break into that car, take out the battery, and fill this flask with battery acid?"

Hailey nodded. He waited for more, but she was back to playing lookout, making sure the sidewalk was still clear. Nick looked from the flask in his hands to the object wrapped in the towel beneath Hailey's arm. He had no idea how these things were connected— but he'd gone this far already.

When things go sideways…

Nick headed toward the car.

CHAPTER SEVENTEEN

Five minutes later, Nick was again two steps behind Hailey, and the vague discomfort he'd felt on the street outside had shifted into something truly palpable as they crossed the cavernous lobby of 77 Massachusetts Avenue, a grand space that was mostly vertical, with pillars rising a hundred feet from the polished marble floor to that glowing, hollow dome. There were two balconies ringing the atrium and a glass skylight directly overhead. From the inside, the obscenely tall windows overlooking Mass Ave. behind Nick had an almost church-like feel to them, and even the air in the vast room felt crisp and serious.

"They call this Building Seven," Hailey said, as she led him forward. "It was actually built twenty years after most of the rest of the campus, because they wanted to add an entrance on Mass Ave. It's not quite as domineering as Building Ten, which is the one behind this one, with the bigger dome. People sometimes call that one 'the center of the universe.'"

"Sounds charming."

It wasn't just the scale of the place that made Nick want to turn and head back toward the comforting alleys of South Boston; the air itself was heavy on his skin, and he half expected someone to come running out from behind one of the pillars, pointing and screaming at him that he didn't belong.

Hailey must have noticed the way he was lagging behind, because she gave him a quick look over her shoulder, an expression he hadn't seen from her before. *Sympathy.*

"Everyone feels like that the first time they walk in here. Especially the new students. They call it impostor syndrome. The sense that you've fooled someone, that any minute you're going to be found out and asked to leave."

Nick was surprised she'd read him that well. He was usually better at hiding what was going on inside. At Shirley, it had been a survival mechanism. Cons would use anything they could against one another, and insecurities were like fault lines. Apply the right amount of pressure on an insecurity, and the hardest criminal would shatter like cheap glass.

"You're a student here?"

"After a fashion. I'm in the graduate school. Applied mathematics."

Nick wasn't sure what that meant, other than that she was probably damn good with numbers. Then again, the bar for him was pretty low. He'd dropped out of school somewhere between the first and second week of ninth grade.

"A lot of MIT grad students spend their nights at the casinos?"

Just like that, the sympathy was gone, and she was once again leading him across the open lobby, toward the far side where two huge pillars embraced the entrance to some sort of interior hallway.

"You'd be surprised."

They passed through the pillars, and Nick found himself peering down what appeared to be an endless corridor, lined on either side with doors to various classrooms. The corridor was lit by fluorescent tubes hanging from the ceiling, and seemed to be a place of constant motion; there were people, mainly students with backpacks, going in both directions, keeping to one side or the other, depending on direction. It was like some sort of human traffic experiment, along some endless stretch of enclosed highway.

"This is the Infinite Corridor," Hailey said. "It runs over eight hundred feet and connects a large part of the campus. There are five levels, including one underground. It's kind of the spine of the university, and it's like this most of the time. Everyone going somewhere, all at once. But a few days a year, everything stops; because of a quirk in geography, the setting sun is in alignment with the corridor and the sunlight shines down the entire length of the place. It's pretty cool. The kids call it MIThenge."

Hailey noticed his expression.

"It's cooler than it sounds. Or maybe it's not. But some of us get off on that sort of thing. A happy confluence of design and accident."

Nick tried to think of something smart to say back at her, but instead shrugged.

"You people have a lot of time on your hands."

Hailey turned, but not down the hallway—instead she headed toward an elevator right past the entrance and hit the down button with the heel of her hand.

"Basement level?" Nick asked.

"A little deeper," she said, as the elevator doors whiffed open.

———

Fifteen minutes later, and Nick had thoroughly lost his bearings.

Initially, he'd been correct; they'd taken the elevator to the basement level of the Infinite Corridor, and followed the long, industrial lit hallway at least a hundred yards under the MIT campus—but that was only the beginning. From there, Hailey had pointed him through an unmarked doorway to a stairwell that had led even deeper underground; when that stairwell had ended in another unmarked door, Nick had been surprised to find it locked. Hailey had pushed him aside, then produced a key from her purse. A moment later, they were in another hallway, very different from the bustling corridors above.

This hallway had smooth cement walls and an unfinished floor. There was visible ductwork running along the ceiling, and there were steam pipes riding up junctures in the walls. Even so, there were more doors along either side, some with numbers, many without.

"Research laboratories, storage rooms, data centers, electrical stations," Hailey had explained. "But I couldn't tell you for sure. There are so many of these tunnels, literally miles of them. They run under the entire campus, and there are multiple levels. They go on forever."

Nick had looked behind them, then ahead. They seemed alone; the only sound had come from their own shoes against the cement floor.

"Do other students come down here?"

"On occasion. Actually, it's kind of a rite of passage—*hacking* the tunnels. In fact, one graduating class put a partial map of the system on their class ring. But I don't think many people have explored all of it. Some of these tunnels go back decades, or longer.

And there are plenty of secrets down here. This is MIT, after all."

They had taken a hard right turn and descended down a narrow ramp, to another stretch of tunnel.

"Beginning before World War II," Hailey continued, "MIT developed a very close relationship with the Department of Defense. A lot of advanced weapons and war technology was developed here, in secret labs, often using student research. Radar came from MIT, and tons of work on radiation. There's even a nuclear reactor somewhere on campus."

"For real?"

"A lot of these doors don't have labels or nameplates for a reason. Things have changed over the years, but you don't shed a history like that overnight."

They'd gone the next ten minutes in near silence, Nick wondering how close they were to that nuclear reactor while Hailey followed some internal compass to wherever they were going.

When she finally came to a stop, Nick found himself in front of another unmarked door. Hailey worked the lock with a second key from her purse—and then ushered him inside.

———

Hailey hit the lights, bathing the rectangular space in a fluorescent glow. Even so, it took Nick's eyes a moment to adjust, not because of the flickering ceiling tubes, or the fact that there were obviously no windows so deep below the campus; but because there was just so much to see, all at once, a visual barrage that had his rods and cones playing twister.

The room was long and split-level; the area closest to the door looked like some sort of engineering lab, with low metal tables and shelves cluttered with computer equipment and electronics gear. Nick recognized a few of the items, from laptop computers—some opened up and in pieces, others in more respectable form—to what appeared to be a collection of antique ham radios that had been taken apart and put back together. But deeper into the room, the place got more confusing. The central area seemed like some sort of library; embraced on all sides by tall, corrugated shelves filled with books. The titles that screamed out at Nick all had something to do with math and physics; and not the sort of math or physics that he'd have had any chance of recognizing, let alone understanding. No algebra or geometry; this was all high calculus, quantum theory, strings and quarks. There were also shelves lined with books that looked much older than the rest—some with tattered, yellowed covers, some with no covers at all. They looked antique, even older than the ham radios.

Beyond the library, there was what appeared to be a small bedroom. A futon on the floor, a set of drawers, and then in the far corner, a sink in front of a pair of vanity mirrors. And beyond the mirrors— that's where things got really strange.

Hailey was already stepping past the futon— where she gently deposited the eagle, still wrapped in its towel—as Nick heard the door shut and lock behind them. It was only when she stopped in front of the mirrors, checking her face and hair, that Nick finally found his voice.

"What is this place?"

Hailey laughed. Then she reached up and took off her blond hair, placing it gently on a mannequin head behind the sink.

Nick raised his eyebrows. In all the craziness, he hadn't even realized that Hailey had been wearing a wig. Her real hair was wavy and brown, and ran down past her chin. She was working on her eyelashes, now, softening her look.

"I think it used to be a lab," she said. "Something to do with early computing hardware. Big consoles, the kind that used to use punch cards. A lot of that kind of electrical stuff was here when I found the place. The newer stuff, I brought in over the years. Kind of a hobby. Well, multiple hobbies."

"You live here?"

She finished with her eyelashes, then started on her makeup, using a sponge to take some of the color out of her lips and cheeks. Nick took the moment to look past the sink to the farthest reaches of the room, toward an alcove with one wall lined with hangers, holding what appeared to be costumes. Clothes for all sorts of different settings and occasions, from shiny, sparkly gowns to leather and lace. There were more wigs, lining a waist-high shelf covered in more mannequin heads. And in front of that, a full-size blackjack table, complete with a casino-level shuffling machine. Scattered about were dozens of decks of cards, some opened, some still pristine.

Nick turned back toward Hailey. Without the wig, with some of the makeup gone, she looked more natural, vaguely, perhaps partly non-white, though Nick couldn't have guessed her heritage without more to go on. Her cheekbones were still high and sharp, but there was something softer about her. Maybe it was this place. She clearly felt at home here.

"Who are you?" Nick asked.

Hailey smiled again, briefly, at the mirror.

"Does it matter?"

"You're a professional gambler? That's what you were doing in the casino? Playing cards?"

"I play cards, but I'm not a gambler. I'm a card counter."

Nick knew a lot of gamblers; everyone in prison gambled, one way or another. Like the cons and the redheaded kid. Card counting, he knew, was a little different.

"So you cheat. But it's still gambling."

Hailey ran a brush through her hair.

"Card counting isn't cheating, and it isn't gambling. It's math. You keep track of the cards and take advantage of the moments when you have a mathematical advantage over the house."

"Yet when I met you, you were being chased through the Encore by a couple of casino goons."

"It's not illegal, but that doesn't mean the casinos like it. They can throw you out, and sometimes they go further, get a little rough."

She nodded her head toward the costumes hanging from the rack, and all the makeup around her.

"You need to disguise your play, and sometimes yourself. The casinos have an idea of what a whale looks like, so you need to play the part. Card counting is almost as much acting as it is math. There's a lot of strategy, a lot of cat and mouse. You need to keep track of everything that's going on around you, not just the cards. To be successful, over time, you need to be able to see things that other people miss."

She finished with the mirror and retrieved the wrapped eagle from the futon. Then she moved past Nick back to the front of the room, and cleared off one of the metal workbenches. She carefully unwrapped the eagle, placing it on the open towel. Then she pointed to Nick's pants.

"The book," she said, simply.

Nick took it out of his back pocket and handed it to her. She held it up between them.

"What do you notice about this?" she asked.

"The pages are blank. And covered in metal."

"Copper, yes. But what else?"

Nick shook his head.

"It's surprisingly heavy," she said, answering her own question.

She hefted it up and down. Nick realized she was right. It weighed a good few pounds.

"There's something else beneath the copper," Hailey said. "A heavier metal. Maybe lead."

"That's what got you so excited?"

She turned back to the eagle, and gently turned it over onto its back. She gestured for Nick to come closer, then pointed a long fingernail at a spot near the base of one of the eagle's wings.

Nick looked closely—and saw two tiny symbols etched right into the bronze.

"What are these?" Nick asked. "Egyptian hiero-glyphics?"

Hailey headed toward one of the bookshelves in the center of the former lab. It took her a minute to find what she was looking for—one of the antique looking tomes, with a soft, leathery cover. When she brought it back to the workbench, Nick saw that it was more bound manuscript than book, with yellowing pages tucked inside, most of it held together by bands of string.

The title on the cover was as strange as the manuscript itself:

Principia of Chymistry

"My foster father was a scientist and a collector," Hailey said, "and he had an extensive library of this sort of thing. I guess I picked up some of his habits, and over the years I've gathered a pretty sizable collection of my own. Mostly books on mathematics going back to Newton, but also a fair number of books on related sciences. This one I found in an antique bookstore in Harvard Square. I took it for my shelves as more of a curiosity than anything else."

There was a lot to unpack in what Hailey was saying, but Nick tried to stay focused.

"I think they spelled a couple of those words wrong."

"'Chymistry' was a term that came about between the Middle Ages and the late seventeenth, early eighteenth centuries; a sort of prescience discipline that rose out of earlier, more mystic endeavors. Basically, it was the predecessor to modern chemistry, the science of elements and compounds, and how they interrelate."

"This is going somewhere, right?"

Hailey began untying the strings holding the antique manuscript closed. A moment later, she was leafing through the yellowed pages, then held the book open to a page filled with tables. On one side of each table was a vertical row of symbols, and next to each, a few lines of text. The text wasn't English—

Nick guessed Latin, but then again, they hadn't quite gotten to Latin by the second week of ninth grade.

"Here," Hailey said, pointing with one of her nails.

It was the first symbol that was etched into the eagle.

"This is the pre-chemistry symbol for sulfur."

"Sulfur," Nick repeated.

"It's one of the basic elements. You remember your periodic table?"

When Nick didn't respond, she continued.

"It's a very common element—the fifth most common substance by mass on earth, actually—found almost everywhere in nature. Historically, very important, because it has a lot of unique properties. For instance, it's very flammable; in the Bible, it's what they mean when they refer to 'brimstone.'"

"And this symbol, on the eagle—it means something to you?"

Hailey began flipping yellowing pages again.

"Not on its own. But that second symbol—"

She stopped on another page in the old manuscript. Another table of images; halfway down, Nick spotted the curved second symbol, which seemed more familiar than the first.

"Libra," Hailey said. "It's an astrological sign. On the Zodiac it's supposed to represent a balanced scale."

Nick had been in plenty of courthouses up and down the commonwealth; he'd seen more than his fair share of statues meant to represent that particular astrological sign.

"Scales of justice," Nick said.

"But here, it also means something else."

She had her finger on the text next to the picture in her book.

Sublimation.

"You might have learned the term in chemistry. OK, maybe you didn't. But it's when something solid dissolves directly into a gaseous state. The way dry ice goes straight from being a solid to a gas, without turning into liquid water in between. It was an important pre-chemistry lab technique."

Nick turned from the book to the two symbols on the eagle. They were so small, so seemingly inconsequential, he was amazed Hailey had even noticed them, let alone guessed at what they might mean. Even so, he was still completely in the dark. But Hailey was gripped by something, now. As he watched, she rummaged beneath the workbench and came back with two pairs of clear safety goggles.

She handed one pair to Nick, while donning the other. Nick looked at the glasses with suspicion, but Hailey wasn't slowing down to explain.

She held out a hand, nodding toward Nick's front pants pocket, where he had her flask, now filled with battery acid from the Ford Taurus outside. Once he'd handed it over, she carefully opened the diary from Gail's trunk to the first page, revealing the slim sheet of copper, which flashed in the fluorescent light.

"The thing about solving really difficult puzzles," she said, as she carefully opened the top of the flask, "is that it's all about context. These two symbols on their own don't really mean much. But when you put them together—and look at the context—things begin to connect."

She held the flask above the copper page, then glanced at Nick, who was finally securing his own safety goggles over his eyes.

"Gail told us her father stole this book from Paul Revere's house. If we can assume that it's from Revere's era, that would date it around the late eighteenth to early nineteenth century. Which would make sense, if it's somehow connected to the eagle—which we know was molded in 1814. Now I didn't study much history growing up, and I don't know much about Paul Revere or the postrevolutionary war period. But I do know a lot about math, and where it intersects with history. The era of Revere and the original American patriots was a golden age of cryptography."

She glanced at him through her goggles in a way that made him feel small again. She obviously assumed he had no idea what she was talking about. She was mostly right, but he was going to go down swinging. He'd picked up things over the years—sometimes he even surprised himself. Breaking into places wasn't always as easy as jimmying a car door, matching some wires to pop an electronic trunk, and unscrewing a car battery. He wasn't an expert safecracker like some of the hoods he'd met at Shirley, but he could work a tumbler and short a keypad.

"Codes. Secret messages."

"Exactly. People think that World War II was the high point of cryptography, with so many stories about German encryption methods, the famous Enigma project—especially here, at MIT, where a lot of sophisticated methods of code-hacking were developed. But the Germans didn't hold a candle to the Founding Fathers. The Revolutionary War was fought over a backdrop of secret messages, complicated spy networks, and fairly complex systems of encryption. George Washington, for one, was famous for using an invisible ink he'd had developed by his own 'scientists' to communicate with his personal spy networks. Thomas Jefferson created something called the 'Jefferson disk,' which was a cipher for encoding messages that could be passed through the mail. So there's good reason to believe that Paul Revere—who was basically a spy, if I remember correctly—might have been similarly possessed."

Nick raised his eyebrows beneath his goggles.

"You think this book was Paul Revere's?"

"Apart from riding around on horses shouting about the British, he was known for being a metalworker and an engraver. And he definitely worked with copper. But it doesn't really matter who made this book if we can't read it."

She carefully unscrewed the top of the flask. Nick got a whiff of the battery acid, and even with the goggles, his eyes began to water.

"You're going to want to lean back," Hailey said.

She started to tilt the flask toward the open copper page.

"The liquid in a car battery," she said, as the

first drops left the flask, "is about thirty-five percent sulfuric acid."

The drops of liquid hit the copper—and suddenly, a loud hiss filled the room. The liquid bubbled up against the copper, and a sharp, intense stench ripped through the air. The fumes coming off the copper were so strong Nick could almost feel them pressing him backward. He started to cough.

"Probably should have told you to hold your breath, too," Hailey said, between gasps. "Sulfuric acid is an oxidizing agent. When it meets copper, a redox reaction occurs. The acid gets reduced to sulfuric dioxide, a nasty, toxic gas."

Nick staggered back a foot, still coughing.

"Libra. Sublimation."

"You're a fast learner," Hailey said.

She poured a few more drops onto the page. More hissing, more noxious fumes rising up—but this time Nick stayed a healthy distance away. Even so, he could see Hailey open her eyes wide behind her goggles.

He looked down at the copper page again, and where the acidic liquid had touched the metal, he could now clearly see—the page was no longer blank. It was covered in letters, etched right into the copper.

"How—" he started, but Hailey was already ahead of him.

"It's pretty simple, actually. You write the letters right onto the copper using something impervious to sulfur. Any oil would work. In Revere's time, that would most likely be whale oil, which also happens to be very stable. Once the oil dries, it would be invisible against the copper."

As she was talking, Nick was looking at the page. The noxious fumes had dissipated enough for him to clearly see what was written across the copper. At least a dozen lines of text, running from the top of the page to the bottom. Amazing, how just a moment ago the book had been blank. And now it was filled with—

"Gibberish," Nick said. "It just looks like random letters. No words, no punctuation."

Hailey studied the page for a moment. Then she signaled Nick to back up again, and went to work on the next page with the flask and the battery acid. Carefully, she continued through the book. By the time she'd reached the end, the air in the room was thick with vapor. Nick's lungs felt tight from coughing, and his eyes watered at the edges.

"Lucky for us, the filtration systems in these old labs are made for this sort of thing," Hailey said, as she tightened the cap back on the flask.

When Nick had recovered sufficiently from the sulfuric dioxide, he joined her back over the book, as she leafed through the rest of the pages. Like the first, they were all filled with row after row of what seemed like random letters. There were no spaces to indicate words, no periods or commas or numbers.

"It's an alphabetical code," Hailey said. "These letters all look random—but there's an order to them, you just can't see it without a key. Thomas Jefferson and a mathematician consort of his named Robert Patterson worked on something similar—what they called a 'perfect cipher.' It's actually foolishly simple to construct. In Jefferson's version, you just wrote your message vertically, then broke the text up horizontally, shifted the lines around, and added random letters to each horizontal row. What you were left with looked like—well, this. But all you needed to decipher it was a simple mathematical key that told you where the horizontal lines belonged, and how many random letters were added to each row."

Nick wasn't going to pretend he'd followed most of what she'd said; but he understood enough to know that her trick with the battery acid had only been a first step toward understanding whether the eagle and the stolen copper-paged book were more valuable than just antique curiosities.

"You can crack this, right? Use some of that card counting magic of yours?"

"Math isn't magic, even though sometimes it can seem pretty close. And yes, this sort of code is theoretically crackable. A cryptographer at Princeton did manage to break an example of Jefferson and Patterson's perfect cipher a few years ago. But it would involve a lot of computing power and more importantly, a lot of time."

As she spoke, she continued leafing through the book—when she suddenly stopped, her fingers hovering over the final copper page. She looked closer, which made Nick lean in as well. There was an image halfway down the page, etched by the sulfuric acid right into the copper:

Nick stared at the picture a good, long beat. Above the picture were more lines of what seemed like random text—but even so, Hailey was running a finger above one particular line directly above the picture:

leserreursnesontpasdanslartmaischezlartisan

"More gibberish," Nick said. Hailey shook her head.

"That's not gibberish like the rest. It's French."

She didn't say more. She was back to staring at the image, seemingly racking her memories.

"It looks almost like some sort of tomb?" Nick tried. "Maybe something Roman or Greek? Or even Egyptian? That strange vase on top—"

Hailey's eyes lit up. She lurched from the book toward one of the laptop computers on the workbench.

"I need to do a little research—but I think I know what this is."

A second later, she had the laptop open.

"If I'm right—that image, it's not from Egypt, Italy, or Greece. It's something right here in Boston."

CHAPTER EIGHTEEN

You sure about this? From where I'm standing— that doesn't look anything like the picture in the book."

Hailey felt an excited tremble move through her shoulders as she stopped next to Nick on a corner of manicured grass, facing an open, sloping glade speckled with tourists, groups of schoolkids, refreshment carts hawking hot dogs, pretzels, and bottled water, and the odd uniformed park ranger. Even with so many people about, Hailey wasn't worried that anyone was going to notice them; one of a card counters' most important skills was the ability to take advantage of natural—and unnatural—distractions. It wasn't hard to hide your play when there was a drunk at the end of the table, making a scene. Your disguise didn't need to be perfect if there happened to be a famous rock star sitting at second base.

And it wasn't likely anyone was going to pay attention to a couple of fugitives strolling across a lawn, with a goddamn 220-foot granite obelisk looming over them, two-and-a-half-ton, pyramid-shaped capstone piercing the midmorning sky.

"Now *this* definitely looks Egyptian," Nick continued. "I mean, other than the guy with the hat and the sword up front."

Hailey wasn't interested in the statue resting on a pedestal a few yards in front of the massive obelisk; William Prescott might have been an important enough figure during the American Revolution to warrant a bronze effigy in such a premier jag of real estate along Boston's vaunted Freedom Trail— the two-and-a-half-mile historical stroll that snaked through many of the city's neighborhoods, showcasing touristy sites with even the faintest connection to the events of the War of Independence—but Hailey knew, from her research, that the statue was a late addition to this last stop along the trail. Molded in Italy in 1880, shipped to Boston a year later, Prescott's sculpture was an irrelevant detail, like an extraneous puzzle piece tossed into the box to throw her off balance.

Hailey was well past the point where she could have been swayed to break focus; from the moment she'd noticed the two symbols engraved into the bronze eagle, something inside of her had flickered to life. A familiar drive—a need, really—had kicked into gear. It was the reason, she supposed, that she'd gone into mathematics in the first place; an unfinished puzzle, an unsolved equation, an answer just out of reach— these things could cause her real, physical distress.

"The design is Egyptian. It's called an obelisk. The Egyptians used to put them at the entrance to their temples. But this one wasn't designed in Cairo; it was made right here in Boston."

Technically, they were in Charlestown, Boston's oldest neighborhood, a residential stretch of peninsular land that used to be mostly brick town houses and Irish bars but was now sprouting full-service luxury apartment buildings and high-end restaurants like it was suffering from an infection of expensive fungus.

Hailey had been to Charlestown before—to that exact spot, actually—during a handful of self-guided tours down the Freedom Trail; when you were responsible for your own schooling and you had aspirations that involved a college degree, the city had to be your classroom. Forging public school records wasn't difficult; but knowing she'd one day be competing with students who had access to textbooks, teachers, and parental guidance had given her the incentive to try and cover as much ground as she could.

But she hadn't been back to the Bunker Hill Monument since her early teens. As impressive as the giant, nearly two-hundred-year-old obelisk was—as well as the adjoining Masonic lodge that sat on the far side of the monument from where they were standing, housing Revolutionary-era memorabilia—for Hailey the site didn't hold the appeal that some of the Trail's other highlights offered. At Faneuil Hall, there were restaurants, souvenir shops, even street performers. In the Boston Common, there was a skating rink and a carousel, and you could ride the swan boats in the Public Garden. But to Hailey, the Bunker Hill Monument was an anachronistic hunk of granite; even as a historic site, it had never made much sense to her.

For someone who liked the pieces to fit together, the Bunker Hill Monument was intellectually challenging. Perhaps that was why the place had stuck in her memory, enough that the symbol in the copper-leafed book had set her mind roiling. The research she'd done on her laptop before she and Nick had maneuvered back up through the Infinite Corridor and across town had only reaffirmed the contradictory facts she remembered from her earlier visits.

"The idea to build something grand and permanent to commemorate the Battle of Bunker Hill came about after a breakfast meeting of wealthy and prominent Bostonians in 1823," Hailey continued. She saw that Nick was scanning the crowd, probably looking for law enforcement, but she kept her attention on the granite monster straight ahead. "They then held a design competition which gave us—this. The cornerstone was placed on June 17, 1825; a hundred thousand people packed this park, Daniel Webster gave the oration, and the ceremony was cohosted by the Marquis de Lafayette, the French war hero who fifty years earlier had helped the Americans defeat the British."

"French," Nick repeated. He eyed the black backpack slung over Hailey's shoulder, which contained the book and eagle, as well as her purse and a few minor tools of the card-counting trade she always kept packed and at the ready, in case she got the urge to hit one of the casinos a bit farther from home. Like the pair in Connecticut she'd ripped through so many times in the past—they should have both dedicated monuments to *her*.

"That struck me as well," Hailey said. "Lafayette's involvement in laying the cornerstone had always seemed a bit odd to me; he'd had nothing to do with the battle itself—he didn't join the Revolutionary forces until two years after it was fought—and yet not only did he lay the cornerstone of the Bunker Hill Monument, when he died, he was buried with dirt from this very spot, fulfilling his wish that he be interred with ground from both France and the United States. It was the sort of celebrity endorsement that ensured the Bunker Hill Monument would become one of the most famous shrines to the American Revolution, elevating this spot and the battle to historic proportions."

As Hailey finally started forward through the park, toward the stone walkway and steps that led to the entrance to the monument on the other side of the Prescott statue, Nick waved toward the scene in front of them—the obelisk, the adjoining lodge, the museum across the street.

"Seems pretty historic to me."

"Sure—but it's all based on bullshit. Because this isn't even Bunker Hill. This is Breed's Hill. Bunker Hill is about eight football fields that way."

She pointed past the museum across the street, toward a row of nearby renovated town houses.

"And the Battle of Bunker Hill didn't take place on Bunker Hill. A small Revolutionary force had been given orders to fortify a spot on Bunker Hill, but instead they'd decided it would be too difficult to defend, so they set up camp here. The British promptly attacked, and the Americans lost—though the British suffered more casualties. One could argue that the battle was vaguely important because it affected the British strategy of trying to take the hills around Boston, or that it was so costly to the British that it somehow inspired the Americans to fight harder—even though, remember, it was a battle the American rebels *lost*. But these seem like pretty weak explanations."

They were close enough now that the shadow of the great obelisk obscured the stone beneath their feet. Hailey could see the entrance to the monument up ahead, which was connected to the stone lodge next door; there was a large tour group, a mix of families, elderly couples, and school-age kids in frenetic clumps, on its way in from the lodge through the unadorned doorway to the obelisk, which was little more than a rectangle cut right into the granite. At their distance, in contrast to the open-air park, the interior of the obelisk looked dark and ominous, less like a monument—more like a *tomb*.

"So why do you think they built this, then?" Nick asked, as they approached a handicap ramp that allowed them to access the entrance without going through the lodge, putting them directly at the back of the tour group filing into the open doorway. "Why here?"

Hailey took a deep final breath of the fresh air, as she followed the last tourist toward the doorway. Then she adjusted the backpack on her shoulder, feeling the weight of the eagle and the book against her side.

"Because something else was here first."

CHAPTER NINETEEN

It took a moment for Hailey's eyes to adjust as she stepped deeper into the base of the granite monument. It was more than just the shift from the bright sunlight of the park to the dim interior of the hollowed out stone obelisk; the contrast was somehow temporal, like she'd just stepped through a portal back to an era when Paul Revere, Daniel Webster, and Lafayette were more than just names in a book. When the Revolutionary War was still fresh enough in people's memories that it was still real to them, three dimensional, not flat like written history.

The air felt cold and dank against her cheeks as she glanced to her left, where the circular staircase that ascended to the top of the tower, 221 feet above, began, but there was something also electrifying about the thought that perhaps people who had fought in that war had breathed this same air; though she knew from her research that it was unlikely. Though Lafayette had laid the cornerstone in 1825, it had taken another fifteen years for the obelisk to be finished—mainly because the foundation in charge of building the monument had quickly run out of money. They had been forced to sell off plots of land surrounding the obelisk, which was the reason the monument now sat on less than four acres of grass, rather than the eighteen acres originally reserved for the site.

It was clear to Hailey that the brain trust behind the monument had been determined to follow through with their grand ambitions, which again raised the question: Why were they so keen on memorializing a fairly insignificant battle that the Revolutionaries lost?

The puzzle nagged at her, as Nick stepped next to her in the dim light. He was watching as the last pair of tourists—a middle-aged man in plaid shorts and his teenaged son, earbuds in and a bored look on his face—started up the curved steps toward the summit. When Nick moved to follow, Hailey held out a hand, stopping him.

"I'm not a fan of heights. So, it's a good thing that what we're looking for is right here, in the base."

"Thank God," Nick said. "That looks like a long way up. How many steps to the top?"

But Hailey was already pushing him directly ahead. Just a few feet in front of them stood a doorway cut into the interior cylinder that ran up the center of the monument. The doorway was narrow— if a set of iron bars wasn't blocking the way, a man Nick's size would have had to pull in his shoulders to fit through.

To Hailey's surprise, there was someone standing in front of the barred doorway. Even though the man's back was to them, he looked out of place; you didn't see many sightseers—or, for that matter, state park employees—in brightly colored, body-hugging cycling gear. Stranger still, as Hailey moved closer, she saw that the man was carefully working what appeared to be an aging skeleton key into the lock halfway up the bars. When the lock clicked open, the man seemed pleased with himself, drawing the door partially open with a groan of metal against metal—at which he tossed a furtive glance over his shoulder—and saw Nick and Hailey for the first time.

There was a brief, awkward pause. The man eyed them from beneath sweeping locks of reddish gold hair. Then his lips turned down at the corners.

"Can I help you?"

Hailey was at a loss for words, so Nick filled the silence.

"You don't look like a tour guide."

The man's obvious disdain grew as he continued to look them over. As he focused on Nick, his eyes narrowed.

"And you don't look like tourists. In any event, this isn't part of the tour. You'll find the observation deck at the top of those stairs."

Hailey glanced at Nick, then back at the man. She had no idea who this oddly dressed person was, but she didn't immediately read him as a threat. She couldn't begin to guess what he was doing in the base of the Bunker Hill Monument, but she knew that she and Nick didn't have time to wait for him to leave. He clearly wasn't a cop, and he didn't seem to know who they were, or care. Which meant he might be in the way, but he wasn't a danger.

"We're more interested in what's down here," she finally responded, and then started forward.

The man stared at her, but she wasn't stopping, so he had no choice but to open the door the rest of the way—revealing the cylindrical shaft running up the center of the monument. Reluctantly, he then stepped back to give both her and Nick a better look.

"What is this?" Nick asked.

"Originally," the man said, in a tone that made it obvious he liked to hear himself speak, even if he wasn't thrilled that they were interrupting whatever it was he was up to, "this was the shaft for an elevator that ran up the spine of the obelisk. It was built to move the slabs of granite up as they built; when the monument first opened, it was then maintained as a passenger elevator—the first in the country—for a short period, before the curators of the monument decided it was damaging the interior walls, and had it removed."

"And it still runs all the way to the top?" Nick asked.

"The shaft ends in a covered grate on the floor of the observation deck. But as you can see, now it houses something much more interesting than an elevator."

As Hailey moved deeper into the shaft, the lighting slightly improved; the lower section was lit by soft orange light fixtures but it remained mostly shadows. Still, it was easy to see what was inside.

Nick whistled low behind her. Then he touched her shoulder. She knew what he was thinking. *The image from the copper book.* Standing in the center of the shaft was what could best be described as a very old, very weathered, tall, rectangular column, resting on top of a wider stone base.

"Christ," Nick said. "How old is this thing?"

"It was built on this spot in 1794," the man, still holding the barred door open behind them, responded. He seemed to know an awful lot about the Bunker Hill Monument, for a guy in a spandex cycling outfit.

"I thought we established that you're not a tour guide," Hailey said, while still staring at the column inside the shaft. "But you seem quite the expert—"

"I'm the Cabot professor of eighteenth century American history at Tufts. I know everything about—

everything. So go ahead and take your 'selfies' or whatever it is you're here for and leave me to my work."

Hailey glanced back at the man. His expression was mostly one of impatience; but there was something else there, too, something she recognized from her years in the casinos. A professional could always spot another card counter circling the blackjack tables, even before he sat down at the felt. It was the little things; the way this man's eyes moved as he looked at them, the way the skeleton key still hung from the fingers of his right hand, the way his other hand bounced nervously against his side.

From the way the man talked, Hailey could buy that he was some sort of snobbishly eccentric academic. But he wasn't giving off the air of someone who was standing in the base of the Bunker Hill Monument in some sort of official capacity.

"I don't think that door is supposed to be open," she finally said, pulling at the thread. "And I don't think you're supposed to be in here, any more than we are."

The man didn't respond.

"Why are you here, Professor—"

"Jensen. Adrian, if you must. Call it a research project."

It was obvious that wasn't enough for Hailey or Nick, so Adrian continued, his disdain morphing to distaste.

"A colleague of mine was inordinately obsessed with this monument—something I previously wrote off—as he was, to put it kindly, a fool. He came here often, wrote many papers about its provenance, even pushed our historical society to throw its annual conference in the shadow of this granite beast. But now I'm led to believe—perhaps there was something beyond his usual affinity for poppycock behind his interest."

It was more than Hailey had expected. She didn't know how it tied into why she and Nick were there, but she doubted it was simply a coincidence.

"So, you lifted a key—" she started.

"Borrowed," Adrian corrected. "The curator is a former student of mine. If he had been in his office, I'm sure he would have been happy— I don't need to explain myself. I have reason to be here. You two—"

But Nick had obviously already lost interest in Adrian, because he'd moved closer to the cylindrical structure in the center of the shaft. He was focused in on the stone base beneath the wood—which appeared to have writing carved into it. The column itself had a plate with more writing, but unlike Nick's, Hailey's eyes were immediately drawn upward—to the strange object that rested on the peak of the column.

"So, this is the 'memorial' that stood on this spot before they built the obelisk," she said.

Adrian was watching her and Nick—no doubt realizing that they weren't going anywhere, which meant he had little choice but to endure their company. Finally, he stepped into the chamber after Hailey.

"That column is made mostly out of wood and stands about eighteen feet tall. The thing on top is an urn, made of gilded metal."

"You say this was built in 1794," Hailey said.

"Correct. About thirty years before Lafayette laid the cornerstone of the obelisk. When the obelisk went up, they placed this replica of the column in here."

"It's not the original?"

"The column, no. The wood was rotting and wouldn't have lasted anywhere near this long. The urn on top—that's a different story. The Revolutionary fathers were quite adept at metallurgy."

Nick glanced up at the urn as well.

"These important and powerful Bostonians at some fancy breakfast decided that they needed to replace some strange, rotting memorial built on the misnamed battlefield of some minor battle, and they came up with a massive Egyptian obelisk?"

"It's more oblique than that," Adrian said. "The original memorial wasn't for the battle itself, or for some famous war hero, like George Washington, or even Lafayette. It was built to honor Dr. Joseph Warren."

"Who?" Nick asked.

"Exactly. Warren was a physician in Boston who became a spy in the early days of the war. Right before the Battle of Bunker Hill he was made a major general of the fledgling Revolutionary army—and was promptly killed in his first foray, right here on this spot. Not exactly heroic; in fact, his greatest claim to fame had nothing to do with Bunker Hill. He's really known for one thing—on the night of April 18, 1775, just two short months before his death, he was the person who sent Paul Revere off on his famous midnight ride."

"And he gets this monument," Nick said, glancing up toward the granite above them.

"And a tavern nearby," Adrian said.

"And what does Revere get?" Hailey asked. "A poem?"

Nick focused on the column again, and the urn on top.

"Who built this thing, anyway? Twenty years before the obelisk?"

"On top of being a spy," Adrian said, "Warren was also a Freemason. The memorial was built by the local

Masonic chapter, King Solomon's Lodge. If you look closely at the urn, you can see the Masonic symbol—a square and compass, tools of the masonic craft."

"Masons," Hailey said. "It's like a cult, right? Goes back hundreds of years?"

Adrian shrugged.

"Cult, guild, secret society—the kind of people who carve weird symbols into urns and build giant obelisks. The Masons have a strange and complicated history that goes back a long time, and a lot of what you hear about them is probably just fiction, but there's no question that many prominent people who were involved in putting our country together were members. There's a pyramid with an eye on top of it right on the back of a dollar bill."

Hailey moved closer to the structure. A slight tremble was moving through her body, her thoughts coalescing.

"I don't think you can write this entire monument— a massive obelisk towering over the city of Boston—off as a Masonic tribute to an interesting, if barely historic, member."

Nick looked at her. The professor might have been staring as well, but she didn't turn to see— instead, she shrugged, even though she was about to say something crazy.

"What if this—all of this—had a purpose?"

She turned back to the column and focused again on the gilded urn. It was a few yards away, but she could see the way it was knobby and bent, almost like it had been finished hastily. Or perhaps, it had been forged like that, uneven—*intentionally*.

The words that had appeared on the copper page above the image of the urn in the book she still carried in her backpack swam in her head. She didn't need to look at the page again to recite them.

"Les erreurs ne sont pas dans l'art, mais chez l'artisan."

"You speak French," Nick stated.

"A lot of the great mathematicians are from overseas. When I'm translating long texts, I usually need to use an app on my phone. But for this, I could work from memory."

"It isn't Lafayette, is it?" Nick asked.

Hailey was quiet. Adrian continued staring at the two of them, obviously wondering, again, who the hell they were. Then he cleared his throat.

"Not Lafayette. It's Isaac Newton. 'Errors are not in the art, but in the artificers.'"

Nick looked back at him.

"Gravity. The apple. That Newton?"

"Yes," Hailey said. "The father of mathematics and physics. Came up with the laws of motion, calculus, gravity. But he was also one of the main driving forces behind early chemistry. And he was seriously into the occult."

Nick seemed bewildered, as he eyed the urn.

"And you think this is all connected. The picture in the book, the quote from Newton. That urn—"

"What's going on here?" Adrian finally stammered. "Who are you people?"

Hailey ignored him, still staring at that urn, at

the imperfections in the metal. Then at the way the interior of the old elevator shaft was dimly lit, and the darker atmosphere where she and Nick and Adrian were standing. Her mind was spinning, as she worked through the problem.

Suddenly, she unslung her backpack and dug inside. A moment later she found what she was looking for; a small compact mirror, which she often used in casinos to check her face during a heated counting session.

She turned to Nick.

"I need a water bottle. Plastic, the kind they sell outside at those vendors."

"Hailey—"

"Just go."

His face had the look of someone who didn't like to be told what to do, but he brushed past the bewildered professor and headed quickly back the way they had come, out into the park. Once he was gone, Adrian gaped at her.

"Did you hear me? What is this?"

"Like you said, Professor. A research project."

Adrian continued spitting questions at her, his tone more flustered, but Hailey wasn't listening. She didn't care about the professor. She was focused on that urn, her mind churning through what she knew. The copper book and the eagle were somehow connected. The eagle had been molded in 1814 and had two prescience symbols engraved above its claws. Those symbols had enabled her to reveal the hidden letters in the book. The letters were encrypted—except for a line from Newton, translated into French above a picture of this urn—which had been placed here, with a massive obelisk built on top of it, the cornerstone laid by a French Revolutionary Wars hero.

She believed that all of it was somehow significant. But her mind kept coming back to Newton. He hadn't been chosen by accident.

Nick burst back in through the doorway, breathing hard, and held out a plastic water bottle. Hailey took it from him. She opened the top and spilled out just enough so that the bottle was a little less firm in her hands. Then she squeezed the plastic with her fingers, adding crinkles, angles, and curves.

Both Nick and Adrian were staring at her as she held the bottle in one hand, then opened the mirror and stepped a foot back. Extending her arm, she moved the mirror until she found a spot where the soft glow from outside reached into the monument.

The mirror flashed in the stream of sunlight.

"What do you do," she asked, as she played with the angle of the mirror, flashing that sunlight into the elevator shaft, "if you want to preserve a secret for a very long time?"

"You hide it in a monument?" Nick tried.

Hailey moved her wrist a few more inches. The light was now flashing against the replica column inside.

"I think it's the other way around. The engraved symbols on the eagle must have coincided with or come after the book. The eagle was molded in 1814. The memorial to Warren was erected by the Masons in 1775—just a couple months after Paul Revere's ride. But it wasn't until 1825 that it was moved here, and then the obelisk was built on top of it."

She shifted the mirror another inch, playing the reflected light up the column—until it reached the gilded urn. The urn flashed in the light. She could see the little imperfections more clearly, now. *Errors of the artificer.*

"You want something to stick around a long time, you make it unique, and you make it sacred. Maybe you build a monument over it that nobody's ever going to knock down. Nick, come over here — I need your help."

Nick moved next to her, and she handed him the creased and crinkled water bottle.

"Besides gravity and motion, Newton's most famous discoveries had to do with light. One of those discoveries was that what appears to be a uniform beam of light is actually made up of many different wavelengths."

"The colors of a rainbow," Nick said, surprising her.

"Correct. The thing is, historians of Newton believe that he came to this conclusion not by pure scientific experimentation, but because of his beliefs in prescientific, occult endeavors, which posited that everything in nature — from metals, to consciousness, to the universe itself — could be broken down to a handful of 'base' constituent parts."

She could tell she had just lost Nick again, but it didn't matter. He was about to see what she was heading toward for himself.

"Hold the bottle up to the light where it comes off the mirror."

Again, he did what she asked, moving the bottle carefully in front of the glass. As the light hit the angles of the crumpled plastic bottle and then passed through the water, it spread out the other side in a subtle cascade of color. *Like a rainbow.*

"The angles of the bottle and the refractory properties of the water act as a makeshift prism, which separates the wavelengths of light," she began, but Nick's expression made her stop.

He was staring through the bars and into the

elevator shaft, his eyes aimed up at the gilded urn. Where the colors of the prism hit it, the surface of the urn suddenly looked different. Clearly visible in the metal right beneath the rim were two rows of numbers.

"Christ," Adrian whispered, behind them.

"No, Newton," Hailey said. Even so, she could hardly believe she had been right. "That urn is gilded—maybe bronze, which is mostly copper—or maybe gold. When you shine regular sunlight on it, it appears to reflect the light back evenly—but it doesn't. Both gold and copper reflect the red wavelengths in light well, but blue and green wavelengths poorly. But if you lace in another metal with different reflective properties—say, wisps of silver, or rhodium—when you use a prism to break the light up into its constituent parts, you get a much higher contrast in the green, blue, and violet spectrum. As you can see."

"So those numbers were always there," Nick said. "Written in tiny amounts of silver or rhodium—but you can't see them unless you use a prism."

Nick was staring at the urn like he was witnessing magic. But it wasn't magic at all, it was science. And the numbers on the urn—

"It's the key, right?" Nick said. "To decipher the letters in the book."

"Jefferson's perfect cipher," Hailey said.

"*Thomas* Jefferson's cipher?" Adrian gasped.

Hailey nodded.

"One row of numbers tells you how to reorder the lines of text, and the other number tells you how many random letters were added to each line. So simple, and yet nearly impossible to crack without this key."

While still holding the bottle with one hand, Nick had his phone out of his pocket and took a quick picture of the urn. After making sure he could read the numbers off the picture, he finally lowered the bottle—and, abruptly, the effect ended. The urn was again just an urn.

"I need to go somewhere," Hailey said, her excitement rising, "so I can get to work on the book."

"What book?" Adrian stammered. "You're saying those numbers—a Jeffersonian key—"

But Hailey had already returned the mirror to her backpack and was heading through the doorway. Nick was right behind her, and after barely a beat, the professor raced after both of them, trying to catch up. Hailey could barely feel her feet as she moved; she had no idea what they would find in that book, but she knew it was a secret that had been kept for almost two hundred years. And now *she* had cracked it—with a little help from Nick—and Isaac Newton.

Hailey was close to a jog as she reached the open doorway leading back out into the park—but suddenly, Nick grabbed her arm and yanked her back so hard she nearly lost her balance.

"Shit," he hissed.

He pulled her to the side, pushing her back against the granite wall at the base of the curved stairs leading upward. Adrian nearly slammed into them—then stepped back, more bewildered.

"What is it?"

Nick ignored him, speaking to Hailey.

"Feds, I think. Or undercover cops. Two cars, on the far curb. At least three badges already on foot, heading this way."

Hailey's chest constricted.

"You're sure?"

"The way they're dressed. The way they're moving. The make of the cars. Definitely law enforcement.

Which is better than whoever took out the warehouse and Jimmy the Lip, but not by much."

Adrian's eyes widened.

"You're criminals?"

Hailey's fingers clenched against the cool granite behind her back. If they were caught by the police or the FBI, they would lose the eagle, the book, and any chance at understanding what they had stumbled into.

She looked past Nick and the professor, at the spiral of steps leading up to the top of the obelisk. She didn't like heights, but there wasn't much choice.

"Two hundred and ninety-four," she said.

Nick followed her eyes and realized what she meant.

"We'll be trapped up there. One way up, one way down."

"We'll start with the way up," she said. She took the lead, and the two of them lunged past Adrian, leaving the professor, stunned and alone, by the bottom of the steps.

CHAPTER TWENTY

For a brief moment, Adrian's entire world seemed frozen; the interior of the base of the monument around him was imprinted on his retinas like painted images splayed across static glass. He had his back against the granite wall, and was still facing the bottom of the stairs where the two fugitives had just bounded upward, away, wrapped in a swirling cloud of mysteries—*Isaac Newton? A Jeffersonian cipher? Some sort of cryptic book?*—and part of Adrian wanted to race right after them, chasing answers, while an equal urge demanded that he turn the other way, seek out whatever law enforcement the man in denim had seen coming, and point them in the right direction. No doubt, the two strangers were indeed criminals; Adrian had no idea what they had done, but it seemed to have something to do with what they'd just discovered on the urn on top of the original Warren shrine—

Adrian shook his head, breaking himself free of the frozen moment, shattering the imaginary glass.

Ridiculous.

Insane.

Charles, what the hell have you gotten me into?

And yet, Adrian was there, in the monument, for

reasons just as ludicrous as the thought of invisible writing on a 250-year-old urn.

After Adrian had come to the conclusion that the bell in King's Chapel was not the bell in the engraving from Charles's paper, and he'd thought back to the hint Charles had given him, in the guise of the coaster from the Warren Tavern, he'd had no choice but to head back to Charlestown. As he'd told the fugitives, that fool, Charles, had always been obsessed with the Bunker Hill Monument, and had advanced the idea many times, in papers and in lectures, that he'd believed the monument was hiding something. He'd pushed the topic so much, in fact, that one academic reviewer had actually referred to it as "Walker's Phallacy"; but it had never dawned on Adrian—until he'd been standing in that chapel listening to the wavering bell—that it was perhaps more than simple fantasy.

So he'd come to the monument, not knowing what he'd been looking for. Still, it was no surprise he'd found himself driven to the Warren memorial in the base; the ancient totem had always been a curiosity, even in academic circles.

But Adrian could never have imagined what the urn on top of that memorial had been hiding; a message, carved into the metal by some Revolutionary-era hand. It was a find, alone, that would rock the academic world. And the girl—how she'd figured it out, presumably from that Newton quote, derived from some sort of book? Perhaps something the two of them had stolen from a museum or the private collection of a library.

A Jeffersonian cipher—code hidden on Warren's urn. Adrian shook his head again.

Truly, he should have headed outside and found the police. But he knew, if he did turn the two fugitives in, they might never reveal what they were chasing—or what secrets the writing on the urn might unveil.

He had come to the Bunker Hill Monument seeking answers, just like them. Though it could be coincidence, the more reasonable assumption was that somehow, their search and his were related.

He took a deep breath and came to a decision.

The two fugitives had run upstairs, toward the observation deck at the top of the monument: a literal dead end. But the woman seemed smart. The man appeared to be a day away from handcuffs, but the woman, the way she'd figured out the writing on the urn—she just might have a chance.

So Adrian decided—the best decision, for the moment, was no decision. He would wait, and watch, and see what happened next.

CHAPTER TWENTY-ONE

Hailey's calves were burning, and she was pulling the dank air in through her teeth by the time they had rounded the last curve. But she figured they still had a pretty good head start on whoever Nick had seen outside in the park. She knew she was going to feel every one of those 294 steps when her heart rate returned to normal, but at the moment her mind was in full flight mode.

She leapt over the final step and found herself in the crowded observatory at the top of the granite monument. The space wasn't large; the tour group ahead of them was huddled around the viewing windows cut into the walls, the tourists mostly gathered in groups of two and three, taking in the 360-degree views of Charlestown, the river, and Boston beyond.

Hailey didn't have time for the view, and she planned to stay as far away from those windows and the vertigo-inducing panorama as she could. Instead, her eyes were tearing around the small space, looking for some way to turn what was obviously a dead end into a way out.

Even a quick assessment told her there wasn't much that hadn't been there from the time the capstone was sealed to the top of the great obelisk, in 1843. Other than what appeared to be some sort of fire alarm control box where the wall met the ceiling directly above her head, the place was a living museum. Aside from the viewing windows, there wasn't much to work with.

Attached to the far wall, behind a family of four taking selfies with a cell phone, was an empty metal frame Hailey remembered had once held the Adams cannon—a Revolutionary-era weapon that had been stolen from a British gun post overlooking the harbor in 1774—which she knew now sat in a glass case in the adjoining Masonic lodge. It looked as though some work was being done on the granite where the cannon had once been affixed; on the floor by the posing tourists Hailey saw a couple bottles of cleaning solution next to a toolbox bristling with different-size chisels and stone-working paraphernalia.

"That's the top of the elevator shaft, right?"

Nick had stepped forward a few feet past her to the edge of a circular grate cut into the center of the stone floor. Peering past him, Hailey could see down into the lip of the shaft—which ran in a stomach-churning straight drop all the way to the ground 221 feet below. When she craned her head and fought back her fears, she could see a hint of the orange light that bathed the column and the urn at the base of the long drop, but other than that the shaft was devoid of light. Even so, Nick went down on one knee for a closer look.

"I think I see iron rungs, starting a few yards down. Maybe for maintenance, when it was still operating."

Hailey shook her head. Even if they could somehow pry the grate loose, Hailey knew it would be pointless effort. Whoever Nick had seen outside would be entering the stairwell by now—which meant they'd get to the top before Hailey and Nick had made it a quarter of the way down the shaft. They'd be even more trapped than they were right now.

"You're right," Nick said, rising back up from the grate. "This is hopeless."

But Hailey had already moved on from the shaft, continuing to search for something else that could help.

On the other side of the circular grate, by a viewing window on the farthest wall from where they were standing, she caught sight of one of the uniformed park rangers; mid-thirties, with a mustache and glasses, in the middle of explaining something about the view outside to an elderly couple in matching red sweaters. Hailey's attention moved to the man's belt; he had a walkie-talkie next to a flashlight— which meant they had even less time than Hailey had thought. Any minute he could get a call from below to look out for them.

At the same time—a thought hit her. Truth was, she'd been in similar positions before, as a card counter. Trapped in a casino by security, desperate to get out. The stakes were higher now, but she had trained for this. Keeping track of the cards was only one component of beating the house.

A plan was forming, puzzle pieces slipping into place. It wasn't going to be easy, and they'd need to get lucky—but there was a way forward. She did her best to steady her nerves, as she unslung her backpack from her shoulder.

"It's not hopeless. But the only way down is the way we came up."

She unzipped the backpack and dug past the eagle and the book. The flask was there, too, still half full of battery acid, as was her purse, tucked into an interior fold of the pack. But the rest were all tools of her trade.

"Hailey, if it's law enforcement, they probably have our pictures from the cameras in the casino. Which means they know who we are."

"Not who we are," Hailey said, "who we *were*."

She started to pull out items. First, a baseball hat, which she tossed to Nick. He eyed it, shrugged, pulled it down low over his eyes.

"And lose the jacket."

Unfortunately, the shirt beneath was denim, too, but she had him roll up the sleeves and pop the collar.

Then she was back to her pack. Her hair was already different from her photos, so it wouldn't catch anyone's attention. But she retrieved a pair of heavy plastic glasses without lenses.

Then she reached deeper into the bag, and withdrew a plastic case, which she flipped open, revealing her heavy artillery: a fist-size ball of puttylike material she'd gotten off the Internet when she'd first been made at Foxwoods, after taking their blackjack tables for five digits.

She tore the rubbery material in half and handed part of it to Nick.

"It goes in your mouth, against the cheeks. Changes the contours of your face. Doesn't seem like much—but sometimes it's even good enough to fool the facial rec software."

Nick watched as she pushed her half of the putty into her mouth, using her fingers to mold it to the inside of her cheeks. He eyed the result, then shook his head.

"Yeah, OK, maybe in the dark—"

"It's pretty dark in that stairwell—"

"And maybe it can fool a camera. But a cop, up close? No way."

Hailey knew he was right—the odds were, a

good law enforcement officer would see right through different hair, a pair of fake glasses and some cheek plumping. But if there was one thing a card counter understood, it was all about changing the odds until they tipped to your advantage.

"The disguise is only part of the plan."

Before he could respond, she turned back toward the stairs—looking at the fire alarm attached right below the ceiling. Then she turned to her left, toward where the cannon was once affixed to the wall. Then to the park ranger. And then to the grate over the elevator shaft, right behind where Nick was standing.

It would work.

It had to work.

"They're only going to see through this if they're looking in the right direction," she said.

Then she started forward.

"The key is to make sure they aren't."

CHAPTER TWENTY-TWO

ish in a barrel," State Detective Marsh grunted as he sidled next to Zack Lindwell at the entrance to the monument, while the second officer—a BPD homicide detective who'd accompanied the puggish statie from the crime scene at the warehouse—remained a step behind. "You might want to stay out of the way, Lindsy. Wouldn't want you creasing that pretty suit if things get physical."

Zack wasn't sure which was bothering him more, the eager look on Marsh's face or the way the man's right hand rested on his sidearm, still thankfully holstered beneath his jacket. Zack doubted the rough-and-tumble cop would be able to restrain himself much longer. The stocky man's deep-set eyes flashed with violent anticipation—or more accurately, anticipation of violence. No matter that they were in a very public setting—a goddamn tourist spot on the Freedom Trail—surrounded by innocent civilians, or that the suspects included a young woman with no prior arrests and an ex-con whose record, though admittedly long, showed no indication that he'd ever carried anything more dangerous than a pocketknife. It was clear that Marsh intended to bring this case to a rapid conclusion, and if bullets needed to fly to get him there, so much the better.

To be fair, Marsh had just come from a crime scene that included two young men lying dead on the floor, victims of some gruesome, paralytic agent. And that dead fence with the missing fingernails was now slowly bloating in a cabinet at the morgue. Marsh was under a fair amount of pressure to make a collar—and by some stroke of fortune, the opportunity had just been handed to him on a silver platter.

Zack still hadn't decided whether they'd just gotten ridiculously lucky, or if they were overestimating their quarry. His tech team at the Boston Bureau in Chelsea had barely had time to begin their phishing operation on Hailey's phone when a source at the BPD had called him with the news: although Marsh hadn't gotten around to alerting him, the two fugitives had been spotted on surveillance footage coming out of an Orange Line subway train at a stop in Charlestown, and then had been picked up on foot crossing past three more cameras on their way to Bunker Hill. As a final nail in their proverbial coffin, a camera mounted on the museum across the street had caught them in real time entering the monument itself, and as of that moment, they'd yet to reemerge.

Marsh hadn't been pleased to see Zack arrive at the scene a minute after his own unmarked car had skidded to a stop by the grassy park in front of the giant obelisk; and he'd been even less his agreeable self when Zack had tried to talk him into waiting for backup arrive before they rushed the monument on their own. Although Zack was FBI and could—given enough time to make the proper phone calls—have attempted to take control of the situation, all they had so far were dead bodies, which meant Marsh, on homicide, was still officially in charge. Unless they were to find a couple of Renoirs on the other side of that entrance cut into the monument, Zack, on art crimes, had to continue to play backup quarterback.

Still, glancing up toward the peak of the massive, jutting granite tower, it wasn't thoughts of Renoir that pulled at the corners of Zack's mind; instead, his thoughts were immediately tipped toward one of the French Impressionist master's contemporaries: Vincent van Gogh. Of course, he knew, logically, that a giant obelisk rising up into the sky should have had him thinking of a different Dutch artist— Govert Flinck, one of Rembrandt's pupils, whose painting *Landscape with Obelisk* had been one of the objects stolen from the Gardner Museum that fateful night—but somehow Van Gogh seemed to him more appropriate. Not merely because Van Gogh had often described the cypress trees that had dominated many of his paintings as reminiscent of these emblems of Egyptian archaeology, but because the huge monument dominating the sky seemed so much like something out of a fevered dream, the sort that Van Gogh was famous for capturing.

The setting defied logic, which was fitting, because Zack could think of no logical reason why Hailey and Nick, apparently on the run from two separate crime scenes, had come to a crowded tourist spot on the Freedom Trail and then cornered themselves inside.

"One way in," Marsh said, nodding toward the BPD officer, "one way out. Detective Karp, you head up the steps to the top. You see 'em along the way, you leave 'em be and radio down. If they're still all the way up—"

Before he could finish the sentence, a sudden blaring alarm tore through the air. The noise was coming from inside the monument, a rising and falling electronic wail that reverberated off the granite and echoed out through the entrance in ear-shattering waves.

"What the hell?" Marsh hissed.

"Fire alarm," Zack said.

And then he heard the footsteps—echoing beneath the wail, from somewhere high above. A controlled stampede of people making their way down the circular stairwell, he assumed.

"So that's their plan," Marsh grunted. "Must have spotted us. Now the fools think they can get past us in a crowd. Karp—plan stays the same. Go!"

The police officer leapt forward into the monument and jogged to his left, toward the stairs. Zack followed Marsh after him.

Once they were past the entrance, the air got a little cooler, a lot darker, and a hell of a lot louder. Caught in the blare of that alarm and the narrow walls of the obelisk, Zack had a moment of sudden claustrophobia; he'd never loved small, enclosed spaces, but he'd been in enough hidden art vaults and aging, guarded museum chambers to know how to control the feeling. Once it had passed, he let Marsh direct him to the bottom of the winding, ascending steps. The pounding of feet coming down toward them was louder, now, and growing by the second.

"You take the left side; I'll take the right. It's very narrow, so it's mostly going to be one or two at a time coming through. We go slow, and we lock eyes with everyone who passes. Got it?"

Marsh had the snaps of his holster open now, and his fingers were on the grip of his .38.

"There could be kids in here," Zack said.

"I'll aim high."

Before Zack could respond, the first pair of tourists

came jogging down toward them around the curve of the stairs. Both looked to be in their mid-fifties and were breathing hard. Zack moved aside to let them through, but Marsh was really giving them a once-over. He might have been a thug, but at least he was thorough.

Once they'd passed, another group came around the curve—and Zack could see the stairwell behind them was crowded with people now, all jumbling together as they rushed down. The blare of the fire alarm was so loud in the confined space it made it hard not to panic, and the tour group was almost one on top of the other as they pushed their way down toward the entrance.

Marsh was cursing under his breath as he continued to try to look everyone over while not blockading their path; Zack, for his part, was quickly parsing the crowd by height, weight, and age. Some he could rule out immediately. Others, he had to look a little closer. The few right in front of him were older—two of them at least sixty, wearing matching red sweaters— but behind them, higher on the stairs, he caught a glimpse of a woman who fit the right age. At that distance and in the darkness her features and hair didn't seem right, and she was wearing glasses, but maybe as she got closer—

Suddenly Marsh was grabbing at him, cell phone jammed against his ear.

"It's Karp—he made it to the top. Guess what? They're not coming down the stairs."

"What do you mean?"

"Follow me," Marsh snarled, and he barreled upward, pushing his compact body through the rush of tourists coming down.

Zack followed, pushing after him. The tunnel grew darker as they moved up from the bottom, and within a few steps it was hard to see anything. If any of the people he was pushing past were Nick and Hailey, he would have had to have gotten right in their faces to have seen—but Marsh was moving like a man possessed, shouting for Zack to keep up. Within a few minutes they'd passed the tourists, and now it was just the two of them churning up the spiral staircase.

By the time they reached the top, Zack's breaths were coming in bursts. He pushed himself out into the observation deck a foot behind Marsh, who now had his gun drawn and out in front of him.

The detective's square head swiveled on his thick neck, back and forth, but it was obvious—the fugitives were nowhere to be seen. The only two people in the room were Karp and a uniformed park ranger. Karp was down on one knee, in front of what looked to be a circular opening cut into the granite floor. A grate that had apparently covered the opening was bent halfway back, a chisel of some sort on the ground next to it. The BPD officer was leaning into the opening, while the park ranger aimed a flashlight over his shoulder.

"I think I see one of them," the officer hissed back at them, "about ten yards down. Wearing denim, hanging from one of the rungs."

Marsh rushed forward to take a look.

"What the hell is this?" he snarled.

"The nation's first passenger elevator," the park ranger answered, a little too proudly. "Well, now it's just the shaft. But in 1843—"

"Shut the hell up, Ranger Smith, and get your ass down to wherever that shaft opens up. Now!"

The park ranger rushed past Zack and hit the stairway at full speed. Marsh was still next to Karp at the edge of the shaft.

"How did this happen?"

"The ranger said after the alarm went off, he quickly corralled the tourists and led them into the stairwell. He'd gotten a few yards down the steps when he'd heard noises from up above. He'd come back up to find this. They must have used the chisel to get the grate loose."

Marsh shook his head.

"You still think we're dealing with a couple of geniuses here, Lindsy? It's a long way down. From fish in a barrel to rats in a hole."

Zack stepped closer to take a look for himself. The shaft was dark—the deeper he looked, the darker it got—but Karp had been right, down about thirty feet Zack could barely make out what looked like a denim-clad shape. It wasn't moving—maybe Nick and Hailey weren't trying to escape, maybe they were just trying to hide. Either way, Marsh had a point. *From Van Gogh's magnificent cypresses to Botticelli's bottomless pit.*

Still, Zack couldn't shake the feeling that they were missing something. Maybe someone with Nick's background, just out of prison, would have panicked and chosen an elevator shaft over a narrow stairwell. But from what Zack knew about Hailey, she was adept at running, and she thought things through. She would have known that the shaft was as much of a dead end as the stairwell—and that it would take much longer to get down those rungs than the steps. The park ranger would be at the bottom well before she and Nick; and if they were simply trying to hide—well, that was hardly likely to work either. Everything about this situation seemed off.

"Why here?" Zack asked, putting words to his thoughts. "Why get themselves in this position in the first place? How does this place connect to the Gardner theft? What were they looking for?"

Marsh rolled his eyes, then glanced from Zack to the Boston police officer.

"Wrong questions, Lindsy. Only one question matters now."

Marsh grinned, nearly salivating, as he turned back toward the dark shaft.

"Which one of us is going in first?"

———

Zack was breathing hard, the sweat spreading across the material of his tailored shirt, as he worked his way deeper and deeper down the shaft. The metal rungs felt cold and rough against his hands—some of the bars were so rusted through, he thought they might crack under his weight—but minute by minute, he continued downward, the light dimming the farther he moved from the opening above.

The air in the shaft felt dense and thick in his throat; he tried not to think about the sort of microbes he might be inhaling, molecules trapped in this narrow, current-less hole for more than two hundred years. Molecules once exhaled, perhaps, by some Revolutionary-era soldier, visiting the site to honor some fallen comrade, maybe a famous soldier, a Lafayette, a Washington, a Revere—

The radio on Zack's belt coughed to life, and he paused against the rungs, pressing the receiver against an ear.

"What the hell is going on down there?" Marsh's voice burst out into the shaft, echoing off the stone walls. "From here it looks like you're right on top of him."

Zack glanced down between his feet—and realized that Marsh was right; he'd traversed the distance faster than he'd thought, and he really was now only a handful of yards above Nick Patterson's denim jacket. No doubt, at that distance, Nick—and presumably Hailey, below him—had heard the radio. And yet the man hadn't moved any deeper down the shaft. Perhaps he had realized that it was futile—that there would be officers at the bottom of the shaft as well as the top, that they were indeed trapped?

Zack hooked the radio back to his belt, and carefully undid the snaps on his holstered .38, while lowering himself the last few rungs—

By now, it was so dark he could barely see more than the shape of Nick's shoulder.

"It's over," he said, into the darkness. "I'm Agent Lindwell with the FBI. Nobody needs to get hurt—"

He paused, because even in the darkness, he could see that something was wrong. The way Nick's shoulder seemed to hang off the rung—the angle wasn't right. Slowly, Zack stretched out his leg, reaching with his shoe until he could touch the denim—then gave it a little kick—

And the material gave way beneath his shoe, because that's all it was, material. The jacket came loose from the rung and fluttered downward, spinning and twisting like some sort of denim gull until it was lost in the blackness of the shaft.

Zack redid the snaps of his holster. It had taken him at least ten minutes to climb down there, which gave Nick and Hailey a pretty good lead. Marsh would be fuming, no doubt, but if Zack felt anything, it was a slight pull of admiration.

Then he reached for his radio and started back up the rungs.

CHAPTER TWENTY-THREE

I think we can slow down," Nick coughed, between breaths, as he jogged behind Hailey down a narrow, poorly paved alley. He considered himself in pretty good shape, but the mad dash up the steps of the monument followed by the nerve-racking journey back down, mixed in with the stream of evacuating tourists, had taken more out of him than he'd expected. And once they were through the park and out of the shadow of the great obelisk, Hailey had set off at a pace that had him gasping by the time they'd moved through the more residential and pricey Charlestown neighborhoods, and into the warren of older, run-down buildings that ran along the commercial docks behind the better-known shipyards.

Hailey finally slowed, halfway down the alley. There was a chain-link fence to her right, separating them from a series of floating docks on the edge of the harbor. On her other side, a jumble of bait shops, convenience stores, supply outlets, but no foot traffic that Nick could see.

Hailey came to a stop by a trash can in front of one of the convenience stores. With some effort, she spit the thick putty out of her mouth and into the can, then removed her fake glasses and unzipped her backpack. As she put the glasses back in the pack,

Nick saw a flash of metal—a few furls of the eagle's wing visible from the open pack—and he shivered, still breathing hard.

His head was spinning, and not just from the jog. Everything that had happened in the past twelve hours had his thoughts tangled up, and for the moment, he believed his best strategy was to focus on the things he *did* understand.

The misdirection with the elevator shaft had been simple and elegant; once Hailey had set off the fire alarm, all they'd needed to do was wait for the park ranger to usher the tourists into the stairwell—giving Nick the opportunity to noisily get the grate loose. Tossing his jacket down toward one of the lower rungs embedded in the wall of the shaft had been his own idea, to help sell the story Hailey was writing. When the ranger had come storming back up the stairs to investigate, they'd been waiting on either side of the entrance—and had easily slipped out while he was occupied with the open elevator shaft. Then it had only been a matter of mixing themselves into the stream of evacuating tourists.

Hailey had assumed either the ranger would walkie-talkie down to the base about the open shaft, or the officers would send someone up—but either way, the misdirection had been designed to give Nick and Hailey the edge they needed. Even in the darkened stairwell, a face-to-face encounter would have ended badly for them; but as Hailey had predicted, once the open shaft had been discovered, they might as well have been invisible.

Still, Nick had endured a moment of true panic as the two officers had squeezed past him in the stairwell. The first had come through like a bull on steroids, and Nick had nearly taken a shoulder in his chest letting the cop through. But the second man had moved more carefully, and Nick had no doubt that if he hadn't been rushed by the thug in front, he'd have nailed Nick right there against the granite wall.

"Worked better than I thought," Hailey said, as Nick caught up with her. She was still moving forward but scanning around them for anywhere that looked sheltered enough to give her time to go to work on the book. "If we're lucky, they're still down in the shaft, trying to arrest your jacket——"

A sound behind them stopped her midsentence. Nick whirled—and to his surprise, saw a familiar figure a half dozen yards down the alley. The professor from the monument—Adrian Jensen—climbing off a bicycle, which he then carefully leaned against the chain-link fence. As Nick and Hailey watched, the man affixed his helmet to the bike, retrieved a leather shoulder bag, and then hurried toward them.

"You kidding me?" Nick said. "You followed us?"

Adrian ignored him, focusing on Hailey.

"The urn at the Bunker Hill Monument—you implied that it was a key to a Jeffersonian cipher?"

"This doesn't concern you," Nick said, squaring himself in front of the foppish man. He didn't think the professor was a threat; if the man had really been following them from the monument, he could have turned them in to the police at any point with a phone call. But his interest was unnerving, and they didn't need a third wheel—even an overeducated one.

"Everything about this concerns me," Adrian responded. "That urn is a piece of Revolutionary history, and you've found something——"

He stopped, staring toward Hailey's backpack. The wing of the eagle was still visible above the open zipper, and Adrian's eyes widened as he seemed to recognize what he was seeing.

"The eagle."

Hailey glanced at Nick, then shrugged.

"It's the finial from the Gardner—" she began.

Nick tried to quiet her with a look, but Adrian was already stepping forward.

"No. *Paul Revere's* eagle."

He reached into his shoulder bag and retrieved a thick envelope. With trembling hands, he pulled out a sheaf of pages and turned to what appeared to be the last page. He showed the page to Hailey, and Nick peered down at it from over her shoulder.

The image was strange—black and white and gray, shaded like the negative of a photograph, or something that had been taken by an X-ray machine. But the shape at the center of the image was un-mistakable.

"Where is this from?" Hailey asked.

"It's a radiograph of an original engraving, taken through the wood of a trunk once owned by John Hancock—carried off and hidden by Paul Revere during the battles of Concord and Lexington."

Nick felt like laughing. But the look on the professor's face was entirely serious. Paul Revere. John Hancock.

"This engraving is of a mold created by Paul Revere."

"Paul Revere made Napoleon's finial eagle?" Nick asked.

"That's the point. He didn't make it. To my knowledge—which is, to say, to the best of any-one's knowledge—there are no Revere eagles. My colleague—Charles—believed this mold was never meant to be fired."

"Why construct a mold for an eagle you never intended to make?" Nick asked.

Adrian didn't respond. There was no question—there was more that Adrian wasn't telling them. But the engraving and the eagle were connected, which meant somehow Adrian was connected to them.

Nick didn't like the thought of involving someone else he didn't know. And he damn well wasn't going to trust this stranger. But the man did seem to be following the same thread of clues as them; he hadn't been at the Bunker Hill Monument by accident. Clearly, he knew things that they didn't, and could probably be helpful.

Hailey seemed to have come to the same conclusion, because she suddenly pointed to a set of steps tucked behind a boarded-up grocery store, mostly lit by the bright green neon shamrock hanging over the convenience store next door.

A moment later Hailey was sitting on the lowest step, the copper paged book unwrapped and open on her lap. She had Nick's cell phone next to her on the step, the screen open to the photo he'd taken of the numbers that had appeared on the gilded urn. Adrian was hovering nearby, watching, and Nick was pacing back and forth, as Hailey went to work.

As she concentrated on the pages, her entire persona seemed to change. It was like a switch being flicked, the way the muscles in her face relaxed, her body gone liquid—as if every ounce of her energy was being funneled toward the task in front of her.

Nick didn't dare say a word, watching as she used a pencil and pad of paper from her backpack to carefully begin applying the numbers from the urn to rearrange the letters from the copper pages into vertical lines, excising out the random fragments along the way. He wasn't sure how much time went by like that—in silence—but he didn't stop pacing until she finally leaned back, the muscles beneath her skin twitching back to life.

She pushed her notepad in front of her; Nick looked down to see sentences, still vertical, but now with spaces and punctuation she had obviously added on her own. Words, not gibberish—except, as Nick stared, he realized he still didn't know what they meant.

Adrian stepped uncomfortably close, almost boxing Nick out as he peered down at the notebook.

"More French," he said.

Hailey nodded, then drew her own phone out of her purse, which was tucked into the pocket in her backpack. She played with the home screen until she'd found her translation app.

"Most of the time I'm translating Russian mathematical papers with this, but it can handle dozens of languages. Give me some time, I'll work through this."

"My French is graduate level—" Adrian began, but Hailey waved him off. The professor seemed like he was going to protest, but then he saw the way Nick was looking at him and only nodded.

It was about ten minutes later when Hailey glanced up from the phone and the book with an expression that could only be described as bewildered.

"It's a diary—not by Lafayette or Paul Revere. It was apparently written by a man named Pierre-Philippe Thomire."

"The sculptor," Adrian said.

When neither Hailey nor Nick seemed to recognize the name, Adrian gave them a stare that Nick guessed was usually reserved for freshmen who were about to fail his class.

"One of the most prominent French sculptors, who worked mostly in Paris during the early nineteenth century. A favorite of the emperor, Thomire also made many pieces for Marie Antoinette. He was proficient with bronze—perhaps the greatest bronzier of his era."

Hailey glanced at her backpack, where the wing of the eagle finial was still visible.

"Indeed," Adrian said. "Thomire was also a noted colleague of Lafayette's. He traveled with the war hero when Lafayette came to the Americas to lay the cornerstone of the Bunker Hill Monument."

"And that's when he put the key on the urn?" Nick asked.

"Presumably," Hailey said. "This diary was written here, too—but earlier, during a short sabbatical Thomire had taken after his sixty-third birthday. It was the summer of 1814—the same year the eagle was made."

According to the diary, she continued, Thomire had come to Boston to spend a week in the workshop of the most famous metalworker in the fledgling American republic.

"Revere?" Adrian coughed. "But there's nothing in the historical literature—"

"I can't speak to that," Hailey said. "But if this diary is real—this is where things get really strange."

According to Thomire's diary, he hadn't visited Revere simply because Revere was the foremost metallurgist in the country—the only person in the Americas who had figured out how to work with sheets of copper, and the top expert on bronze and engraving—but because Thomire and Revere shared another passion.

"'*Le monde secret de l'alchimie*,'" Hailey read, from

the diary. "If the translation software is working correctly, he's talking about *alchemy*."

Adrian coughed again, shaking his head. Nick looked at him, then at Hailey. Alchemy. He'd heard the word before.

"Like, turning lead into gold."

"It's a strange, cultish endeavor that goes back thousands of years," Hailey said. "When I first got interested in science, I read about it pretty extensively. The prescience stuff you and I talked about at MIT— well, alchemy goes back even farther than most of that—farther back than the origins of chemistry, even way beyond chymistry. It began in ancient Egypt but has been practiced throughout time. A handful of famous scientists in history were secret alchemists. Newton was perhaps the best known. When I said he came to his conclusions about light being broken up into more basic elements—that comes from alchemy. But Newton wasn't the only famous historical alchemist—there were many others."

Adrian was still just shaking his head. Nick wasn't sure how to digest what Hailey was saying, but she seemed to be only getting started.

"And you're right, at its most basic, alchemy is about changing lead into gold. But it's much bigger than that. Alchemists believed that once you had the power to transform one metal to another, you had the secret to dominance over the material world. It was considered such a powerful science that alchemists were often arrested, and in medieval times, even killed. Which is why they became so secretive. Began using symbols to hide their work. Symbols like the one for sulfur, other symbols that made their way into the masonic traditions—"

"And Paul Revere?" Nick asked.

"Getting to that," Hailey said. "Thomire had come to Boston because, according to the diary, Revere believed he had uncovered something significant. Thomire couldn't get Revere to tell him what it was, but late one night, alone in Revere's lab, Thomire had stumbled upon a sculpting mold. Except this mold was different; it was the result of many pages—books filled with pages—of mathematical calculations. The mold had been crafted to a mathematical precision Thomire had never seen before. He felt certain it had something to do with Revere's alchemic discovery, so he copied the mold as best he could and took the copy back with him to France."

She shifted around so that she could reach her backpack, and carefully withdrew the bronze eagle. Adrian's eyes went round seeing the entire thing in her hands.

"Why an eagle?" Nick asked.

Adrian's eyes never left the finial.

"The eagle as a symbol goes back a lot farther than Napoleon," he said. "Even farther than the Roman legions, who carried it on their flags as a sign of their empire. Alchemists had been using a double-headed eagle as one of their prime, hidden symbols since before medieval times. That's the real reason you see it as one of the symbols of Freemasonry as well. Many of the original Freemasons were alchemists. In the Revolutionary era, noted alchemists included Ben Franklin, John Hancock—"

"Revere?" Nick asked.

Adrian looked at him like he'd eaten something bitter, but then shrugged.

"Revere was a metalworker by trade. A Mechanic, as he called himself. So, it would not be much of a stretch that he shared such a passion with his colleagues."

"So Thomire brought the mold back to France," Nick said, continuing Hailey's thread. "And then he cast it and used the design for the finial for Napoleon's regiment."

"Yes," Hailey responded. "But according to the diary, and as the professor pointed out—Revere had never meant it to be cast, because the mold wasn't really a mold at all. Apparently, it was a way of hiding a particular mathematical equation—which was supposed to lead to a mathematical *solution*. You see, the shape of the mold was actually an example of a branch of mathematics called 'algebraic topology.' It's like writing an equation, but instead of using numbers, you use shapes. You know how you can use math to figure out the area inside a circle? Or how you can figure out the volume of a cylinder? This applies to more complex shapes."

Nick was having an understandable amount of trouble keeping up. Hailey was so damn smart. Digesting all the information she'd gotten from the diary so quickly—it was boggling Nick's mind.

"Alchemy is math, now?"

"Everything at its heart is math. Physics. Chemistry. And yes, alchemy. Take turning lead into gold. Lead is an element—you remember the periodic table? Gold is also an element. At the atomic level, they're differentiated by three protons. Lead has three more protons than gold. To turn lead into gold, all you need to do is knock out those three protons."

"Which is impossible," Nick said.

"Not at all. In fact, it's been done before. Or something very close to it. Thirty years ago, scientists at the Lawrence Berkeley National Laboratory used a particle accelerator to blast a sample of bismuth, which is right next to lead on the periodic table. The accelerator knocked away two protons, turning the bismuth into gold. It takes an immense amount of power—nuclear-fission level power—to transform metals, but it is indeed possible. Prohibitively expensive, and only on a limited scale, but yes, scientists *can* turn lead into gold. But I wouldn't call a nuclear reactor the philosopher's stone."

Nick raised his eyebrows, until Adrian reluctantly stepped in.

"It's what the alchemists called their Holy Grail: some sort of device or substance that could transform metals. Nonsense, of course. Most alchemists described it as a rock or powder—"

"According to this diary," Hailey interrupted, before the professor could go down a winding path, "Revere believed it was a mathematical equation, not a powder. Thomire was skeptical; how could a mathematical equation turn lead into gold? Even though he'd taken the mold and cast it into this bronze eagle, he couldn't figure out the answer. But he did find one more clue. According to the last pages of Thomire's diary, Revere's experiments in alchemy did not end with the eagle's mold. There was a second part—*'deuxième partie'*—information without which the eagle was useless. Contained in the curves and swirls somewhere within the shape of the eagle was the mathematical equation, the blueprint—but its solution was somewhere else."

She shuffled to the last page of the diary, then looked up at the two of them.

"Thomire believed the clue to this second part could be found in a book Revere carried with him everywhere. When Revere passed away, just a few years later, the book also ended up in the library in his house, but Thomire never made it back to the Americas to retrieve it."

"So, this is a dead end," Nick said.

Hailey didn't answer. He could see she was thinking the same thing. But Adrian was still looking at the eagle, and his hands seemed uncomfortable against the shiny material of his bicycle tights.

"What sort of book?" he asked.

Hailey glanced up at him.

"Thomire only calls it *'le livre avec la couverture rouge.'*"

Adrian was silent. Hailey seemed to be reading his face.

"You know where it is."

Adrian ran a hand through his Medusa-like hair.

"This is more poppycock. Foolishness."

"But you do." Nick could feel Hailey's excitement from a few feet away. "Can you take us there?"

"You're fugitives," Adrian said, suddenly pulling his gaze away from the eagle. "Criminals."

Nick put a hand on his shoulder. Not hard, just to get his attention. Nick wasn't an educated man, like Adrian, but at the moment, he could make an educated guess.

"You want to know the truth about this eagle as much as we do."

Adrian looked at Nick's hand, then reached up and removed the offensive appendage.

"I know the truth. My colleague was chasing fairy tales, and so are you."

Still, he didn't walk away.

"Fine. Yes, I think I do know where we can find 'the book with the red cover.' But we're going to need to get across town. I assume neither of you brought your bicycles."

Hailey was suddenly up on her feet. Nick pulled her aside.

"And you're sure about this?"

"A few hours ago, we were sitting on half a billion dollars in art. Now we've got a bronze eagle that might get us enough to pay for the lawyer we'll need to beat a homicide rap. But if Thomire was right— you could pay for a lot of lawyers with a working philosopher's stone."

Nick nodded. He didn't like the idea of following Adrian—someone he didn't know—but the professor did seem to be an expert on the facts surrounding the eagle, Revere, all of it. And as Nick had surmised before, if the man had wanted to turn them in, he would have done so already. He had no reason to help them beyond his own selfish quest to understand what was going on—but on this, they were aligned.

"The T is out of the question," Nick said. After what had happened at the monument, law enforcement wouldn't be taking any more chances. And Nick knew from experience, once that APB went out, it was, for cops, piñata without the blindfolds, and everybody got a chance with the bat.

Which meant that public transportation of any sort was out. A taxi or Uber wasn't a much better choice; taxi dispatchers would have been warned to look out for people fitting their descriptions, and an Uber left too big an online trail to follow. Who knew what sort of technical tricks the FBI was capable of?

Which meant on foot.

"You say across town," Nick said. "That can mean a lot of things—"

But Adrian was looking past him, at something beyond the chain-link fence directly across the street from them. Nick saw one of the floating docks he'd noticed when they'd first entered the alley, lined with motorized skiffs that bounced against the water.

Hailey stepped next to him.

"You know how to drive one of those?"

"Pilot," Nick said. "It's not that complicated. One lever steers; the other makes it go."

He thought for a moment. The chain-link fence wouldn't be a problem, and the skiff's ignition would be even more simple. He glanced back at Adrian, who nodded. Truth was, it wasn't much of a decision. They were too deep, now, to do anything else.

"But we should wait until it gets dark," Nick said.

———

"Look out. This one's gonna hurt."

Nick braced himself against the low bench that took up most of the aft section of the arrow-shaped skiff, twisting the throttle forward as hard as he could. His other hand was white against the rudder controls, keeping the bow of the little boat aimed directly at the peak of the wave that had suddenly sprung up in front of them, probably churned up by one of the big cargo boats farther out in the harbor.

The motor behind him groaned as the front of the boat hit the wave. Nick felt himself lifted into the air, Hailey holding on to his arm next to him—but he gripped tight to the controls. Then the boat slammed back down with a wicked thud, and a spray of salt water drenched Adrian, up at the bow, his bicycle jammed in next to him. The professor let out a torrent of curse words, and Nick stifled a grin as they hit the next wave, thankfully smaller than the first. He pushed the rudder slightly to the left, steering from memory. It was getting darker by the minute. The moon was now high in the sky, which was just cloudy enough to cast the harbor in a thick envelope of gray on gray. Still, Nick didn't need much light to know where he was going—once Adrian had told him the destination. He'd spent his teens and twenties mucking about the docks and piers that jutted out from the various landfills and cargo depots that spotted this section of the harbor.

At the moment, they were circumnavigating the edge of the city, staying as close to land as possible to avoid the bigger boats out in the harbor while staying far enough from the docks to keep themselves shrouded in that enveloping gray. Despite the circumstances, Nick had to admit he was enjoying himself. The spray of water felt good against his skin, and there was now the littlest bit of hope smoldering inside of him—not the conflagration he'd felt when he'd come so close to the biggest score of his life—but *something*.

He glanced toward Hailey, right up next to him, more for balance than anything else, but still. She noticed his attention, and, he thought, maybe held his arm a little tighter.

"You look pretty comfortable," she said.

He shrugged.

"Spent a lot of time out on the water when I was a teen."

She didn't say anything, and he wasn't sure what made him continue.

"Maybe it was a way of dealing, when things weren't working out."

"That happened a lot," Hailey guessed.

Nick felt himself smile.

"You get used to things not working out. Before he died—my dad used to say, when things go sideways, you go forward."

"Your dad sounded smart."

"My dad was a drunk and an asshole. But he knew a lot of things about going sideways."

Nick shifted the rudder again, and the skiff curved inward, avoiding the wake of a loud party cruise farther out in the water.

"I don't think my father could've wrapped his head around how sideways this has gone. Paul Revere and a way of turning lead into gold. Using math."

"Not just lead into gold," Hailey said. "If he figured this out—it's a lot bigger than that. If you can transform one metal to another, you're talking about restructuring materials at an atomic level. From that starting point—there's no telling what you could do. Sure, you could turn lead into gold. You could also turn it into plutonium. You could use such a technology to engineer an instant, infinite power source. Hell, alchemists believed the philosopher's stone could unlock the secret of immortality. Lead into gold is just a starting place. The applications would be endless. Infinite wealth, yes, but also infinite power."

Nick didn't understand much of what she'd explained—but wealth, power, these were concepts he couldn't ignore.

But alchemy? Paul Revere? Nick wasn't an educated guy; Hailey could swim circles around him in that department. But it all seemed more like magic than science. *And yet here they are—*

Nick's hand suddenly froze against the throttle, and he quickly pushed down with all of his weight, lifting the motor right out of the choppy water. The skiff jerked forward as it slowed, and Hailey nearly toppled over next to him. She stared at Nick, surprised, but he just pointed past her, past Adrian and his bicycle, into the gray on gray ahead of them.

Something was rising up out of the darkness not a hundred yards ahead, something tall and familiar, something that appeared incredibly old. It took Nick a full moment to understand what he was looking at.

The central mast of a Revolution-era sailing ship.

Nick knew that the ship in front of them was actually a re-creation, from its ninety-foot, ornately decorated hull to its multiple masts and riggings. But in the darkness, with only the sound of the lapping water against the skiff, he felt instantly transported back two hundred and fifty years, to one of the most famous and significant moments in American history, something every schoolchild had heard of, even a child who had later turned to crime.

Fitting, he thought to himself, as he lowered the motor carefully back into the water, piloting them the rest of the way forward.

They were already flirting with alchemy.

They might as well add time travel to the mix.

CHAPTER TWENTY-FOUR

Adrian's cycling shoes clicked against the wooden planks of an eighteenth-century wharf as he hurriedly led Hailey and Nick through the darkness, picking his way past stacks of corkwood barrels, snakelike piles of heavy docking ropes and spiderwebs of unfurled rigging. To their right, spread out beyond the wharf as far as Adrian could see, the even darker panorama of Boston Harbor, as it might have appeared two hundred and fifty years ago, marked by a distinct, if cacophonic symphony: water crashing against great, tall ships, the caw of gulls, the odd rumble of thunderclouds gathering high above.

Adrian's lips turned down at the corners as he hurried his gait. He had no time for such foolishness. As good as the re-creation might be, it was all fantasy. The wharf had been constructed by professional set designers with Hollywood pedigrees. The panorama of the harbor was a projection, crafted by a cinematographer with a flair for the dramatic. The sounds were being pumped in through speakers hidden in the ceiling. It might have seemed like he was rushing through the crisp air of December 16, 1773, but it was actually the second week of May, and the air was crisp because some fool had set the air-conditioning much too high. The only thing linking Adrian to that fateful night—perhaps one of the most written about, taught, and referenced events in American history—was the time.

Adrian reached the end of the wharf, slowing a bit to let the two fugitives catch up. Even the thought of them just steps behind him made the skin at the back of his neck tingle in the most unpleasant way—but from the moment he'd decided to follow them when they'd come skittering out of the Bunker Hill Monument, instead of alerting the policemen he'd seen rushing up the steps when they'd first left him, he'd thrown his lot in with them, for better or worse.

In the end, it was all Charles's fault. But once he'd seen what Hailey had revealed on the urn, and especially after he'd laid his eyes on Thomire—and Revere's—eagle, he'd really had no choice. He was a scholar, and this was squarely, now, a scholarly endeavor. If his two "companions" were thieves—and clearly, they looked like thieves—there would be time to deal with that after the mystery had been solved.

Once the bedraggled pair were right behind him again, Adrian quickened his pace. "Griffin's Wharf," the sign hanging atop a suspiciously blank and blackened section of the set proclaimed, even though Adrian was well aware the actual location of that historical spot was now filled in and paved over, at the corner of Congress and Purchase streets a few blocks away. Then the three of them passed through an open doorway that led deeper into the museum.

If you could call it that. From the two ships parked outside—expert re-creations of the shipping schooners *Eleanor* and the *Beaver*—to the exhibits set within the sprawling complex that stretched along Congress Street, the Boston Tea Party Museum seemed more of an amusement park ride than a place you would go to study history.

If it had been up to Adrian, this would not have been a surreptitious visit. If it had been up to him, he would have made a simple phone call to the museum trustees—something he'd suggested while Nick was hot-wiring the skiff before their soggy journey around the harbor. But both Nick and Hailey had refused the offer—and in a way, Adrian had seen their logic. He would not have been able to give many details to the trustees, and they would have been less than enthusiastic to allow him to rifle through one of their rotating collections. No matter that Adrian *himself* had curated that particular collection, two years earlier, when the trustees had finally deigned to acknowledge Paul Revere's participation in the Tea Party, that historic act of hooliganism.

And to be fair, even if Adrian had been able to give them some story about a special project that needed immediate attention—he suspected they might have refused him anyway. He knew that many of the trustees simply didn't like Adrian, because he'd often told them what he thought of their *institution*. It reeked of whimsy. And Adrian felt almost as strongly about *whimsy* as he did about *flights of fancy*.

On the other side of the doorway, Adrian found himself in the main section of the museum, a wide gallery filled with exhibits. There were framed documents on the walls documenting the onerous Stamp Act of 1765, which levied taxes on just about every piece of paper, from letters to playing cards, and the Townshend Act of 1767, which taxed pretty much everything else. Then a print of Revere's engraving of the Boston Massacre, which followed in short order. And after that, the declaration of the Tea Act of 1773, which most historians taught was the parliamentary outrage that led, in short course, to the Tea Party, the British overreaction, Paul Revere's ride, and the start of the American Revolution at Lexington and Concord.

None of that was true, of course, as any of the freshmen who'd remained awake through the lecture Adrian gave at the start of every year to his newest class could have explained. Adrian believed the Tea Party had very little to do with taxation without representation at all. The Tea Act was not a new tax; it was a *repeal* of the heavy taxation inflicted on the colonies up to that point. It was called the Tea Act because the one item exempt from the repeal was tea. But the real indignity of the Tea Act wasn't the continuation of taxes, but that in the same stroke the British gave the foundering East India Company a total monopoly over the tea trade, indemnifying them from shipping duties. Tea itself became *cheaper* for the colonies, not more expensive. But if the people of Massachusetts had no real reason to be upset by the protectionist move, one class of Bostonians became instantly incensed: the *smugglers*. The most prominent smugglers of the time—John Hancock and his friend Sam Adams—realized their tea business couldn't compete with such a monopoly, and decided they needed to do something. So, they turned to their colleague Paul Revere.

It wasn't simply out of patriotic fury that the angry townspeople gathered in the Old South Meeting House that evening to foment an act of rebellion against the crown. They were incited by Revere's Sons of Liberty, or more accurately, his more professional cadre of clandestine operatives: his Mechanics. It was the Mechanics who provided the rabble-rousers with Native American costume, adorning them with war paint and Mohawk feathers. It was the Mechanics who had provided the tomahawks that were used to shatter the lids of the tea crates. And it was John Hancock, the top tea smuggler in the colonies and soon to be hero of the Revolution, who had reportedly led them from the meetinghouse, with the shout: "Let every man do what is right in his own eyes!"

In fact, one could argue—as Adrian often did—that the entire Revolutionary War was the result of a smuggler's attempt to derail his competition. But Adrian's role at the museum had been decidedly limited. He had nothing to do with the main exhibits, or the paintings on the walls of Hancock and others, or what was in the glass case that dominated the center of the exhibit space, which contained an actual crate from the Tea Party itself, rotating under elegant spotlights. The crate, one of only two that remained, had been scooped up out of the water the morning after the event by a fifteen-year-old kid named John Robinson, and had been handed down from generation to generation until it had been offered to the curators of the museum in 2004. Adrian wasn't interested in crates thrown into the water in an act of corporate competition; no, his only contribution to the museum was a second, much smaller, and often ignored display case, right up against the far wall.

Adrian made short work of the distance, followed closely by his two charges. This display case was waist high and only a few feet across, ending right by a door marked "Staff Only" that Adrian knew led to the museum's control center—which itself told you everything you needed to know about the place. *What sort of true historical site needs a control center? What sort of academic institution needs special effects?*

As he reached the case, he pulled a set of keys out

from his bag, which was still hanging from his shoulder. He wasn't sure what had made him make copies of the keys when he'd first been brought in by the trustees to curate this addition to their exhibit room. Probably, it had simply been spite. He hadn't been the trustees' first choice. But *Charles* had been too busy to help out—busy with what Adrian now knew was his insane, secret project.

When the trustees had first informed Adrian that they'd wanted to add a case of Revere artifacts to their collection, he'd actually been in the process of helping to restore a batch of items taken from the basement of the Revere House in the North End. Of course, the Tea Party Museum had wanted Adrian to bring over dramatic memorabilia, maybe something to do with Revere's midnight ride, or maybe a Revere-owned musket or a Revere-made cannonball.

Adrian grinned, more to himself than to Nick and Hailey, as he carefully opened the top of the display case. They hadn't gotten muskets or cannonballs. Instead, he'd brought them a few examples of Revere's delicate metalwork; copper screws, silver plates, a few pieces of well-crafted jewelry, including a little necklace made mostly of silver, with an ornament attached to the links that shined like gold. And a stack of books, most in Revere's own hand. Revere had been an obsessive bookkeeper, writing almost everything down. It was one of the reasons he was still so well known. Often, the most famous figures in history weren't the most important. They were simply the ones narcissistic enough to write about themselves more than their peers, and smart enough to leave those books behind in places that were likely to still be around a couple of hundred years later.

Adrian ignored the copper, silver, and jewelry, and

went right for the stack of books. It took him barely a minute to find what he was looking for: a small, bright red notebook, tucked between an almanac Revere had gotten as a gift from Ben Franklin, and a sheaf of records from one of his foundries.

The leather-bound notebook wasn't particularly impressive to look at, but Adrian knew it by sight. And though he'd mostly forgotten about it before Hailey had read Thomire's description of the thing in that copper-plated diary, the color of its cover had always stood out to him—even if its actual title had never meant anything to him before today.

He turned the book to show that title to Hailey.

"*The Book of Bells*," she said, confused. "What do bells have to do with this?"

Instead of answering, Adrian opened the book and began scanning through the pages. Two years ago, Adrian had only given it a passing glance. He hadn't really read it—if he had, as he did now, he would have realized what it was: Revere's meticulous record of every bell he'd made.

Now, armed with what Charles had discovered, with what Hailey's book had told them—Adrian wondered—was there more to it than Revere's pedantic personality? Maybe this record of Revere's bells was actually a log of experiments, conducted over a lifetime, all aiming toward one goal: his final bell.

Adrian had never given it thought before, accepting the common perception that the last bell Revere had made was the one hanging in King's Chapel. But now—he quickly shuffled through the book, making his way to the last page.

His eyes widened as he reached the final entry.

My God.

CHAPTER TWENTY-FIVE

"Professor," Hailey asked again, more insistent. "What do bells have to do with any of this?"

Adrian looked up from the book, his mind spinning through what he had just read. Hailey was staring at him, her backpack still over her shoulder; Nick seemed more interested in the flashier items in the exhibit case than the red-covered book.

Adrian was still digesting it all himself, but he could see from the wild look in Hailey's eyes that she wasn't going to wait for him to work everything through on his own. After a beat, he pointed to her backpack, then beckoned with a hand.

She glanced at Nick, but he was still occupied by the case. Then she unzipped the pack, and removed the eagle, unwrapping its body from the checkered blanket. Carefully, she handed it to Adrian, who held it gingerly, feeling the cold surface of the bronze against his fingers.

"This was never supposed to actually exist. It wasn't even really a mold—"

"But it does exist. The eagle—"

"Not the *eagle*," Adrian said, shaking his head. "The eagle's *wings*."

Adrian turned the eagle over in his hands, showing her one extended wing. He ran a finger over the curves.

Hailey seemed to understand.

"The mathematical equation," she said, "hidden in the shape of that wing."

Adrian nodded.

"Alchemical, occult, I wouldn't begin to hypothesize—but obviously an equation Revere deemed to be valuable and powerful, so important that he went to great lengths to hide it."

Hailey was watching his fingers move across the curves of the wing.

"Powerful—and incredibly complex. It would take years to solve it from the topography of such an object. Perhaps you'd even need the use of a super-computer. And even then—it might not be possible. Certainly, Thomire didn't know how to solve it—but by making the eagle he did manage to preserve it. But that book—"

Adrian shook his head.

"The solution isn't written in a book. This wing is hiding an equation for a pattern of sound waves. A tone, made by the ringing of a bell."

Hailey opened her eyes wide. But then she nodded, impressed.

"Sound waves. The curves of the eagle's wing represent precise sound waves. It's theoretically possible. Sound waves can affect materials at a molecular level. Everyone knows the right frequency of sound can shatter glass. But using sound for something like this, to generate the perfectly precise tone to *transform* molecules—that would be one hell of a bell."

This finally caught Nick's attention—as he pointed at the necklace in the case in front of Adrian.

"Like that bell?"

Adrian looked down, realizing that in fact the gold-looking ornament on the end of the necklace was indeed a small bell, about twice the size of an acorn. He shook his head, annoyed.

"Don't be foolish. That bell is a trinket. Revere originally made it for a child's dollhouse, then put it on a necklace."

"Well, then which bell?" the man grunted.

Adrian ignored him, speaking to Hailey, who at least showed an appreciable level of understanding.

"At first, I thought it was the bell in King's Chapel. An easy mistake to make. Popular knowledge would have it that the King's Chapel bell, delivered two years before Revere's death—was his last. But I should have known better. Popular knowledge is an oxymoron. People, on the whole, are usually wrong about most things."

Nick and Hailey looked at Adrian with a shared expression he'd seen before on the faces of many of his colleagues and students, but he couldn't have cared less. Because, now having seen the last page of Revere's *Book of Bells*, he knew he was *right*. The textbooks, the tourist pamphlets, the popular conception were all *wrong*.

"In the later years of Revere's life," Adrian continued, now in full lecture mode, "he'd become obsessed with making bells. Over the course of a decade, he cast over three hundred of them. Now we know why."

Adrian noticed that Nick had reached past him into the display case and had deftly palmed the necklace with the gold-looking bell. But Hailey slapped his hand, then took it from him, as if planning to return it to the case. No doubt, she was the brains of the pair.

"Alchemy," Adrian repeated. "Sorcery, magic, whatever you want to call it, he was chasing a fantasy—"

"And the key to it was a precise tone emitted by a perfectly crafted bell," Hailey said.

"My colleague found evidence to suggest that Revere believed he had succeeded," Adrian said. "He'd followed the blueprint that he'd hidden in the wing of the eagle and crafted the solution—his very last bell."

Adrian handed the eagle back to Hailey, then opened *The Book of Bells* to the last page.

"After the King's Chapel bell, he made one more. It was actually a replacement. In 1798, Revere had made a two-hundred-and-forty-two-pound bell for the greatest warship of the fledgling republic. But it had been shot off the boat's deck during a naval battle, at the height of the War of 1812. While the ship was being refitted in Boston, a few years later, in the calm of night, Revere delivered a second bell. His last, crafted right before his death."

Hailey digested his words, her eyes growing wider.

"You're talking about the USS *Constitution*. The tall ship parked in Charlestown. Old Ironsides."

"It was called that because of Paul Revere. It was Revere's factories that plated the sides and bottom of the boat with sheets of copper. When the boat was struck by cannon fire during the war and survived, it was nicknamed Old Ironsides."

"So this last bell is on the *Constitution*?" Nick said. "Why would Revere put it there?"

Adrian chose his most dismissive tone.

"The *Constitution* is basically a floating museum today, but at the time it was one of the most powerful ships in the world, certainly the most formidable in the Americas. It had just returned from numerous victories at sea. It was considered unsinkable. At the time, oceans were dangerous. There were pirates, enemy nations, storms. If Revere had wanted to transport something he imagined to be valuable—

so valuable that the British had essentially started the Revolutionary War over it, if my colleague's theories are correct—how do you think he'd do it? He'd put it on the most powerful boat of his era. But not out in the open, where it could be shot off again. He'd have hidden it there."

"So, he put this bell on the *Constitution*," Hailey said. "And then he died. You think it might still be there? Today?"

Adrian looked back at the book, his mind whirling. It was ridiculous, fantasy. None of it seemed true or possible. But he finally shrugged.

"If Revere's bell actually is still on the *Constitution*, I know where you'd find it."

He held the book up toward them, showing them the last page.

"It's right in the name."

Revere's handwriting was lavish and in script, but readable:

La Cloche Sous L'aigle

"More French?" Nick asked.

"Revere's father was a Huguenot. He grew up speaking both languages."

"But what does it mean?"

Adrian didn't feel a need to respond. He could tell that Hailey understood. And she was about to answer for him when suddenly there was a loud hiss, and something whipped through the air, hitting Nick in his right shoulder, spinning him around. There was a spray of bright red blood, and then another hiss—and the display case behind Adrian exploded in a rain of glass.

CHAPTER TWENTY-SIX

It all happened so fast it seemed like time itself had shattered along with the display case. One minute, Hailey was reading the last page of the book in the foppish professor's hands, and the next everything exploded around her. She saw Nick spinning away, pushed by the force of the bullet that had hit him in the shoulder. She saw the professor diving to the ground and then scrambling on all fours toward a door marked "Staff Only." And then she herself was diving forward, her backpack coming off as she grabbed Nick and pulled him behind the closest protection she could find—the slowly revolving Robinson crate, encased in its envelope of glass.

She looked down at Nick, who was flat against the floor, clutching at his wound. Blood seeped through his fingers and his face was pale, but he was breathing. Hailey risked a glance around the edge of the revolving crate—but she couldn't see the woman who had fired at them. She'd only caught the slightest glance before she'd hit the ground: jet-black hair tied back in a ponytail, some sort of dark vest over a zippered sweat suit, and heels. But there was no sign of the woman, who could be anywhere by now, and moving closer by the second.

She turned back to Nick. His eyes were open, but he wasn't trying to move.

"I'll be OK," he said. "You've got to go. You can't stay here."

"I can't just leave you."

Even as she said the words, Hailey realized she felt them, too. The emotions surprised her; she didn't get close to people easily. They were in this together.

"She's not after me," Nick coughed. "She's after that."

He jerked his head toward the eagle, which Hailey realized she was still clutching. She'd lost the towel, and the bronze glinted in the spotlight from the revolving crate above.

"Then I'll toss it to her."

Nick shook his head.

"She gets that, and we're dead. You saw the warehouse and the hotel room. She doesn't leave loose ends."

Hailey realized Nick was right. She thought quickly, did the math, and came to the only conclusion that she could. It wasn't ideal, but there wasn't any choice.

"I'll draw her away. If you can make it, meet me at the skiff."

She gave his hand a squeeze, then started scanning the room, looking for the best way out. They'd come in through a locked side entrance that had been child's play for Nick, but getting there would take her past where she'd last seen the woman. But as she looked around, she saw another way; an open door leading into a dark hall with wooden planks for a floor.

Hailey took a deep breath, kept low—and took off. Her sudden move gave her a slight advantage; the bullet that came her way went wide by a handful of inches, shattering a framed picture on the wall behind her. Then she was through the doorway and into a much darker space. Not a room, but a wharf overlooking what appeared to be the harbor, except it wasn't, because there were tall Revolutionary War–era ships bouncing up and down on the water. Hailey saw a pile of cork barrels in a corner, and quickly huddled behind them, hiding herself as best she could. Just in time, because as she clutched the eagle to her chest, she heard the distinct sound of heels against the creaky wooden floor.

The woman with the dark hair stood in the doorway, the handgun floating expertly in her right hand. She paused there for a moment, listening. Then she spoke.

"You don't have to die, Katie. You know that, don't you?"

Hailey felt the blood rushing into her cheeks. She hadn't heard that name in a long, long time.

"I just want the eagle," the woman continued. "The people I work for have been chasing that eagle for a very long time. Give it to me, and you can go back to the life you've created for yourself."

Somehow, the woman knew who she really was. But if that was supposed to frighten Hailey, well, it had the opposite effect. She felt anger boiling inside her. This woman had no idea what she'd gone through to get from Katie to Hailey.

"The eagle is worthless," Hailey hissed, from behind the barrels.

"You know that's not true. Something is hidden in the shape of its wings that is more valuable than either of us can imagine."

"You were listening in on the bar."

"I wasn't the only one. Which is why I don't have time to play with you."

Hailey felt her anger building.

"I know why your employers want the eagle. But it just contains the equation, not the solution. I'm a mathematician. Trust me, an equation like this could take years, lifetimes to solve."

Hailey wasn't simply stalling. She was telling the woman the truth. The eagle was a blueprint, but on its own, so complex it might not even be possible to decipher. The end result—the bell, the precise tone that could transform one metal to another, was something else. *Somewhere else.*

But the woman didn't seem to care. She started forward, toward the barrels, one heel click at a time.

"To the people who pay me, lifetimes are cheap. Don't be a fool, Katie. Give me the eagle and you can walk out of here."

The sound of the woman's heels against the faux wooden dock stopped. Hailey held her breath. She glanced up and realized for the first time that the darkness to her right was actually made up of a plane of incredibly smooth black glass. She caught a glimpse of her own reflection in the strange glass—and realized the woman could see the reflection, too.

"It's over, Katie."

Hailey rose to her feet, facing the woman. She held the eagle in front of her, a pathetic shield.

"My name's not Katie," she started, as the woman raised the gun—

And suddenly, two figures sprang up directly behind the black glass. Women, in revolutionary garb, one of them pregnant. As they started to speak, the killer with the raven hair whirled toward them and fired. The bullet hit the glass, shattering it, and the two

revolutionary women vanished in a puff of sparkle—
because they had never really been there at all.
Holograms, Hailey realized, as she dashed full speed
toward a doorway that had automatically opened directly across from her. The professor, she realized, was
at the controls. When he'd scurried through the door
marked "Staff Only," she'd assumed he was running
for his life. She'd misjudged him.

Another bullet crashed past her, but she was already
through the doorway. She found herself in another
dark room, this one with a descending floor separated
into bleacher-like alleys. A vast movie screen wrapped
around the entire front of the room, from floor to ceiling. There was an emergency exit next to the screen,
but before Hailey was halfway there, she heard those
heels again, and dove for the floor.

Just as she hit the carpet, the entire room changed.
The movie screen became a vast green field, and even
the floor seemed to become part of the theme park
vision, so real Hailey could almost smell the grass of
Lexington Common. Smoke rose from panels in the
walls, obscuring the air around her. Then out of the
mist, across the entire front of the room, a phalanx of
British redcoats roared toward her, seeming to come
right out of the screen, muskets and bayonets bristling.
Ear-shattering explosions rocked the room, and the
entire floor started to shake.

The woman with the dark hair seemed momentarily stunned or confused, and Hailey didn't waste
the moment. She flung herself toward the emergency
exit and hit the door dead center with her shoulder.

Cool, night air whipped her skin as she barreled
down what appeared to be a half-covered gangplank.
Ahead of her, she saw the ship: a near perfect re-
creation of one of the three boats that had been

victimized in 1773, now floating in the same water that had once been doused with tea. With a leap, she was on the deck and moving even faster.

In front of her was a row of fake, cubic crates attached to ropes, readied to be thrown into the water during regular museum hours, assumedly by cheering tourists dressed as Mohawks. Hailey lowered her shoulders, tucked the eagle under her arm, and headed for the crates at full speed.

"Katie," she heard from the gangplank behind her. "Stop!"

But she was already over the crates, and over the ship's railing, plummeting toward the dark, cold water below.

CHAPTER TWENTY-SEVEN

Patricia had her gun out in front of her as she stalked back and forth along the railing of the re-created schooner, her eyes scanning the oily black water of the harbor where Katie — Hailey — had gone in only moments ago. As she searched the choppy surface, she used all of her training to siphon out anything that might break her focus; the lapping of the water against the boat's hull, the noise of the light late night traffic on nearby Congress Street, the odd shriek of a seagull in the air above. But it didn't matter — Hailey — Katie — was smart, and obviously a good swimmer. She hadn't broken the surface of the water yet, and there was no way to know which direction she'd gone.

When the young woman had first gone over the side, Patricia had considered diving right after her. Physically, she knew the girl would be no match for her, even submerged; but chasing a motivated target in ocean water — in near perfect darkness — was a low-percentage endeavor. If Patricia had lost her in the harbor, she wouldn't have just let the woman, and the eagle, get away. She would have also lost precious time, and perhaps the ability to regain the girl's trail.

As it was, the girl's dive into the water had only delayed the inevitable.

Patricia gave it one last scan, then pulled her focus away from the water, lowered her gun, and turned back toward the entrance to the museum. She knew she didn't have long before the Boston Police—and the FBI—arrived. Not just because of the gunshots that would surely draw a law enforcement response; Patricia was only steps ahead of the FBI's own hunt for her surprisingly troublesome loose ends.

Though the phone conversations Patricia had intercepted with her StingRay device between the FBI agent in charge—Zack Townsend—and his IT surveillance team had only provided hints toward the fugitives' destination (the Tea Party Museum), which Patricia had been able to fill in with her own knowledge of what they might be looking for, Townsend would eventually make enough connections to point him in the right direction. Though it would take him longer to decipher what he had overheard via his phishing operation into Hailey's cell phone—snippets of her, Nick, and the professor's deconstruction of Thomire's diary—eventually he might zero in on the "book with the red cover" that had led Patricia to the right destination. Which meant, even without the gunshots, she only had minutes to spare. Hailey was in the water, but she wouldn't stay in the water; where she was heading next was the only thing that mattered.

Patricia had no doubt the other two targets were already in the wind. The thief—Nick—didn't matter; he was a lowlife who would surface sooner or later, if he didn't find a way to reconnect with Hailey in the nearer term. The other threat, and thread—the professor—was a slightly larger problem, and a personal embarrassment. A connection to Charles Walker that had slipped past her, to obviously detrimental results. But he wouldn't be difficult to track down.

Still, neither of the two men were more than inconveniences; it was Hailey who drew Patricia's focus. Not only because she had the eagle, but because she was smart enough, and determined enough, to be a true threat.

As Patricia reached the end of the gangplank, she glanced up at the security camera affixed above the entrance to the museum. There would be similar cameras throughout the building; she didn't know if they were wired for sound, but even if they weren't, she had access to sophisticated lip-reading software. Which meant it wouldn't take long for her to piece together where Hailey was now heading, before Patricia erased whatever the cameras had recorded.

Patricia would not underestimate the girl again. The next time they met would be their last.

CHAPTER TWENTY-EIGHT

Two hundred yards away, moonlight flashed against the undulating waves of the harbor, far enough from the museum that the eighteenth-century sailing vessel was mostly shadow. There was a brief moment of silence, broken only by the soft hiss of wind against the water—and then Hailey burst upward through the surface eagle-first, gasping for air.

When she'd finally regained her breath, she swung her head wildly back and forth, her feet churning below to keep her from sinking back down. Her shoes were soaked through, hugging her feet like gloves, and her skirt and top were clinging to her body, pulling at her skin like fingers from the deep. But the adrenaline was fire in her muscles, spurring her farther and farther away from the dock, that woman, and the gun that had nearly ended her life.

Hailey had never held her breath that long or swum that far before in her life; she'd always been a good swimmer, even as a foster kid. Her foster father—before he'd lost himself, became lost from her—had taught her in a lake just over the New Hampshire border from his property, and she'd always loved the quiet, and the freedom, of being surrounded by water. But a lake in New Hampshire in the middle of the day was nothing like the Boston Harbor in the dead of night, swimming for your life while a deadly killer took aim from a nearby dock—

"Hailey? Over here."

Hailey whirled toward Nick's voice—and finally saw the motorized skiff bouncing and bobbing just a dozen yards away. With another burst of adrenaline, she swam toward him, crossing the distance in seconds. He rose from the floor of the little boat to help her over the side, and then she collapsed next to him, her chest heaving with the effort.

At a glance, she could see he was in similar shape; breathing hard, her backpack next to him, his shoulder wrapped in a checkered towel. There was blood soaking through the towel, but he seemed mostly upright, and some color had returned to his cheeks.

"We should get you to a hospital," Hailey said, as she found her voice between gasps.

But Nick was shaking his head, looking back toward the museum.

"She's not going to stop coming. We need to end this."

"I agree," Hailey said. "First we get you fixed up—"

"No," Nick said. "I mean we need to stop. We should call the police."

Hailey paused. Of course, he was right. The woman had shot at her—had shot him. The smart thing to do would be to call the police, probably the FBI. There was something big going on that they were only beginning to understand, something that involved a killer and stolen art and a historical conspiracy going back hundreds of years. And the two of them were so small—a card counter and an ex-con— they were clearly in over their heads.

"They'll lock you up," she said. "You'll be connected to the stolen art, and they'll put you back in prison. They'll take the book away, and the eagle."

They'll take it all away. Whatever this is, wherever it leads—they'll take it from us.

"But we'll be alive."

Hailey paused again. He was right, they'd be alive. But for how long? Would the woman stop coming after them, once the police were involved? And what would happen to Hailey? Was she ready to run again? To keep running?

"It's not enough," she said.

"Hailey—"

"No. And it's not about some big score, not anymore. It's like—the first time I learned to count cards. It was a doorway to a secret world I'd never known existed. I couldn't turn away."

As she said it, Hailey realized—no matter how stupid and dangerous, she was going to see this through to the end. It wasn't about the money anymore. Now, it was the math—that magical power she had over cards, and equations, and anything that involved numbers. And here, too, the skill at cards that had brought her to the casino had also opened a door to a role in recovering what shouldn't have existed: something of incredible power. Paul Revere's bell, his alchemical philosopher's stone—a bell that emitted a tone that could transform lead into gold. Hailey had to see this through.

She looked directly at Nick.

"I can't turn away. Not yet."

"We don't even know if what we're looking for is even real—or if it's been lost to history. We're going to be risking our lives, for something that doesn't even seem possible."

But she could see in his eyes that at least a part of him understood.

She reached past him, toward her backpack — and her phone.

"But you're right, if we're going to do this stupid, dangerous thing — we need to at least try to do it the smart way."

CHAPTER TWENTY-NINE

Zack sank back into the front seat of his unmarked agency car, still cradling his cell phone against his ear. He'd already listened to the message he'd been forwarded from the dispatcher in his office three times, but he was still having trouble digesting what he'd just heard.

Finally, he slid the phone back into his jacket pocket, and stared out through the windshield at the scene in front of him.

Christmas, Fourth of July, the Boston Pops Fireworks Spectacular all rolled into one; enough squad cars flashing lights that the entire section of Congress Street abutting the Tea Party Museum was lit up like Times Square, and still he could hear the sirens coming, so many damn sirens, that the dashboard in front of him was trembling to the tune.

Marsh must have called every unit on the waterfront—if not every cop in uniform available through the entire city—as soon as Zack had informed him of the intelligence he'd gathered from his phishing operation. Unfortunately, it had taken Zack a fair amount of time to decipher the fragmented conversations he'd been able to overhear, between Hailey and Nick and the third party, a history professor he still hadn't definitively identified. What he had gleaned—that they were looking for a book with a red cover, somehow tied to Paul Revere and the stolen finial from the Gardner theft—hadn't been enough to lead him to the fugitives; it had taken some keen triangulation work, using pings from cell towers that Hailey's phone had passed by—correlated with some quick research into the whereabouts of collections of Revere's artifacts throughout the greater Boston area—to give him enough information to make a best guess as to where she and Nick had been heading.

Even so, until the reports of gunshots had begun to come over the wire just under an hour ago, Zack hadn't been certain he'd been on the right track. But when those calls came in—Zack had known they were facing a fourth crime scene connected to the murder from the night before; and Marsh, still fuming from the Bunker Hill Monument, had marshaled a small army to greet whatever they might find.

Which, it turned out, had been very little. Shattered display cases and ruined artwork, bullet casings that had come from an unmarked, unlicensed weapon, and blood on a carpet that hadn't yet been identified by its DNA. Any security video that might have existed had been professionally erased, and since it was a museum, any fingerprints, fibers, hairs, et cetera found at the scene would be hay in the haystack—let alone anything resembling a needle.

And still, the squad cars kept coming. Through the windshield, Zack could see Marsh, now storming back and forth in front of the entrance to the museum, surrounded by uniforms with very little to do but stay out of the puggish man's way. Zack almost felt sorry for him; he knew how frustrating it could be to always be one step behind a perp, how awful it could feel when a case seemed to be getting away, the hit your ego took, especially when it all went down in such a public fashion. But Marsh was a disagreeable human being—and such a remorseless, brute of a cop—that Zack had a hard time gathering together any true empathy for the man.

Which is why, as soon as he'd done a cursory walk through the crime scene, Zack had returned to the solace of his car. When he'd noticed the message indicator on his phone going off, informing him that dispatch had forwarded him a recorded call that had come in via his office number, he hadn't expected much more than a distraction.

Then he'd heard the young woman's voice on the call, and his entire world had turned upside down. And even after listening to the message three times, in succession, he was still having trouble processing the information—and having an even harder time trying to decide what to do with it.

The message had been short and to the point. The girl had explained that she'd gotten his number from her roommate, with whom he had left his card. She had told him that she was caught up in something, that she and her partner hadn't hurt anyone, and that they were in danger. And then she had gotten to the most important part: she had told him where she was heading next.

His phone now back in his pocket, Zack continued watching Marsh through the window, shouting at the nearest officers. He knew what protocol was in a situation like this; although he was an FBI agent with his own authority to follow up leads during an active investigation, now that he knew the potential location of the prime suspects in a case involving multiple homicides, he had a responsibility to inform local law enforcement so that they could make the arrests.

Zack didn't care about the arrests — he didn't care about who got credit for taking Hailey and Nick in, who would make it into the papers for solving the case. But he was certain that Hailey and Nick were only part of the story; and a heavy-handed arrest would likely eliminate any possibility of figuring out what was really going on.

He also knew — the minute he told Marsh what he had just heard, the man would go off like a thunder-cloud. He would arrive at the scene with a dozen cops — if not a hundred — along with SWAT vans and trained snipers. If Hailey was in danger now, on her own — how much better off would she be facing Marsh and a few dozen uniformed men with guns?

The truth was, Zack didn't care about protocol, or credit, or Marsh's ego. He cared about making the right call. And everything was telling him that the right call was to give Hailey the benefit of the doubt — at least for the moment.

He took a breath, then reached for the ignition.

CHAPTER THIRTY

On the opposite flank of Boston's inner harbor, it took all of Hailey's strength and a good bit of leverage to pull Nick the last few feet up the side of the massive, slowly rocking hull of a much bigger, much different ship. Even with the help of the ropes and rigging that dripped like ivy down the side of the great, floating piece of history, it had been an ordeal working her own way up from the skiff, parked in the water some forty feet below. She could only imagine how difficult it had been for Nick, with only one good arm and a fair bit of blood still drenching his shirt and the makeshift bandage they had made from the checkered towel that had once covered the French bronzier Thomire's diary.

With one last gasp of energy, Hailey leaned back and heaved the bigger man over the railing. Then she collapsed back against the polished deck, breathing hard, next to her backpack, which she'd placed on the deck before helping Nick. It was dark out, somewhere between two and three in the morning, but between the moon and the lights from the pier on the other side of the ship, it was easy to see the details. And even from flat on her back the details were beyond magnificent.

The USS *Constitution* was nothing like the

reconstructed trading vessel Hailey had leapt from, that short hour ago. Stem to stern, the massive Revolutionary warship was more than three times as long, and though the *Constitution* had been refitted and restored dozens of times over the centuries, it was still a working vessel, the oldest commissioned ship in the US Navy. Normally, a crew of more than sixty still served on it. In Revolutionary times, it carried as many as five hundred.

Thankfully, at the moment it appeared to only be Hailey and Nick on board. Research on her phone had given Hailey the good news that the *Constitution* was in the midst of a month-long retrofitting and would be docked in its bay by Building Twenty-Two in the Charlestown Navy Yard until it was deemed seaworthy again. Approaching from the water, they'd been able to avoid the guard station on the pier and had made it to the ship's waterline without much trouble.

Before they'd begun the climb up, Nick had briefly, once again, tried to talk Hailey out of the endeavor. He had agreed with her decision to reach out to law enforcement—first, through her roommate, who had told her about the investigators who had been at her apartment, and then leaving a message for the FBI agent who had given her roommate his card—but now that they were actually there, facing the huge ship in all its glory, he had again had second thoughts about them risking their lives trying to find something that probably didn't even exist.

But Hailey's resolve had only grown stronger. She had come too far to turn back, and she had made it clear—she was going forward, with or without him.

And so here she was, on her back on the deck of the USS *Constitution*, on the verge of what could be a history-changing discovery, a feat that made card counting look like a petty child's trick.

She rose from the deck, taking the backpack with her. She'd actually been on the *Constitution* before, during her freshman year at MIT, at one of those social mixers she'd been unable to avoid. Back then, so early in her grift, and her carefully layered new identity, she'd still been concerned about appearances.

A glance ahead told her Nick's piloting of the skiff had been on target; they were very near the stern of the ship. The three masts rose up behind her to dizzying heights—the main mast, to 175 feet—but ahead the deck sloped only slightly upward, ending in a railing that seemed part of the current refitting. Planks from the railing had been removed, beyond which Hailey could see the water, a good forty-foot drop below.

She started forward toward that gap in the railing. Nick followed, his head swiveling to take in the ornate woodworking on either side, the elegance and precision of the ship around them. Usually, visitors to the *Constitution* started in the museum dedicated to the ship on the pier, learning how it had been built in 1794 in a shipyard in the North End—just blocks from Paul Revere's home—and launched in 1797. How the ship had bested numerous pirates off the Barbary Coast, before it had made its name in the great battles of the War of 1812.

Almost at the stern and the break in the railing, Hailey noticed that a row of three of the ship's cannons had been moved up onto the deck from the cannon room below; probably part of the retrofitting, they were huge beasts, squat and heavy in the darkness. All three were on wheeled frames, their barrels facing out toward the ocean. Nick was now eyeing the cannons as well.

"Fake, I assume?" he said. "Nobody's going to use them to sink our skiff on our way out of here, if we manage to find this bell?"

"The whole ship has been refitted and restored numerous times over the years. The cannons, too. Most were recast, iron dummies, not meant to be used. But a couple are active. They don't fire cannonballs. They've been hollowed out and retrofitted as .40-millimeter saluting guns. Packed with gunpowder and saluting shells. They make quite a blast. They fire them twice a day when this thing is up and running."

Nick raised an eyebrow, more at her encyclopedic memory than the mean-looking cannons. But she ignored him because she was already at the break in the railing. She paused, scanning the deck around her, looking for something she could use. Luckily, one was never far from rope on the deck of a ship.

She skirted over to a coil resting by the base of what appeared to be a heavy copper tying post. She grabbed a thick length of the rope and used her weight to drag it back to the break in the railing.

"Hailey, is this really a good idea?"

Hailey handed her backpack to Nick. Then she looked around herself again.

"I'm going to need some sort of tool to pry it loose."

She looked left and right, but there was nothing within range. Then Hailey noticed that Nick had pulled something out from the waistband of his jeans. He held it toward her.

It was a tomahawk.

Hailey judged him with a look.

"I couldn't help myself," he said. "Hey, you were fine with selling the stolen Gardner paintings. What's the difference?"

"There's a big difference between making money off something that's already stolen and stealing it yourself. It's what separates a card counter from a cheat."

Nick rolled his eyes, as Hailey grabbed the tomahawk from him. She slid it into the waistband of her skirt, then took the end of the rope in both hands. Nick moved farther down the line, dropping to his knees on the deck and gathering rope into his own hands.

"Will you be able to handle my weight?" Hailey asked.

"You just hang on to your end. It's a long drop down."

Hailey turned and looked over the ledge. He was right, the water would feel a little like concrete if she fell from that height. But she didn't intend to go all the way to the water. Her gaze focused on a ridge about halfway down the stern, where something wooden and white and ornate had been affixed to the hull.

She clutched the rope with both hands, then climbed over the break in the railing and began her descent.

CHAPTER THIRTY-ONE

Slowly, foot by foot, Hailey clambered down the stern of the boat, using the toes of her tennis shoes to find purchase in the small gaps between the planks of the ship's hull. She could hear the water lapping beneath her, and the grunt of Nick belaying her from above—but she was focused directly ahead on the ornate fixture now just a few yards below.

"Be careful," Nick hissed. "And hurry. This is one big, damn boat, and we're not going to be alone on it for very long."

Hailey worked the muscles of her arms and legs, her hands white against the rope, lowering herself, closer and closer.

"We may not be alone as it is," she whispered back toward him, as she worked. "There's a story that a ghost lives on board. A nineteenth-century sailor, by the name of Neil Harvey. Supposedly, he'd fallen asleep during his watch. The captain had him stabbed in the stomach, then tied him over one of those cannons. Blew him into tiny pieces. Now he haunts the decks."

"Really encouraging," Nick hissed back. "You should hire yourself out to kids' birthday parties."

Hailey smiled as she descended the last few feet, and then her focus was entirely on the white, ornate object affixed to the stern. Up close the thing was huge, much bigger than it looked from the water below. Painted in glistening white, with a bright red eye and a shield across its chest, red and white stripes beneath thirteen little stars. A Revolutionary-era American flag, on a Revolutionary-era symbol— a great eagle, wings unfurled, affixed to the stern of the greatest warship of the time.

Hailey ran her eyes over the eagle's wings. She knew it wasn't part of the original construction of the ship; like the rest of the USS *Constitution*, this part of the hull had been retrofitted many times. This particular wooden decoration dated back to 1907. But the ship's relationship to the powerful symbol went back much further than that. In fact, the USS *Constitution*'s first nickname had not been Old Ironsides. Before that, it had been known by another name.

"The Eagle of the Seas," Hailey whispered to herself.

Before this eagle had been affixed to the *Constitution*, there had to have been earlier versions, Hailey felt sure. Maybe dating all the way back to Revere. He had, after all, made the copper that lined part of the bottom and sides of the ship, as well as many screws and bolts and wedges throughout. He'd also made the giant bell that had once stood on its deck, before the bell was shot to pieces by a British frigate.

And maybe he'd crafted one final item, placed it aboard as well, somewhere only he—and whoever he meant to send it to—would find it.

Hailey pulled the tomahawk out from her waistband and jammed the edge of the ax blade between one of the eagle's wings and the planks of the stern.

"*La cloche sous l'aigle,*" she whispered. *The bell beneath the eagle.* She wasn't fluent, but she recognized enough words to make the translation. If Adrian was right, this was the place to look.

She braced herself with the rope in one hand, then put all her weight behind the tomahawk. There was a groan from the wood of the ornate eagle—and then an edge started to come loose. Hailey leaned farther back—Nick groaning at the strain on the rope— and the edge shifted a little more, there was a light crackling sound, and then the wing pried loose from the stern. The rest of the eagle was still affixed, but Hailey was able to reach behind the wing, to the boards beneath.

These were smooth and strong—but Hailey was determined. She lifted the tomahawk above her head, took a breath, and then swung it forward, hitting the wood with the sharp edge of the blade. Wood splintered around her, but she kept swinging. In a matter of minutes, she was through the first board, and then into another, deeper into the frame behind the ornate stern. Two more swings—and she heard the distinct clang of metal against metal.

She put the tomahawk back in her waistband, then leaned forward, gripping the rope with just her legs, and reached in with both hands. She didn't know what she expected to feel—the smooth curve of an enormous bell, hidden in the wooden frame?— but she was shocked to find something much smaller. There appeared to be a carved-out hiding place in the wood, and in that space, a metal box. Too small for the bell, Hailey realized, but she grabbed it anyway and pulled it free.

The box glinted in the moonlight, and Hailey realized with a start that it was made of what appeared to be solid gold.

"What is it?" Nick hissed, from above. She could

see that he was leaning over the edge, holding the rope, staring down at her.

She shook her head. She wasn't sure. But she needed to find out.

"Pull me up," she hissed.

———

Minutes later she was topside next to Nick. He was still holding the backpack, and they were both breathing hard, but Hailey's mind was entirely focused on the gold box on the deck between them. Before either of them could speak, Hailey dropped to one knee. The box had a clasp, but no lock; she wouldn't need the tomahawk this time.

With trembling fingers, she undid the clasp and opened the box.

Inside there was a small bit of yellowed paper, very old. Written across the paper were words in sweeping cursive, by the hand of someone who had died very long ago.

"What does it say?" Nick asked.

Hailey read the words with difficulty.

"'From she who made the box.'"

Her heart was pounding in her chest. *From she who made the box.* The golden box. Hailey was about to read the words out loud again, when she noticed that there was something else in the box, beneath the paper. She carefully moved it aside—and saw a piece of narrow metal, carved and polished, longer than her hand and wrist. The shape seemed vaguely familiar.

"I think it's a clapper," she whispered. "Or part of a clapper. From a bell. A very big bell."

"There's something written on it," Nick said.

Hailey realized he was right. There were words

inscribed along the edge of the clapper. She had to squint to make them out.

Proclaim Liberty

Hailey stared at the words. It took a moment, but then she recognized them.

"What does it mean?" Nick asked.

"It's part of a longer inscription. 'Proclaim liberty throughout all the land unto all the inhabitants thereof.'"

She shook her head, her mind whirling. *Was it possible?*

"Nick, this clapper, I don't know how—but I think it's from the Liberty—"

She never had a chance to finish her thought. There was a flash of motion from behind her and then something hit Nick from the side, yanking the back-pack out of his grip and then sending him toppling backward to the deck. He landed, sprawling, next to the coil of rigging rope as his head hit the heavy copper tying post with a terrifying crack.

Hailey leapt to her feet, trying to pull the toma-hawk out from her waistband, but the woman with the pitch-black hair was too fast. Her foot, still in heels, came up and the tomahawk spun away, harm-lessly. Hailey took a frightened step back and felt cold iron against the small of her back. She glanced behind her and saw the curved base of one of the heavy black cannons, its barrel pointed out toward the ocean. Then she turned forward again to see the woman facing her, just a few feet away. She'd dropped Hailey's backpack—but now the eagle, which she'd retrieved from inside, was in her left hand. Her right hand, still at her side, held the gun.

The woman looked at Hailey, then at the golden box on the deck between them.

"You've got what you want," Hailey said. "Let us go."

The woman's expression changed, just a fraction. Hailey had never read a face so cold, so controlled, so practiced. There was pity there, but it was overwhelmed by something else: *the needs of her mission.*

"Unfortunately," the woman said, "that's not how this works."

She raised the gun. Hailey pressed back against the iron of the cannon, felt the wheels beneath its frame give a little, but she knew there was no time to do anything, nowhere to run. She thought about closing her eyes, but decided she needed to keep them open.

Suddenly, out of the corner of her eye she saw the slightest rush of movement, then something flashed in the darkness.

A bullet hit the woman with the dark hair just below her ribs. Her gun spun out of her hand, and she crumpled forward, clutching at the wound. A man rushed toward her from the direction of the bow of the ship. He had his own gun drawn and was flashing a badge with his other hand.

"Zack Lindwell," he shouted, "FBI."

He kept the gun trained on the woman, who was still barely on her feet, but hunched all the way forward, almost to the deck. Then Zack turned toward Hailey.

"You OK?" he started, but he never finished the question.

In a flash of motion so fast Hailey couldn't digest what she was seeing until after it had happened, the woman with the dark hair leapt forward, holding something she'd slipped out of the heel of her right

shoe. Before Zack could react, she'd jammed the thing
into his extended arm, and, in an instant, his entire
body contorted. The gun fell from his fingers and
he collapsed onto the deck. He rolled onto his back,
trying to regain control of his limbs, but then every
part of him went rigid, like his muscles were turning
to bone.

The woman stepped away, kicking off her other
shoe so that she was now barefoot, still pressing the
gunshot wound beneath her ribs with one hand. The
bronze eagle, now flecked in her blood, was still tight
in the other. She turned toward Hailey, took a step
forward. Hailey stumbled backward, felt the cannon
again—but then noticed something else. The base
of the cannon wasn't as smooth and curved as she'd
thought. She reached back, touched it with her hand.
There was an opening near the top of the cannon that
shouldn't have been there.

A gasp emerged from the stiffening FBI agent on
the ground.

"What did you do to him?" Hailey asked.

As the woman glanced toward Zack, prone against
the deck, Hailey reached behind herself and grabbed
the cannon with both hands, then pulled as hard as
she could, spinning the enormous thing around on its
wheeled frame. When she looked up, the barrel was
aimed directly at the woman, who was staring at her,
a mixture of shock and amusement on her face.

Hailey looked down at the cannon. As she'd felt,
there was an opening in the iron where the back
of the tube had been shorn off and replaced. From
within the opening, Hailey caught the faint scent of
packed powder.

As the woman watched, still amused, Hailey drew
something from a pocket in her skirt. It was the

necklace that Nick had tried to take from the display case in the Tea Party Museum. Hailey had grabbed it from him, meaning to return it to the case. Whatever else she was, she wasn't a thief. She was a mathematician, a card counter. And just maybe, a *Mechanic*.

She took the little bell that flashed like gold at the end of the necklace in her hand, and held it over the opening of the cannon.

The woman with the dark hair smiled, the blood from the wound beneath her ribs seeping through her fingers.

"It's not a real cannon," she said. "None of this is real. It's history. It's an illusion. And Katie—even if it was real, you can't get fire from gold."

Hailey smiled back at her.

"My name's not Katie. And this isn't gold. It's pyrite. Any idea where it gets its name?"

With a flick of her fingernail, she shaved a tiny segment of the pyrite from the miniature bell. The second the flake touched air, the oxygen reacted with the iron sulfide in the pyrite and a tiny ember fluttered down into the opening in the cannon.

The woman with the dark hair had barely enough time to widen her catlike eyes before the packed charge within the refitted cannon ignited, the 40 mm signaling shell exploding through the barrel with immense force. The blast from the cannon hit the woman direct center, a cone of fire mangling the bronze eagle and crashing into the woman's chest like a balled fist. She staggered backward, screaming, flames leaping from her clothes. Then she reached the opening in the railing behind her and toppled backward—plummeting to the water below.

Hailey's ears were ringing as she rushed toward the two men lying on the deck. Nick was stirring, rubbing at his head where it had hit the copper tying post. She went to him first, helping him up to a sitting position, checking his eyes, the wound on his head and shoulder. He looked reasonably lucid, so Hailey turned quickly to the other man. He was in much worse shape. The FBI agent's eyes were wide open, staring straight upward. His arms and legs were rigid, and his chest was barely moving as he struggled to breathe. His lips opened as if he was trying to speak.

Hailey heard sirens coming from somewhere beyond the pier, and she knew help would be there soon, but she doubted it'd be soon enough. She needed to help this man, but she didn't know how. The woman had stuck him with something, some sort of syringe. Hailey looked past Nick, to where the woman had been standing just moments ago—and saw one of the woman's high heels lying on its side, close to the break in the railing where she'd gone over into the water.

Hailey ran to the shoe. She grabbed it with both hands, flipped it over. Beneath the heel, she saw a little compartment—and a second syringe. There was no way to know for sure. But, Hailey thought to herself, if you were in the business of poisoning people, you were likely to carry an antidote.

She grabbed the syringe and rushed back to the prone FBI agent. Then she unrolled one of his sleeves.

"You're going to be OK," she said, praying it was true.

She jammed the needle into his arm.

Several long seconds passed, the sirens from the pier growing louder. Behind Hailey, Nick was trying to sit up, now, looking her way. But Hailey was watching the FBI agent. His gaze had suddenly shifted, the stiffness of his cheeks loosening. He looked back at her, his mouth finally moving.

"The paintings," he started.

Hailey shook her head.

"Never saw any paintings. Had the eagle for a while, but that's gone now. Maybe you can fish it out of the water with whatever is left of that woman."

She stood, then looked toward Nick. There was still blood running from his scalp and the wound in his shoulder, but he was smiling at her, and she smiled back. She knew he could hear the sirens, too, but he made no move to rise. He seemed resigned to the moment. Maybe they'd take him back to jail, maybe they'd let him go. Heck, maybe they'd give him a piece of that reward, for getting so close. A part of her wanted to go to him, again, be by his side for whatever happened next. But she pushed the thought down, into the protective cage she'd built up over her years as a runaway, the cage where she kept most of her feelings.

"It's been fun," she said, toward him. "But I think this is where we go our separate ways—at least for a while."

The last part was hard to say, but there wasn't much of a choice. That woman, the killer with the sable hair, had known Hailey's real name, which meant the FBI assuredly had figured out who Hailey was as well. Her carefully crafted house of cards had fallen, which meant it was time to pack it up and start over.

Being Katie again wasn't an option. Katie was nobody; scared, broken, alone.

Hailey pulled away from Nick, retrieved her back-pack, and started toward the rigging that would lead her back down to the skiff, intending to get as far away from all of this as she could.

"Hailey."

It wasn't Nick calling her back, it was the FBI agent, Lindwell, behind her on the deck. She turned slightly, to see that though he still looked like he could barely move, he was now focused on the golden box, containing the strange clapper. "You don't have to keep running."

Hailey looked at him. The FBI agent didn't understand. It went against every grain in her being, standing still. It was something every good card counter knew: when the cards got cold, you got up from the table.

But for the briefest of seconds, she didn't take that next step. And it wasn't the FBI agent she was now looking at, it wasn't just Nick again — it was that gold box, containing the strange clapper.

A clapper, Hailey believed, made for the most famous bell in the world.

Proclaim liberty throughout all the land unto all the inhabitants thereof. Hailey had recognized the inscription immediately. It was carved into the bronze of the Liberty Bell, the ultimate symbol of American independence.

It seemed insane, impossible, but the math was leading Hailey to one conclusion:

The Liberty Bell wasn't just the most famous bell in the world. It was quite possibly the most powerful object in existence. A bell designed by Paul Revere to produce a tone that could, for a start, transform lead into gold.

No matter how badly Hailey wanted to keep running, she knew this wasn't over yet. She started toward the gold box and toward Nick, across the deck of that famous, aging ship, racing the sirens as they grew louder and louder — melding together into one insistent note, sounding almost like the peal of that distant bell.

CHAPTER THIRTY-TWO

It was the third whiskey that finally did the trick.

Adrian Jensen felt his limbs turn to rubber as he sprawled back against the velvet-lined Louis XV fainting couch in the corner of his well-appointed office, tucked in a deserted stretch of the third floor of East Hall on the Tufts University campus. The matching Napoleonic goblet that he'd bought at auction along with the couch—both of which, he'd been assured, had traveled with George Washington's command tent to not one, but *two* vaguely important battles toward the end of the Revolutionary War—in celebration of his tenure appointment a decade ago, had somehow, between whiskeys one and three, traveled from his right hand to the corner of his George III mahogany writing desk, which was now shoved up against the door leading out into the hallway.

Blockading the door with the heavy desk had been no small feat, especially considering how hard Adrian's arms and legs had been shaking when he'd first returned to his office from the evening's ordeal. It hadn't helped that he'd biked home—in the dark—at a speed he should never have contemplated sober; twice along the route, he'd nearly been killed by oncoming traffic, and only a truly heroic maneuver over an unexpected pothole in Davis Square had enabled

him to arrive at Tufts physically—if not mentally—
intact.

He reached out toward the goblet on the desk, but
quickly realized that it was now beyond his grasp—
and rising from his prone position on the couch no
longer seemed an option. He considered trying to
reach the bottle from which he'd poured the whiskey,
which still sat in the open glass display case behind
where he was lying, next to a half dozen other items
of various historic importance and value—but that,
too, seemed an impossibility. He was all out of heroic
energy.

His only solace was that he was in the place he
normally felt most secure. Everything around him in
his academic throne room, as he liked to think of it,
had been carefully curated to highlight his intellectual
journey over the past two decades. From the desk
to the display case—which contained mostly artifacts
once owned by Paul Revere himself, including a
flint pistol, accompanied by its bag of powder and
lead shot; one of Revere's retractable walking sticks,
a technologically impressive bit of metallurgy which
he'd used in his senior years, the handle made of
carved walrus ivory of the same sort he'd chiseled into
numerous pairs of false teeth; a collection of Revere
spoons, shined to near perfection by the man himself;
a pair of boots similar to the ones Revere wore on his
ride to Concord; and the remains of the fifty-year-old
spirit that Adrian had just begun to consume, which
had once been owned by a fellow Revere collector,
who had thrown in the dusty bottle along with a
fife and drum that had survived the failed Penobscot
Expedition, which had led to Revere's court-marshal
and discharge from the Continental Army.

That display case, along with the high oak bookshelves brimming with Revolutionary history books and original manuscripts—some centuries old—that lined every wall of the office, had rightly intimidated numerous grad students and undergrads who had dared trouble Adrian during those loathsome hours the university forced him to mingle with the student body between his lectures. They'd also cowed a fair number of visiting scholars who had come to seek his input on usually trivial questions of Revere lore.

Charles Walker, for his part, had never visited Adrian at Tufts; if he had, Adrian would have tried his best to talk some sense into the fool, and perhaps he could have steered him in a direction that wouldn't have ended with bullets flying through the Tea Party Museum. Then again, try as he might, Adrian couldn't hold Charles *entirely* to blame for his present state. Although Adrian still had no reason to believe Charles's thesis was more than the fictitious ramblings of a fanciful mind—there appeared to be people taking it very seriously.

The eagle from the image in the walls of Hancock's trunk was real, and someone was apparently willing to kill for it. If Adrian hadn't crawled into the control room and tinkered with the museum's special effects, Hailey and Nick would already be dead; or perhaps, Adrian had only bought them a little time—for all he knew, their bodies could right now be floating in the harbor, waiting to be fished out by the local authorities.

Adrian supposed that he should have waited around the museum for the police to arrive. But even as he'd dialed the 911 operator to report what had happened, he'd been heading to his bicycle. Sure, his efforts in the control room had been brave— but any student of history knew that the difference between a hero and a fool was not in the act, but in the aftermath. Five hundred brave Americans died at Penobscot; Paul Revere walked away and into the history books.

Just maybe, the pair had managed to escape with the eagle; and perhaps they had actually made their way to the great tall ship in the Charlestown Navy Yard, and found Revere's final bell, if it had really remained hidden aboard that two-hundred-year-old vessel. Adrian simply didn't care. He wasn't going to risk his life to prove Charles's absurd thesis wrong.

Because of course that's what they would discover, even if they had indeed found that bell. A flight of absurd fancy that Adrian should have discarded the moment he'd read it—and the fact that someone was willing to kill over it didn't make it any more believable. People had been willing to kill for fiction since the dawn of myth and religion.

Adrian exhaled dramatically, now intent on only one thing: marshaling enough heroism to reach that goblet for a fourth shot of that foolishly expensive whiskey—

Before he could move a rubbery limb, there was a loud knocking on the door to his office.

Adrian's eyelids shot open, and his spine suddenly straightened, the effects of the alcohol no match for the burst of fear in his veins. He stared at the door, and at the desk in front of it—hoping that it was enough. The knocking started up again, even louder—and then was followed by the sound of metal against the door's lock.

"Go away," Adrian shouted. "I've already called the police."

The lock lasted less than three seconds; the knob twisted, and then someone was pushing at the door with a shoulder. The desk moved an inch, then another.

"I said go away."

"Professor Jensen," a voice he recognized echoed through the crack in the door. "We found something we need to show you. On the *Constitution*."

Jensen swallowed, then coughed.

"How did you find me?"

"Google," Hailey, undoubtedly still in her tennis skirt, said. "You have kind of a distinct look. Wasn't hard to track down your office. If you weren't here, we planned to wait for you. Figured you'd show up sooner or later."

Adrian closed his eyes. He didn't want anything to do with this anymore. Maybe Charles had seen himself as some sort of swashbuckling historian, but Adrian was a serious scholar. He thought about redialing the police—but then he realized, with a start, what the woman had just said.

"You found something on the *Constitution*?"

There was a grunt from the other side, presumably the man in the denim shirt, still leaning on the door.

"Are you going to open this thing?" Hailey said. "Or do we have to break it down?"

Adrian exhaled again, even more dramatically—then struggled up from the couch and went to work on the antique desk.

———

"'And ye shall hallow the fiftieth year,'" Adrian whispered, half to himself, as he leaned over the object in the gold box, which was now sitting on the mahogany of his antique desk, "'and proclaim liberty throughout all the land unto all the inhabitants thereof...'"

"The Bible, right?" Nick said. "It was the only book my dad owned, though he didn't read it often."

Adrian didn't look up, though he was mildly surprised the denim man had placed the quotation.

"Leviticus 25:10," Adrian said. "Though I think just as many people know it from the bell as they do from their trusty King James."

Adrian ran a finger down the side of the heavy clapper, feeling the cold of the bronze. *From she who made the box.* Hailey had shown him the note as well. In a lab, with the proper tools, he might have been able to authenticate both items—the note and the clapper— and perhaps date them to within a few years of their origins. For the clapper, he might discover physical metallurgic signatures that would point to the hands that had crafted it so long ago. But here, in his office, the best he could do was conjecture; and to Adrian, conjecture was only a bare step above fancy.

Still, it was intriguing. Revere's *Book of Bells* had led them to the USS *Constitution*; a clue written in Paul Revere's handwriting had guided Hailey not to another bell—Revere's final bell—but to this clapper. *From she who made the box.* It was not unusual for a craftsman to refer to a bell in the feminine vernacular. Adrian could forgive the clever young woman and her shifty friend for making a leap and calling it logic. But to Adrian, despite the circumstances, it still seemed a leap. Though if one were to have to choose a landing place fit for another flight of fantasy, one could do worse than the Liberty Bell.

"Such an emblem of freedom, the ultimate symbol of American Independence—when in fact, the Liberty Bell had absolutely nothing to do with the Revolution. A mundane, though sizable, chime installed in the steeple of the Pennsylvania State House twenty years *before* the War of Independence, by government administrators who were perfectly happy under the yoke of British rule; even the inscription had less to do with vague notions of Liberty, and more to do with timing, as the bell was being commissioned to commemorate the *fiftieth* anniversary of William Penn's signing of the Pennsylvania Charter."

Hailey was close to him now, as he continued to study the clapper. He had no idea what she'd endured on the *Constitution* in her efforts to secure the clapper—but he could tell from the way she was breathing, and the slight tremor in her arms, that the Tea Party Museum had only been a first act. Nick looked like he'd been through a war. His shoulder was wrapped, and there was dried blood on his scalp. But somehow, he was still standing.

"The Liberty Bell," Adrian continued, "wasn't even originally crafted in the Americas. It was first ordered in 1751 by the Pennsylvania Assembly from Whitechapel Bell Foundry in London. The bell was raised into the steeple of the State House two years later, in March of 1753—but on the very first ring, the bronze cracked right down the middle, rendering the bell useless."

Adrian could hear Nick rummaging around the office behind him, but he fought the urge to turn away from the clapper, because Hailey was concentrating on what he was saying; she, at least, seemed to rightly value his expertise.

"Two local metalworkers named John Pass and John Stowe—their names now adorn the bell, smack in the middle—were tasked with crafting a substitute. They melted down the original bell in their foundry in Philadelphia, recast it to new specifications, and added a higher concentration of copper to the mix, hoping for a better result. But when the new bell was brought up into the steeple of the State House and rung again—it emitted a sound so awful, the entire town complained. Once again, the bell was broken down to be recast."

"And that bell is the one we now call the Liberty Bell? The one that's hanging in Philadelphia today?"

"Yes and no," Adrian said. "Because Pass and Stowe failed again. The second bell sounded no better than the first. The assembly, so disturbed by the process, ordered a new bell from England. But when that bell arrived, it, too, sounded awful. So, the good people of Philadelphia were now blessed with two terrible sounding bells. They hung the British bell in the State House cupola, and the Pass and Stowe bell—which we now call the Liberty Bell—in the steeple. The British bell was rung multiple times daily to count the hours. The Liberty Bell was saved—most likely due to the awful sound it emitted when rung—for special occasions. Such as, to celebrate when King George III took the throne in 1761."

Nick had arrived at the glass display case behind Adrian and was eyeing the contents. But at least he'd been listening carefully enough to comment.

"Not exactly a moment of great liberty. When did the new bell get the crack?"

"Nobody's certain; at some point over the next decade the bronze started to show strain. But its last ringing was on George Washington's birthday in 1846—as the final peal reverberated over the city, the bronze fractured in the way we see it today. And it was never rung again."

Hailey seemed to be going over the facts. Her expression was inscrutable—or maybe it was just the whiskey—but Adrian could imagine some sort of calculations taking place in her head.

"Before it cracked, wasn't it also rung on July 4, 1776? To announce the Declaration of Independence?" she asked.

"That's what children are taught," Adrian answered, "but no. That comes from a fictional story published by the *Saturday Courier* in 1847. Sort of an early example of 'rebranding.' Twenty years before the story in the *Courier*, the bell had fallen into disuse. In fact, in 1828, someone in the Philadelphia State House had tried to sell it to a local foundry for four hundred dollars, to be broken down for scrap. But the foundry decided it wasn't worth the effort. It wasn't until the leaders of the abolitionist movement took notice of the inscription that graced the bell—Leviticus 25:10 is considered one of the strongest biblical passages against slavery, or at least permanent slavery—in the mid-1830s that the bell got its more current name, and mythology. Overnight, it went from being a strangely awful sounding bell hanging in the Pennsylvania State House, to an emblem of freedom known across the nation."

Adrian stepped back from the desk, wobbling a bit on his feet. But Hailey didn't move from where she was leaning over the clapper, still studying the shape of it.

"A bell and its clapper go together like parts of a mathematical equation," she started, quietly. Then she looked up at Adrian.

"This clapper connects somehow to Paul Revere. But Revere didn't cast the Liberty Bell, did he?"

"Of course not. If he had, the Liberty Bell would likely have a shrine to it in Boston by now, the way people salivate over everything the man touched. The Liberty Bell has only been to Boston once, in point of fact—in 1903. It was brought to town by train to commemorate the hundred and twenty-eighth anniversary of the Battle of Bunker Hill. Briefly trotted out to the monument, before it was shuttled back to Philadelphia.".

Hailey glanced back at Nick, but her colleague was still busy running his hands over Adrian's display case. Nick had paused at the flintlock pistol.

"Does this thing work?"

"I have papers that say it does," Adrian responded.

Before Adrian could stop him, Nick had reached into the case and was handling the antique weapon with one hand, while admiring the ivory-handled walking stick with the other.

"Do you have any idea what those are worth?" Adrian snapped.

"I figure this might come in handy," Nick said, lifting the gun out of the case.

"That's because you've never tried to fire a flintlock pistol," Adrian sniped back.

"Professor," Hailey interrupted. "The bell. Revere's foundry didn't cast it — but does that mean he couldn't have been involved? You said it was recast locally — twice. And that Pass and Stowe added more copper to the mix, trying to solve whatever was wrong with it. Wasn't Revere the premier copper worker in the country at the time? Wasn't he the sort of technological expert they might have turned to for help? Couldn't Revere have been involved, without the history books taking notice? As you said, it wasn't a remarkable bell until many years later — in fact, the only remarkable thing about it was that it sounded strange."

Adrian tried to ignore the bitter taste on his tongue. Conjecture, again. But he'd gone this far.

"Revere did make multiple trips to Philadelphia in the time period. The day after the Boston Tea Party, he raced to the city to inspire the Philadelphians to a similar act of defiance. Interestingly enough, it was written at the time that he was "greeted with the ringing of bells." More famously, a year later he was sent to Philadelphia to deliver the Suffolk Resolves, a treatise protesting the local arm of the British government. The Resolves were written by Joseph Warren, and it was Warren who ordered Revere to Philadelphia—which began the spread of the Revolution—"

"Warren?" Nick said, at least momentarily stepping away from the display case and the antique pistol. "The same Warren from the Bunker Hill Monument?"

"The point is," Hailey said, ignoring Nick, "it isn't impossible that Revere had something to do with the bell. It wasn't a particularly famous bell, it had an odd and disturbing sound, and it was tinkered with multiple times. The clapper that hangs with it might not be the clapper that was designed *for* it."

An almost feral intensity spread across her countenance, as she turned to face Adrian and Nick.

"The sound a bell makes isn't just written in the curves of its design; it's also the result of an interaction with the striking mechanism. The density—the chemical makeup—of the clapper is as much a part of the resulting tone as the metallurgy of the bell. There might be a reason the Liberty Bell never sounded right, no matter how many times it was recast from its mold. If that mold was designed to work with a specific clapper—"

She whirled around and lifted the artifact out of the gold box.

"This clapper," she said—and then she shook her head.

"But where does that leave us? I'm guessing the Liberty Bell isn't something you just walk up to, is it?"

Adrian felt suddenly the slightest bit sober. Maybe it was Hailey's passion; maybe it was the fact that the adrenaline from the events at the museum had finally begun to fade, replaced by the more stoic elements of his personality. But for some frightening reason, this woman's conjecturing was starting to make the tiniest bit of sense.

"It's kept in a bulletproof glass pavilion, surrounded by security checks and X-ray scanners, dozens of cameras, with armed guards watching twenty-four hours each day."

Hailey's shoulders seemed to sag as she lowered the clapper. Adrian looked at her, opened his mouth—then closed it. He shook his head. Did he really want to continue this insanity? An image from inside Hancock's trunk, a two-hundred-year-old eagle stolen from the Gardner Museum, Paul Revere and alchemy, the Liberty Bell.

Adrian shook his head. He was a scholar. An academic. Not like Charles, not some sort of treasure-hunting swashbuckler.

And yet, the thing in Hailey's hands was real, a piece of history.

Finally, despite his most basic instincts, Adrian found his voice.

"There's another way," he said. "And we don't need to go to Philadelphia."

"There's another Liberty Bell?" Nick asked.

"No," Adrian said.

And then he smiled.

"There are fifty-five."

CHAPTER THIRTY-THREE

The blue and red lights of a dozen police cruisers splashed like spray paint against the man-made embankment rising above the dark water of the harbor, intermittently catching Curt Anderson in their technicolor glow. Curt was seated comfortably on the top of the low wall, his legs dangling down against the stone. He was still wearing the tailored electric-blue suit, but he'd draped a dark gray overcoat around his shoulders against the mist and had pulled a black knit cap low above his eyes. The knit cap barely concealed the molded white wireless buds that rested comfortably in his ear canals. The buds on their own were not remarkable; more than a few of the odd predawn joggers that sped past along the wooden planked pathway winding behind where Curt was sitting sported similar devices, Bluetoothed to phones strapped to their wrists or swinging in the pockets of their jackets.

But Curt's earbuds were not paired to a phone. The device in his lap, about the size of a mailbox, was a bit more conspicuous, if anyone had felt the urge to look his way. Though there were unidirectional mikes with smaller footprints available, Curt had always been finicky about the tools of his trade. If it wasn't

military grade—preferably American or Chinese—
he wasn't going to waste his time.

Not that any amateur spy with an Amazon account couldn't have found a listening device capable
of handling the two hundred yards that separated
Curt from the staging area in the corner of the navy
yard adjacent to the bow of the *Constitution*, where
the bulk of the Boston police officers, Massachusetts
state troopers, and harbor cops had been gathering for
the past forty minutes—ever since the EMTs had first
lowered the FBI agent in the stretcher down from the
deck of the great ship.

From that distance, FBI Agent Lindwell didn't
look particularly injured; though his legs were still
strapped in, Lindwell was sitting up as the EMTs
took his blood pressure and pulse. From the snippets
of conversation Curt had already picked up through
the mike as the man had been lowered down from
the ship, the FBI agent was eager to continue his
pursuit of the two fugitives—who had apparently
acquired another item of importance in place of the
stolen eagle. Lindwell hadn't yet given any details
about the new item itself; but now that he'd reached
the ground and was furiously trying to brush off the
emergency personnel tending to his health as he spoke
in quick bursts to a heavyset state detective who'd
arrived moments before—Curt was sure it was only
a matter of time.

A noise from directly ahead, out in the harbor,
interrupted Curt's surveillance; for a brief second, he
shifted his attention to the pair of Coast Guard cutters
turning tight circles in the harbor, a hundred yards
in front of the *Constitution*. They'd been working
their way outward from the ship's hull since Curt
had arrived on the scene, and they didn't seem close

to giving up the search. The divers, however, had already returned to the surface, probably to change out their oxygen tanks. If any of them had seen any sign of Patricia's body or the eagle that had gone with her into the water, they hadn't advertised it yet—and from what he'd already overheard from Lindwell's account of the confrontation, Curt doubted they'd find much of her intact.

For a brief moment, Curt's lips tightened against his teeth. Then he forced his muscles to relax. Patricia had been a competent asset for many years, with a terrifying capacity for violence; but she had gotten sloppy, perhaps overeager. She had been overpowered by a pair of civilians and an art crimes investigator. If it hadn't been for the tracking device Curt had slipped onto her when they'd met in the Public Garden, her failure might have given them an insurmountable head start.

The Family had been correct to task him with overseeing her mission; and in a way, Hailey, Nick, and Lindwell had done him a favor by taking her out of the picture, saving him the effort of having to do the job himself. The Family didn't respond well to disappointment. No doubt, Patricia would have been a worthy adversary, and part of him regretted that he'd never have the opportunity to test his training against hers. He knew, from Patricia's dossier, that she'd been through hell as a child in Russia; but if skill was the end result of torment, he had no doubt that his own scars would put hers to shame. The tangled, knotted web of suffering that had honed him was not the sort of thing that could be encapsulated in a dossier.

Curt turned back toward the staging area, listening as Lindwell began to describe what the girl—Hailey—had found. It was clear the FBI agent was still far away from understanding what he was investigating; to him, this was still about the Gardner Museum, and he had no way of processing the new information.

But Curt was beginning to understand what Patricia had missed. Nick had set things in motion, trying to fence the eagle that had gone missing for so long; but now things had moved beyond that narrative. It appeared as though their "loose ends" were putting pieces together in ways that Patricia—and the family—had not foreseen.

Hailey seemed to be a step ahead of all of them, which made Curt's job even easier. She wasn't going to go to ground; if anything, she was going to take more risks now that she was so close to solving the puzzle.

Hailey had a head start; but Curt had threads to follow. If the Coast Guard found the eagle, Curt would be able to retrieve it from them with minimal effort. If they didn't, the Family would dredge the harbor themselves. But in the meantime, Curt had a more immediate path: earlier that evening, the Family's contacts at the BPD had intercepted a 911 call from a cell phone pinged to the Tea Party Museum that would provide direction.

Hailey was smart, and obviously determined. If Curt could mimic her and likewise figure out where the pieces fit—he could turn Patricia's failure into the Family's success.

CHAPTER THIRTY-FOUR

The sky above Beacon Street had gone from pitch black to gunmetal gray by the time Hailey found the professor where he'd told them he'd be waiting, when she and Nick had first left his office twenty minutes earlier: poised in moderately drunken repose, an overcoat now slung over his skintight, near-neon cycling outfit, his back against the wrought-iron fence that ran the length of the Boston Common behind him, just a few feet from his shiny, professional-grade bicycle, which was chained to a parking meter by the curb.

It had been Adrian's idea to go separately, and Hailey and Nick hadn't argued with him. Hailey hadn't been convinced that Adrian, in the state they'd found him in his office, would make the four-mile trip from the Tufts campus to the base of Beacon Hill by bike intact—but he didn't seem the sort of person who lost arguments very often, and Hailey didn't have the time to waste. By now, half the police officers in Boston were probably out searching for them—and law enforcement was the least of her worries. The woman who'd nearly killed her twice was obviously working for someone; whoever it was, they were after the same thing Hailey was—and had already killed multiple people in the pursuit.

Hailey shook off the thought of the woman with the sable hair—that ice-cold look in her eyes, as she'd aimed that gun, the way her body had shattered when the cannon had gone off—with a violent shudder, and leaned up against the fence next to Adrian, feeling the cold iron against her shirt.

Adrian had already given her and Nick a two-minute history lesson on the park behind them on the way out of his office. The professor liked to lecture, that was for sure, and something as simple as giving directions had been an opportunity for him to tell them more than they'd ever need to know.

"The Common is the oldest public park in the country," he'd intoned, as he'd led them out of 14 Talbot. "Dates back to 1634, when it was bought from the commonwealth's first settler by the Puritans. Fifty acres in the heart of the city; over the years it's been used as everything from a cow pasture to a dumping ground to a gallows to a center for protest. It was also one of the main encampments of the British army at the outbreak of the Revolutionary War. The regiment that raced Paul Revere to Lexington and Concord in 1775 started their night there."

Now, after the dash from Tufts to that iron fence, partially on foot but mostly in the back of a taxicab, her face and Nick's shielded as best as possible—it seemed fitting that things had come full circle, in a way. The impetus for Revere's midnight ride had begun here, and perhaps, close to this same spot, the man's true legacy would soon be revealed.

Adrian finally acknowledged Hailey's presence with a limp wave directly ahead, toward the building that stood across the two-lane road in front of them. Of course, Hailey recognized the building immediately. Also surrounded by an iron fence, which sprouted upward from a low stone wall, the Massachusetts State House was immense and regal; designed directly after the Revolutionary War by the great Boston architect Charles Bulfinch in his signature American Federalist style, the building was boxy and multitiered, its exterior consisting mostly of sturdy brick and ramrod straight Corinthian columns—and as impressive as it was, all of it overshadowed by the signature gilded dome on top, which could be seen across Boston for miles.

"Originally it was shingled in wood," Adrian said, as he noticed where Hailey's gaze had landed, on the curves of that dome that glinted even in the predawn haze. "But they soon discovered that the wood leaked when it rained, so they contracted Paul Revere to sheath the entire dome in copper. He did such a competent job, they didn't think to gild it in gold leaf until seventy-odd years later. The original copper is still down there, beneath the gold. Pretty ostentatious, the gold, if you ask me. During World War II they painted it gray, to make it less tempting a target for the Germans. They could have just left it Revere's copper, saved them the expense and the trouble."

"Revere certainly got around," Hailey said. "The *Constitution*, the dome—"

"If you needed something done in copper, he was the man to call. But the State House was more than a simple contract for Revere. He also presided over the laying of the cornerstone. Some of his furniture and silverware made it into the offices and meeting rooms where the governor and the state senate still preside. And, of course, Revere and his friend Sam Adams, who was governor of the state at the time, buried their time capsule here in 1795."

"Seems like the only thing he didn't leave here was one of his bells."

Adrian gave her the slightest of smiles, as he swayed against the fence behind him.

"The bell came later. A lot later."

Instead of a wave, this time he pointed toward a spot right up against the base of the building, in a small stone courtyard adjacent to the front steps leading into the grand entrance. Hailey squinted but could only make out shadows—something large tucked behind another fence, right up near the orange and red bricks of the first floor.

"The Liberty Bell," Hailey whispered.

"In a sense," Adrian said, expounding on the broad strokes he'd given them before they'd left his office, a lecture that had even included photos from one of the books from his overflowing shelves, which he'd left open on his desk. "In 1950, the US treasury was looking for new ways to squeeze donations out of the weary, post–World War II American public. So they came up with the idea to prick at the nation's sense of patriotism. They commissioned the molding of fifty-five exact replicas of the Liberty Bell, down to the smallest detail—and delivered them to every state and territory in the country. The bells arrived to much fanfare, parades, speeches—raising millions for the National Savings Bonds. Many states still display their faux bells in prominent places."

"Boston seems to have taken a different approach," Hailey said, shifting her gaze from the courtyard where the bell presumably sat, to the locked front gate directly across the street. Despite the inarguable curb appeal of the State House, the front entrance had been locked to visitors for nearly two decades.

"Originally, the Boston Liberty Bell was part of

the State House tour. But after 9/11, when the front entrance was locked down, the bell became off-limits. There've been some movements to get it properly displayed—including a bill brought up to the Senate a few years ago—but for now it's one of the State House's many secrets."

"But the bell itself," Hailey said, trying to focus on the positives, "it's really a perfect replica?"

"The foundry that designed and cast it brought in a team to measure the original Liberty Bell down to every curve and ding. It's the exact same proportions. Four feet tall, two thousand and eighty pounds. Seventy percent copper, around twenty-four percent tin. The Boston bell has one marked difference—which you'll see when you get close."

Hailey's lips pressed together—from where she was standing, getting close to the bell looked like an extremely difficult task, if not impossible. And she didn't just need to get close—she needed to get right up to the damn thing, near enough to affix the clapper that was still in the gold box, now in her backpack.

It wasn't just the locked fence, or the fact that the bell was tucked right up against the building. Because just walking over along Beacon Street to where Adrian had been waiting, Hailey had spotted at least four uniformed state troopers patrolling the grounds behind that fence. There were also two cruisers at the corner where Beacon met Bowdoin Street, with officers inside.

Hailey didn't know if the police presence had anything to do with her and Nick—but then again, they'd been involved in two separate incidents at famous Boston tourist spots, and the State House certainly qualified as a third. It was a little after four in the morning, so the police weren't there to tend to tour groups or State House office personnel. There was a good chance they were patrolling out of an excess of caution, spurred by a fire alarm at the Bunker Hill Monument and a cannon firing on the USS *Constitution*.

The only other possibility had to do with the scaffolding Hailey had seen along Bowdoin Street— which ran perpendicular to the State House—when she and Nick had first arrived, before he'd gone off to case the building, something he'd described as "force of habit," which Hailey hadn't felt the need to question. Adrian hadn't had to explain the scaffolding; Hailey had walked past the State House enough times living in Boston to know that the aging building was in an almost constant state of refurbishing and repair. The gold leaf on the dome had been replaced multiple times, the bricks painted, repainted, and restored. Even the building's many columns, which had once been carved out of wood, had been replaced by replicas in iron. There was always some sort of scaffolding near different portions of the building, and that usually meant more cops, more cameras, more complications.

Whatever the reason, the police presence was going to be hard to get past; and every minute that went by, the sky lightening through different shades of gray, their goal became more and more remote.

"This isn't going to be easy," Hailey said.

"Yes—*you're* going to need a hell of a plan," Adrian responded, sinking deeper into the fence. "I'm going to get back on my bike and find my way back to my whiskey. Even heroes have their limits."

He was interrupted by a shape jogging toward them down the sidewalk. Hailey could tell that it was Nick even before his face, beneath his hat, was visible;

the way he held his hurt shoulder, his arm stiff against his side, made her wince in empathy.

But if Nick was bothered by the injury, he didn't let it show. In fact, his expression was almost beaming.

"The police," Hailey started, as he got close enough to hear, but he was already ahead of her.

"Going in from the front is out of the question. They'll have us in handcuffs before we get five feet from the bell. But I've been around the perimeter twice, and I think there might be another way."

He glanced at Adrian, who was looking at him with only a modicum of disdain, but a fair amount of disbelief. Then Nick turned back toward Hailey.

"But I'm pretty sure you're not going to like it."

CHAPTER THIRTY-FIVE

Nick clenched his teeth against the throbbing in his shoulder as he hoisted himself over the low railing that separated the roof of one of the rear wings of the State House from the levered tiles that ran up toward the peak of the main building. The trek along the rooftops of the massive complex that extended back behind the State House—like the workings of some sort of reverse peacock, all the plumage up front, the utilitarian giblets hidden behind—had been mostly easy going up to this point, once they'd made it up the twenty feet of scaffolding to the top of the car park. But now that they were nearing the front of the structure, with its multiple eaves, slanted tiling, and columned balconies, each step had to be carefully chosen. One poorly placed foot could send him sliding the few feet to the edge—and beyond that, the fifty-foot drop to the ground below.

A scuffling sound from behind told him that Hailey had reached the railing as well, and he paused to offer what little help he could as she swung herself over to the slanted roofing next to him. Her backpack swung against her side at the motion, and he wished he could have carried it for her—but the only part of his right shoulder that didn't hurt had gone worryingly numb. He'd kept as much of the pain that he was feeling away from Hailey, but as soon as this was over, he'd need to find a quiet source of medical attention.

It was a strange and unnerving sensation, getting shot. He knew he was lucky; he didn't think the bullet had hit anything important, like bones or arteries, and he'd still been able to make short work of the scaffolding.

Nick's plan had been simple from the start. Going in from the front, unnoticed, would have been impossible. The locked gate and the state troopers posed too many risks, and he and Hailey would have been exposed all the way to the courtyard where the bell was kept. But Nick had been breaking into places since he was fourteen. And there was always security to contend with, locks and bars and uniforms. Not usually troopers and police cruisers—but Nick had found, if you cased a target well enough, you'd always find a way in.

Or in this case, a way *over*.

Though the scaffolding and construction work above the car park had nothing to do with the State House proper, it had provided just enough of a weak spot for them to gain the advantage. Where the scaffolding met Bowdoin Street, Nick had counted a handful of security barricades and one more police cruiser. But walking by, Nick had realized that it would be a straight shot up to the rear roof of the complex, and then an easy sprint over the various ledges and balconies to the main building.

The hardest part had been timing the first part of their ascent to when the closest trooper had turned the corner on Bowdoin during his walking patrol of the parking area. Once he and Hailey had gotten to the second story of the rear building, they were beyond anyone from the street's field of vision. Minus the shoulder, it wasn't even one of the more difficult illicit entries Nick had attempted; the bank gig that had landed him in Shirley had been infinitely more complicated and had included a roof hop as well as some intricate alarm rewiring. Sure, that job had ended with Nick locked up in a prison cell, but that had been the result of bad luck — not bad planning.

Hailey now safely behind him, he clambered to the top of the slanted roof, and started working his way toward the front of the main building. It was still just dark enough out that he didn't feel the need to crawl, but he did keep himself as low as possible without touching his knees to the tiles. When he glanced back over his bad shoulder, he could see that Hailey was following his lead, crouching down beneath her backpack. She was breathing hard at the effort, but to Nick's surprise, he realized that she didn't look scared, or even anxious. She looked thrilled.

She noticed his attention and gave him a little smile.

"You thought I wouldn't like this? Look where we are."

Nick cast a glance to his right, down the sloped tiles to the ledge of the section of roof they were crossing. They had just turned the corner from the rear of the building to its facade, and now the Boston Common was spread out in front of them, glades of grass interrupted by the dark shapes of trees of various shapes and sizes, from huge, mature elms to more spindly beech and birch, even a redwood, all of it stitched together by the paved paths that crisscrossed the park from one end to the other.

And to Nick's left, he could see past the edge of Beacon Hill toward the lights of the financial district; straight ahead, past the park were the low buildings of the Back Bay and the South End beyond, still asleep in the shadow of the angled, spear-like Hancock and the glimmering Prudential, its blinking lights rising up until they were swallowed by the clouds.

"It's beautiful," he said. "But I know you don't like heights."

And then he realized—Hailey wasn't looking out over the city. She was facing the opposite direction. Because since they'd climbed up the slanted roof, they were now positioned right below the base of the golden dome. Its curved haunches began just a few feet beyond where they were standing, rising up like an onion on its head. So close, in fact, that Nick could have reached out and touched the shiny, plated surface, but something made him resist. It looked so smooth, so pristine, and he felt—*unworthy*. And yet, not small; something about the quest they were on, the path they were following, made him feel like he was finally doing something important. This wasn't just another gig, he wasn't just chasing another score, and Hailey wasn't just another partner.

He watched as Hailey rose from her crouch, enough to see more of the dome. She pointed up toward the structure at the top—a strange sculpture made of wood but covered in gold.

"People think it's a pineapple," Hailey said. "But it's actually a pinecone. The pine tree was one of the area's most important resources at the time, and the golden cone was supposed to symbolize the importance of lumber to the fledgling commonwealth. Rich people all over the state used to have statues of pinecones atop their estates."

Nick smiled.

"The professor?"

"Actually, I remembered that one on my own."

Her voice drifted off, as she peered closer at the

dome itself. Nick noticed that there were places where the gold plating was scuffed by weather, muddled in spots so profusely that the gold seemed burnished, a different shade.

"I think that's the original copper," Hailey said. "Paul Revere's copper, where the gold plating has worn away."

In the past, Nick might have considered trying to chip some of that antique copper loose—let alone, a few tiles of that twenty-four-carat gold—as a little insurance against what still seemed like the impossible treasure they were chasing. But he knew that Hailey would never have let him, and that alone kept him moving forward. And he had to admit; now he was as determined as she to see this through to the end.

"I'm glad you changed your mind," he said. "On the *Constitution*. When the FBI agent asked you to stop running—you were going to leave me there—and I understood. But I'm glad that you didn't."

Hailey was close enough behind him to reach out and touch his hand. It was a small motion, almost nothing, but Nick felt it all the way through his body.

They started forward again, moving around the lip of the dome. Another handful of yards and they would be directly above the small courtyard where the bell was held. The way down would be trickier than the way up. There was no scaffolding on the front of the building, but there were a couple of low balconies that would make the climb possible. The last ten feet would involve gravity and a hard landing. The only real problem would be the exposure—even coming over the top from behind the building would mean they would have to get to the bell in full view of the troopers patrolling the main grounds; but Nick's plan had taken that into account as well. Or more accurately, he had borrowed a bit of strategy from Hailey and her card counting—*distraction and misdirection*. If things went according to plan, they would get to that bell unnoticed.

After that—Nick would leave the rest to Hailey. It was still hard to imagine what they were on the verge of discovering, but Hailey had gotten them this far already. Nick glanced back at her again, marveling at how confident she looked as she edged along after him, framed like a silhouette against the gray sky—

There was a sudden flash of motion behind her, and Nick froze, his feet coming to a stop against the slanted tiles. Hailey saw the fear in his face and whirled in time to see the angled, thin man in the tailored suit lunge over the railing they had just climbed. He landed on his feet a few yards in front of Hailey, his narrow frame casting an even narrower shadow up the curve of the golden dome to his left.

"Thought I might find you here," he said. "It appears that Professor Jensen's quick thinking—and extensive library—saved us both a trip down the coast to Philadelphia. You've done some amazing work, friends. But I think I'll take it from here."

And then he was moving forward, his body light above the tiles. The man didn't have a gun drawn, but he didn't look like he needed one.

Nick started to move as well, but Hailey was between them, and the man was close, too close. Hailey looked stunned, but then Nick saw that one of her hands had moved into her backpack—and then everything happened at once.

Hailey's hand tore free of the pack and Nick saw the dark metal of her flask between her fingers. The man in the suit lunged, but Hailey was faster; she ducked down low as one of her fingers flicked the flask open, her hand swinging in a wild arc. The battery acid sprayed out toward the dome next to her, the noxious liquid hitting the gold plate covering the dome, splashing across the spots where it was scuffed down to the copper beneath.

There was a sudden hiss as the toxic gas billowed upward; Hailey was low enough that most of it missed her, but the man in the blue suit caught it full in the face. He staggered back, coughing violently, grabbing at his burning eyes.

Nick seized the moment and hurled himself forward past Hailey, then lowered his good shoulder and hit the man straight in the chest. The man teetered backward, his shoes sliding against the slanted tiles, and then he was right at the edge of the roof—but somehow caught his balance. One hand still covered his eyes, but the other hand was now reaching into his jacket, and Nick saw the grip of a handgun.

But Nick was on autopilot, now. He reached into his own belt and his fingers touched cold ivory. In one motion, he yanked the retractable walking stick from Adrian's display case free, whipped it open with a flick of his wrist—and then swung at the delicate man with all his strength. The stick hit the man full force in the jaw, sending him toppling backward— and then he was over the edge of the roof, plunging downward. Inertia almost sent Nick after him—but Hailey grabbed the back of his shirt, catching him before he, too, went over the edge.

Nick peered down. Where the man had gone over, the drop was sheer brick for at least fifteen feet, ending in another slanted roof, and then a longer drop to the stone steps below. Nick could see dark marks on the lower roof that was almost certainly blood, but no body. It was still too dark to see all the way down, but as far as Nick could tell, the man had hit the first ledge and probably rolled off and gone the rest of the way.

"Is he?" Hailey started, but she didn't seem to want to finish the thought.

Nick shrugged. He didn't know if a man could survive such a fall, but if there was a body down there, it was only a matter of time before one of the patrolling state troopers noticed it. Which meant he and Hailey had to hurry if they were going to finish what they'd come for.

Nick turned back to Hailey. She was putting the empty flask back in the backpack. Her eyes were red, and she was coughing a little—but most of the fumes had dissipated into the air. Her fingers trembled as she zipped the backpack closed, but when she looked up, her eyes still flashed.

There was no chance she was going to turn back now. The killer with the dark hair, the man in the suit, even the FBI agent—they'd all underestimated her. Nick wasn't about to do the same.

"We need to keep moving," Hailey said. There would be time to digest what they'd been through later, but for now she was right.

Nick started forward again, his mind already whirling ahead. In a moment, they'd be in position, right above the courtyard where the bell had been stashed. But that would be as far as Nick could take them.

The rest of the plan was out of his hands.

CHAPTER THIRTY-SIX

I hope you're happy, Charles, wherever you are…

Adrian muttered to himself as he stumbled down the brick sidewalk as fast as his current state allowed, one hand on the seat of his bicycle for balance and the other guiding the handlebars to keep the damn thing aiming straight. He would much rather have been riding, in the saddle, than walking the bike along the narrow street, bordered on both sides by three- and four-story town houses, but the Hill here was steep, and he wasn't going very far. In fact, another yard, and he'd reached the corner of Mount Vernon and Joy—and a quick glance at his Tag Heuer sports watch, fit snugly beneath the wrist of his tight biking shirt, told him he was right on schedule.

He took quick stock of his surroundings. The intersection between the two streets—the much wider and more stately Mount Vernon, with its multimillion-dollar homes, private garages, and fenced greenery, and the more claustrophobic Joy, where the town houses seemed close enough to touch each other, were often split between multiple units, and the garages were nonexistent—was deserted and mostly bathed in shadows, save for the warm glow coming off a single, wrought-iron gas lamp jutting up from the closest curb.

In the grimness of predawn, staring up at the gaslit, two-centuries-old buildings, Adrian imagined the scenery looked very much as it would have at the turn of the nineteenth century when these houses had been built, and when the people who roamed these streets had names like Cabot and Lodge and Hancock and, yes, Revere.

It seemed a fitting spot for what was to come next. Adrian walked his bike the last few feet, then leaned it up against the lamppost. No lock, because if things went the way they were supposed to, he was going to need to beat a hasty retreat. Down the back slope of the hill—the area that in Revere's time was known as Mount Whoredom, a term coined by the sailors and British soldiers who traipsed through these narrow streets before the Cabots and Lodges finally chased them away. Then he stepped back, straightening his overcoat. He took one last look up at the town houses on either side; the windows were all dark, most of the shades drawn. The timing was right, the location perfect. Deserted, close enough to the State House for the desired effect, but far enough away to give Adrian a fitting head start.

"Now or never," Adrian whispered.

Then he reached into his overcoat and pulled out the flintlock pistol from his display case, along with the small hemp firing sack. The gun felt surprisingly heavy in his hand; he'd held it before, of course, when he'd first purchased it at auction and a handful of times when he'd showed it off to particularly annoying undergraduates and visiting scholars. But of course, he'd never taken it out of his office, and he'd never even considered doing what he was about to do.

And yet, despite the tremors of fear moving up his spine, he couldn't ignore the second sensation growing inside of him as he tilted the pistol back, eyeing the long barrel and the firing mechanism behind it: a palpable surge of excitement.

He chased the feeling away, because it wasn't becoming of his stature or the moment, and because he had work to do. Carefully opening the hemp bag, he withdrew a small powder flask and carefully tilted it over the opening of the barrel of the pistol. He could only guess at the appropriate amount of gunpowder to pour down the barrel; if he'd had the time to peruse his office library, he could have been exact—but heroism, it seemed, was an inexact science.

Once he'd added what he hoped was enough shot, he made sure the powder had settled up against the base of the firing mechanism. Then he retrieved a small section of thick cloth from the bag and placed it over the opening of the gun. After that, came the bullet; it took a moment of searching with his fingers to find the round piece of lead. Originally, the sack had held four bullets, but he'd only needed one for the job ahead.

He placed the bullet on top of the cloth, then carefully removed the ramrod from where it was attached beneath the barrel of the pistol. He used the ramrod to push the bullet and the cloth into the barrel, all the way down to the powder. Because of the cloth, he could be sure that the barrel was properly plugged and airtight; when the firing mechanism went off, the bullet would only have one way to go.

He reaffixed the ramrod, then put the sack back in his pocket. Now the pistol was loaded and ready. All he needed was the proper target.

It only took a moment for his eyes to rise up the iron lamppost, to the rectangular glass fixture at the top, maybe ten feet above his head. The gas-fed fire flickered within the glass, its orange glow toying with his optical nerves.

Adrian took a deep breath, then extended his arm, aiming the pistol at the light.

"To you, Charles. And to you, Mr. Revere."

He pulled the trigger.

The explosion ripped through the air, a cone of fire bursting out of the end of the pistol. Adrian was lifted off his feet by the recoil, his body flung backward until he landed on his haunches in the middle of the street. In the same instant, there was the sound of shattering glass as the light fixture burst into a thousand pieces, the flickering fire inside leaping upward.

Adrian sat dazed on the pavement, staring up at the destroyed gaslight, his head throbbing from the sound still reverberating through his ears. The pounding was joined by a cacophony of car alarms, set off by the report—and as he watched, the lights in the windows of the town houses on either side started to go on, one after another. And then, in the background, the sound of sirens, cutting through the night.

Adrian whistled low, staring down at his hands. They were covered in soot and smelled of gunpowder, but all his fingers were still there. It took him a moment longer to find the pistol, which had skidded almost to the curb. And then another moment to get back on his feet, and hurry over to his bike.

Next time, he'd use less powder. But even so, Nick's plan seemed to be working perfectly. Distraction, misdirection, whatever the man had called it— Nick and Hailey would have their chance.

But for Adrian, there was no time to waste. He pulled the bike off the iron of the post, which was still reverberating from the gunshot, and slung his leg over the seat. He was going to ride like he'd never ridden before.

He believed it was Emerson who had once said: A hero is no braver than an ordinary man, but he is brave five minutes longer. Adrian would have added; a minute more, and he'd cross that line, from hero to fool. And Adrian Jensen was nobody's fool.

He kicked off the pavement with a heel—and a moment later he was pedaling down the brick sidewalk as fast as the bicycle's well-oiled gears could carry him.

CHAPTER THIRTY-SEVEN

He actually did it," Nick whispered, as the last echoes of the gunshot reverberated through the air. "Gotta admit, I'm more than a little surprised."

Leaning forward over the brick ledge of the first-floor balcony where they were crouched, Hailey could see the nearest state troopers scrambling around the front of the State House, in the direction of the noise. She knew the distraction would only give her and Nick a little time; Nick had told her that the officers would circle back shortly after they'd assessed the situation—but it was the only chance they were going to get. Adrian had done his part; now it was up to them.

Hailey swung her legs over the ledge and turned herself around so she could lower herself down as far as she could with her arms. The backpack almost snagged on the stone detailing at the lip of the balcony—but Nick helped her free. She cast one last glance toward the ground below; it was still pretty high, maybe eight to ten feet—but there was some grass and shrubbery leading up to the low stone steps to the courtyard that contained the bell. Even if she landed wrong, the foliage should keep her mostly unbroken.

She gave a last look up at Nick, then released her grip.

She landed with a soft thud, her knees bending low

to absorb the impact. Nick came right after her, hitting the ground so close that he nearly took off some of her toes. If the drop had exacerbated his shoulder, he didn't let it show. Instead, he just nodded toward the courtyard. A moment later they were racing up the stone steps.

The courtyard was actually more of a low balcony, similar to the one from which they had just dropped. The ground was stone, the walls and pillars brick. There was a row of curved windows along one side, looking into the first floor of the State House, but the lights inside were out. Nick was trying to look through the glass panes, to see if anyone might be there to see them—but Hailey's attention was already fixed on their quarry.

"It's incredible," she whispered.

The bell stood between two brick pillars, bordered on one side by a fence made of shoulder-high metal bars. The bell was much larger than she had imagined; suspended on an authentic-looking metal frame, it was as tall as she was, and though burnished by time and weather, it looked to be in near perfect condition. In fact, it looked—too perfect.

"The crack," Hailey said. "There's no crack."

Nick turned away from the windows and stood next to her.

"Adrian said the Boston bell was different than the rest. I guess that's what he meant. They didn't add the crack. So, it's not a perfect replica."

"Actually, it is. A perfect replica of the bell as it was cast, before it was rung."

She unslung her backpack, reached inside, and retrieved the golden box containing the clapper from the *Constitution*.

"The Liberty Bell was rung many times over

almost a century—and it never sounded right. Maybe because it was never rung in the way that it was intended. A part of it was missing."

She opened the box and lifted out the clapper, then placed the box back into her backpack. The clapper was heavy in her hands, made of what appeared to be the same bronze as the bell.

She crossed the courtyard to the metal fence. She gave a cursory glance to the plaque hanging halfway up the metal bars, describing the bell and how it had arrived in Boston; then she moved around where the fence met one of the brick pillars, and she was right up next to the bell itself.

She dropped to her knees and peered underneath. To her surprise, there was no clapper inside, just the setting where one should have been attached. She wondered if all the replica bells had come this way, or if the Boston clapper had been removed at some point in the past seventy years. Perhaps people had gotten tired of listening to what had been described as a noxious sound.

It took Hailey a few minutes to attach the clapper from the *Constitution* to the setting. By the time she stepped back, there were beads of perspiration on the back of her neck, making the breeze shifting over Beacon Hill feel like fingers of ice against her skin.

"Ready?" she asked.

And then she reached beneath the bell, took the clapper in her hand, and gave it a hard swing toward the bell's bronze interior wall.

The sound hit her like a solid wave, and she rocked back on her heels. The tone was deep and strange and intense, riding right into her bones. Her stomach felt like it was dropping out, and she gasped—she'd never heard anything like it before.

Metal against metal, but something else, something beyond what her ears alone could detect, something that seemed to make the very cells in her body start to vibrate. She looked back at Nick, and his face had gone completely pale, his eyes like saucers. She turned back toward the bell; the clapper had traveled back to the other side of the bronze interior, and a second tone joined the first—the strange noise growing and growing, deeper and more powerful, disturbingly so, riding right through every inch of her body—

"Hailey, look!"

She whirled back around toward Nick. He had his hand out, and in his open palm, she saw he was holding the three remaining bullets that went with Adrian's flintlock pistol. Except, they didn't look right at all, because they weren't dark gray lead anymore. They were glowing, shining even in the dim light—

They had turned to gold.

"This isn't possible," Nick whispered.

But Hailey knew he was wrong. It wasn't just possible, it was real, it was happening. It was—

It wasn't. Because suddenly the three bullets darkened against Nick's palm, and a second later, they'd returned to their original state. *Cold, unremarkable lead.* The tone from the bell was still echoing around them, but the feeling Hailey had felt just a moment before—the intensity, the internal, almost cellular vibration—was gone.

"They were gold," Hailey said. "For a second, they were gold. But it didn't last. It wasn't permanent—"

A sudden rending sound interrupted her mid-sentence, and Hailey turned back toward the bell. She saw, in awe, the crack as it appeared, working its way down the front of the bronze, all the way to the bottom. The bell was fracturing right in front of her.

And as it did, the tone changed even more, bending toward something dull, unpleasant.

Hailey took another step back. And then she realized, there were other noises beyond the sound of the bell. It took a moment to recognize that they were sirens.

"The police are on their way back," Nick said. "We have to go."

The clapper was slowing now, in its arc within the bell, and the tone, unpleasant as it was, grew softer as the sirens grew louder. Hailey was trying to understand what had just happened. Revere's equation— the sound curve he'd molded into the eagle's wings— had been made real, translated by the Liberty Bell. The secret, holy grail of alchemy, the philosopher's stone, that could transform lead to gold—but it had only been a temporary effect. It hadn't *transformed* the lead—it had only momentarily *rearranged* it.

She shook her head. It didn't make sense.

The box in her backpack that had held the clapper was made of gold. The note that had been inside the box along with the clapper had read: *From she who made the box.* Hailey had thought the note had referred to the Liberty Bell itself. But she wondered— what if it didn't?

What if the bell wasn't the end of Revere's alchemical inquiry?

"A mathematical proof," she whispered.

"What?" Nick asked.

He was staring down at the lead bullets in his hand. He looked bewildered. Something incredible had happened, they had gotten so close to something immensely powerful. But then, just like that, it had slipped away.

"In math, a proof is an argument that shows the undeniable truth of a theory," Hailey continued.

"Revere's bells were experiments. The Liberty Bell, his true, final bell, was his proof; what he was trying to do was indeed possible. But the Liberty Bell didn't make that golden box. *Something*, or *someone*, else did."

"Revere's philosopher's stone—" Nick started.

"It's still out there."

Nick's hand closed over the bullets. Then he looked at her in a way she hadn't seen before. Maybe it was because they had come so close, or because he'd seen the unthinkable, if only for a moment. But something had definitely changed. Before, he'd told her that everyone was in this to get paid. For the first time for Nick, she believed, that was no longer true.

"This isn't over," he said.

Hailey retrieved her backpack and slid past him. Considering they'd just climbed the State House itself, getting out of the courtyard and over the fence surrounding the front facade of the building wouldn't be difficult. But beyond that—Hailey wasn't yet sure.

Even so, as she led Nick down the stone steps toward the fence, Beacon Street, and the Boston Common beyond, she realized she was smiling. She and Nick had just witnessed something earth-shattering, and incredibly powerful; a mechanism that, however briefly, could transform lead into gold. But they also had evidence—the box in her backpack—that somewhere, there was something even more powerful and permanent waiting for them. Paul Revere had started this journey more than two hundred years ago, but now Hailey felt certain she was hot on his trail.

"I thought the Liberty Bell was the solution to Revere's puzzle," she said, as they moved. "The culmination of his work. But I was wrong."

The bell wasn't the solution to the puzzle.

It was only the first piece.

EPILOGUE

Five miles away, Curt Anderson limped deliberately down the long private dock toward the figure standing at the far end, backlit by the sun rising up from beyond the harbor. Curt's right leg throbbed with pain as the dock swayed with the water that crashed and cavorted against the wooden pylons holding it up, but Curt refused to acknowledge the pain, his long, taut muscles reacting instinctively to keep his balance perfect, his motion pure. Along with the leg, which might very well have been broken, two of his ribs were undoubtedly bruised. Every breath was a challenge, but Curt knew, in this moment, that his wounds were irrelevant. Given time, they would heal. In this moment, the fact that he had failed was much more of an existential threat; so despite the pain, he didn't walk so much as *glide*, his joints perfectly tuned to overcome the damage by a near lifetime of physical training.

But even with all that he had been through at the State House, and despite his *education*, the years he'd spent plying his unique profession—something about the man at the end of the dock still filled him with trepidation.

Strange; as Curt moved closer, he could make out the man's features, and there was nothing unusual or terrifying about them. Middle-aged, handsome, thin but not gaunt, with short hair slightly silver at the edges, and maybe just the hint of a scar above his left eye. If anything, the man looked like a banker, or someone who started companies in Silicon Valley. There was nothing inherently frightening about him.

But as Curt stopped a few feet in front of the man, bowing slightly, he could feel the palpable surge in the nerves of his spine, overcoming the needles ricocheting out of his ribs. All of his senses were going off, warning him, and it took much of his energy just to push the feelings away.

"Mr. Arthur," Curt finally said, when he'd regained his composure. "I have unfortunate news to report."

The man sighed. Curt could see, behind him, the leather-lined tender tied to the end of the dock, piloted by a sailor in a crisp gray uniform. The exterior of the tender was sleek and mostly pitch-black fiberglass, without markings or numbers. The interior was likewise dark, the leather imported and expensive. Curt knew that the tender was one of the fastest of its kind, ridiculously expensive, with a price running into the millions. But it was nothing compared to the three-hundred-foot yacht it served, anchored just beyond the harbor.

Curt had been on the yacht once before, when he'd first been hired to shadow Patricia. The yacht was something quite incredible: two helicopter pads, multiple swimming pools, an indoor theater, and a lower level that could only be described as an art museum, filled with Picassos, Van Goghs, and probably now, at least one Vermeer. The yacht flew a flag of a small European country, but the family that owned it had a different provenance, one shrouded in mystery. Even Curt didn't know their full history. And he didn't intend to research the matter. There were certain stones you did not turn over, no matter how curious you were.

"Both Patricia and I failed," Curt started, not mincing words, but Mr. Arthur stopped him with a wave of his hand.

"It doesn't matter. There's a new thread to pull, Mr. Anderson. A promising thread."

Curt instinctively recoiled as Mr. Arthur reached into his jacket pocket, then relaxed as the man retrieved a small photograph, and handed it across to him.

Curt looked down at the picture. It was of an engraving; one he'd never seen before. The signature at the bottom of the engraving was instantly familiar: Paul Revere. Revere was in the image on the engraving as well, but he wasn't alone. A second man was there with him. Heavyset, mostly bald but with curly, longish hair at the sides—and circular, metal-framed spectacles resting on the ridge of his nose. The two men were standing in what looked to be a workshop, with a table between them. On the table was what appeared to be an eagle, made of what might have been solid gold. But strangely, the eagle wasn't the focal point of the engraving. The focal point was something else, an object hanging between the men, above the table.

A kite. With what appeared to be a key, dangling from its tail.

Mr. Arthur held out his hand, and Curt handed him back the photograph. Then Arthur turned toward the tender, beckoning Curt to follow.

"We'll be in Philadelphia by the morning," he said.

So, Curt realized, he would be making the trip down the coast after all.

He and Patricia had failed, but the hunt wasn't over. In fact, it was about to begin all over again.

ACKNOWLEDGMENTS

When the *Boston Globe* first approached me—at the height of the pandemic—with the wild idea of me writing a serialized novella to run, daily, over a period of two weeks in the pages of my hometown newspaper, I was both excited and terrified. I'd always wanted to do this sort of book—a modern thrill ride built around an epic-scale mystery going back centuries into real history—but the thought of crafting a chapter a day for a waiting audience of readers seemed more than a little ambitious. Thankfully, a delusional sense of adventure won out over reason; *The Mechanic,* which has now evolved into a full-size novel, *The Midnight Ride,* ended up being one of the best writing experiences of my career. For this, I owe an enormous debt of gratitude to the wonderful readers of the *Globe* all over New England and around the country, who followed me daily on what turned out to be only the beginning of an incredible journey.

Likewise, immense thanks to the brilliant Linda Pizzuti Henry and the dedicated Brian McGrory for taking a risk on something like this, for all the right reasons. Special thanks to Mark Morrow at the *Globe* for helping shape the chapters that appeared in the newspaper and Heather Hopp-Bruce for the amazing artwork that appeared with each installment.

Turning *The Mechanic* into a full-size thriller was a labor of love, which I could not have achieved without the incredible help and genius of my editor, Wes Miller; I'm very lucky to be working with someone as skilled as Wes, and the entire team at Hachette, including Autumn Oliver and Andy Dodds. I'm also thankful for the wonderful help from our team at Amblin Partners, Jeb Brody and John Buderwitz; can't wait to see these characters on the big screen.

As usual, immense thanks to my incredible agents, Eric Simonoff at WME and Matt Snyder at CAA. And to my family, Tonya, Asher, Arya, Bagel, and Bugsy, who were around for most of it—I couldn't do this without you. *The Midnight Ride* opens a new chapter for me, and I can't wait to see where this adventure leads.

ABOUT THE AUTHOR

Ben Mezrich is the *New York Times* bestselling author of *The Accidental Billionaires* (adapted by Aaron Sorkin into the David Fincher film *The Social Network*), *Bringing Down the House* (adapted into the #1 box office hit film *21*), *The Antisocial Network*, and many other bestselling books. He has sold more than six million copies worldwide.

Learn more at:
Benmezrich.com
Twitter @benmezrich
Facebook.com/BenMezrichAuthor
Instagram @benmezrich